*02
Falling
I0727206
Via Lactea

Falling

An imprint of Via Lactea Ltd.

Author: Yu Cheng
Translators: Arien; Yun; Hobbitsflower
Editor: Moca
Proofreader: OWL
Layout Designer: Ayan

CONTACT:
Customer Support: info@vialactea.ca
Wholesale & Distribution: market@vialactea.ca
Other Cooperation: https://vialactea.ca/pages/cooperation
Discord Channel: https://discord.gg/vialactea

Follow us on X/Instagram/Facebook: @ViaLactea_Ltd
Official Website: www.vialactea.ca

ISBN 978-1-77408-521-9 (pbk)
Printed in Canada

LOCATION:
Shops At Waterloo Town Square
#27, 75 King Street South, Waterloo, ON
Canada
N2J 1P2

"I don't want another snowman.
I want you."

CONTENT

Chapter 09 ·························· 001

Chapter 10 ·························· 026

Chapter 11 ·························· 061

Chapter 12 ·························· 089

Chapter 13 ·························· 118

Chapter 14 ·················· 149

Chapter 15 ·················· 181

Chapter 16 ·················· 217

Chapter 17 ·················· 251

Glossary ·················· 284

Volume 02

Falling

CHAPTER 09

FOR the week-long May Day holiday, Ye Jinxiang planned to take the whole family to a small island in the south of China.

Ye Qin didn't want to go, but it was rare that Ye Jinxiang would be so proactive in preparing for a family trip. He got all his luggage packed several days in advance, and bought a new swimsuit for each family member.

Considering the fact that Ye Jinxiang had always brought gifts or flowers for his family whenever he returned from a business trip, Ye Qin deduced that irregular attentiveness from Ye Jinxiang must come from guilt. This time, Ye Qin sensed something wrong as well. He decided to go in case his mother were to be treated unfairly when he was not around.

Fortunately, his father didn't do anything that would trigger him. He spent most of the time eating, sleeping, and swimming. He even took Luo Qiuling to the local mall once. Ye Qin's heart fell to where it belonged. The sun outside was too bright for him, so he stayed in the hotel and chatted with Cheng Feichi via text messages. Running out of anything serious to discuss, he just kept sending lame jokes to him. Anyway, they couldn't lose track of each other, not even for a single day.

Cheng Feichi couldn't reply instantly to his messages because of work. When Ye Qin received his serious reply, he would have to try to recall what he had sent him before.

For instance, last night he sent, "Lu You was a poet in the Song Dynasty. During that period of time, the Jin troops invaded Song territory and made the whole country suffer like hell. Lu You was furious, and then..."

Cheng Feichi replied, "And then he wrote a poem: The long Yellow River is dashing eastwardly to the sea, and the high Mount Hua reaching high up to the sky. Adherents of Song Dynasty suffer under the invader's heel, hoping the lost territory could be retrieved soon."

...Mr. Cheng really had the qualities of a good teacher.

Ye Qin was speechless. He replied with the right answer: "And then the internet went down."

Cheng Feichi soon got back to him: "Hahahaha"

Ye Qin read the joke again and found it hilarious too. "Lu You" and "router" were homophones in Chinese, which made the basis of the pun. He rolled back and forth on the bed, laughing like crazy. Knocking at the door to his own room in this family suite, Luo Qiuling asked him whether he wished to surf with his father. Ye Qin turned her down without even thinking about it. He continued sending Cheng Feichi messages: "Are you off from work now?"

Cheng Feichi replied: "Yep."

"Can you connect to Wi-Fi network now?"

"Yes."

Ye Qin invited him to join a video call.

Half a minute later, Cheng Feichi answered the call. Ye Qin saw the ceiling first, then the wall. At last, Cheng Feichi's face appeared on camera.

Seeing that Cheng Feichi moved closer and was looking at

him, Ye Qin suddenly moved away his hand, which was blocking his own camera. Cheng Feichi was caught off guard by his grimace, only letting go of himself when he heard Ye Qin's laughter. Resigned, he admitted, "You've really got me."

"Sure! Of course I did!" Ye Qin finally got himself under control and continued, "You've never had video calls with other people?"

"No," Cheng Feichi was walking, so the camera was a bit wobbly. He removed the dangling facial mask from his ear and looked at the bell hanging on the wall of the lounge. "Have you had lunch?"

"Yeah...what about you? You just finished your shift?"

Cheng Feichi nodded and took off the apron. "Yes, I'm going home now."

Ye Qin adjusted his posture. He lay on the bed and held his cellphone up in the air so that his whole face could be seen in the video. "So you haven't had lunch?"

"I'll have it soon." Cheng Feichi changed the subject. "Are you having fun there?"

Ye Qin pursed his lips. "Not really. What fun could I have with the elder generation? It's not even as good as being with you in the restaurant..."

Cheng Feichi smiled. "Next time I'll take you to the dessert bar upstairs. We won't need to wait in line."

Ye Qin was skeptical. "The restaurant's working with the dessert bar?"

Cheng Feichi wouldn't tell him now. Ye Qin turned over another several times and didn't feel like finishing the call.

"Well, I'm gonna get changed now." Cheng Feichi put the cellphone on a table, his fingers raising towards the buttons of his uniform.

Ye Qin sucked in a sudden breath and abruptly ended the call.

Afterwards, he thought he was being too sensitive. He and Cheng Feichi were of the same sex. If they were to go to the public bathhouse together, they would have to see each other fully naked. So what was the big deal about watching Cheng Feichi get changed, especially when he could only see his upper body?

He lay on his stomach and buried his face in the pillow. He bit his lips as if he could still feel the other boy's temperature on them.

It was all because of the kissing! Ye Qin couldn't believe that he had let Cheng Feichi take the lead. Thumping the pillow twice, he thought to himself: *Next time I have to take control of everything! Have to let him know who gets to make the calls!*

The seven days, indeed too long to bear sometimes, had finally come to their end. Setting his feet onto the campus, Ye Qin was welcomed by the same line on the billboard outside the teaching building and on the black board in the back of the classroom: Only 396 Days until the College Entrance Examination.

The students entered the school gate while chatting about their holiday activities with their friends. The next minute they became upset, sitting down in front of the textbooks. Even Zhou Feng, who never took studying seriously, felt nervous and began furiously copying Liao Yifang's notes.

Ye Qin slept through a class and nearly continued sleeping during the break. He got up and looked around with his sleepy eyes, only to find that everyone was still seated in the classroom. Some were busy doing exercises, while others were trying to memorize English vocabulary, their books shut. He was the only one who was not affected by the countdown at all. He was even dreaming about eating the meals that Cheng Feichi made for him and drooling in his sleep.

Zhou Feng was still working on the notes. Ye Qin patted

him on his back. "What are you doing?"

"I'm trying to rescue myself from the falling sickle of the Grim Reaper."

"How do you know it for sure that it'll fall on you after 396 days?"

Zhou Feng roared in desperation. "I'm not like you. You can go abroad if you don't get a good result in the CEE. There are still millions of dollars waiting for you to inherit. But if I don't do well enough, I'll be sent to the army. That must be my own personal hell."

Ye Qin thought about the soldiers he saw on TV shows. Indeed, that life was not easy. They had to endure torrential rain and dirty mud, or stand under the scorching sun—these would be unbearable for a rich and well-protected playboy like Zhou Feng. Surely, he would pass out in no more than three minutes under the sun.

After lunch, Cheng Feichi took out a book on Olympiad challenges and some scrap paper. Before he could dive into the ocean of mathematical problems, Ye Qin slightly kicked him. "Do I have a chance of getting into the same university with you?"

Cheng Feichi hesitated and handed him an English textbook. "Let's start from memorizing the vocabulary from unit 1 to unit 5."

Ye Qin was so bored that he actually took the book and started memorizing the words. Yet he kicked Cheng Feichi again after getting only two or three words down. He asked Cheng Feichi which university he planned to get admitted to.

"It depends on my performance in the Olympiad in the second half of the year," Cheng Feichi answered. "If I did a good job, I would be more likely to get in there through independent recruitment."

Cheng Feichi didn't give him a direct answer, but Ye Qin could tell that it must be some university that he couldn't possibly enroll in. He somehow felt upset and asked Cheng Feichi, puffing out his cheeks, "Aren't you planning on studying abroad?"

This was referring to the trip to the International High School. Cheng Feichi answered, "At a moment, I don't have plans for that. I went there to broaden my horizons, that's all."

Ye Qin had expected that. How could Cheng Feichi afford to study at foreign universities? Even if Ye Jinxiang wanted to send him overseas, he would have to persuade Cheng Feichi in the first place.

Cheng Feichi seemed to be a nice gentleman, but in truth, he had strong self-esteem, just like all other poor people. Otherwise, he wouldn't prefer doing part-time jobs to receiving Ye Qin's financial help.

During the days spent with Cheng Feichi, Ye Qin knew this for sure. Thinking that Ye Jinxiang might have been rejected by Cheng Feichi over and over again, he felt unparalleled joy.

Joy was followed by spiritual emptiness. All of a sudden, his classmates and friends acquired their short-term goals. They either prepared to get into a good university in China or planned to study overseas. Even Liu Yangfan and Zhao Yue stopped hanging out with him—they were forced to study for TOFEL at home, so that they could be sent to the U.S. straight away in the autumn.

Compared to his peers, Ye Qin was living the easiest life. He was insulated against all the anxiety, tiredness, and desperation around him. He couldn't even find a proper reason to memorize some English words.

The warm sunshine in the middle of the day made Ye Qin drowsy. He rested his head and arms on a book on the desk, his fingers aimlessly pointing at Cheng Feichi's notebook as if he was still trying to read it. When he was almost falling asleep, he heard Cheng Feichi saying to him, "You...do you really want to get into the same college as I do?"

Ye Qin was still unconsciously savoring the taste of the sweet and sour pork ribs remaining in his mouth. The delicious ribs that Cheng Feichi made for him. At this moment, his only wish was to have Cheng Feichi continue cooking for him. And it would also be great if they could sit at the same table and breathe the fresh air by each other's side for a longer period of time.

So he told Cheng Feichi about the feelings that he had at this exact moment. He yawned and murmured without even opening his eyes, "Yes, for real."

Not even half a month later, Ye Qin was already wishing that he could eat his words.

The long break in the morning used to be "Game Time" for him, but now he had to study during this period. Cheng Feichi would come to his classroom each Monday, Wednesday, and Friday with lollipops and exam papers prepared by himself, where all the questions that once tripped up Ye Qin were included. These were for Ye Qin to finish before the end of the day, and then he would check the results.

Two days were all it took for Ye Qin to start complaining. He didn't finish the paper last Friday. When he returned it to Cheng Feichi, he tried to please Cheng Feichi with a lovely smile and a kiss on his face. Cheng Feichi accepted both, but still made him stay right in the classroom until he completed the assignment.

Plus, as consequence, Cheng Feichi came with merely a piece of exam paper this Monday. Ye Qin searched all his pockets for a lollipop in vain, so he blinked. "Where's my lollipop?"

Cheng Feichi said, "There's no lollipop for you. You didn't get the task done last time."

He sounded not in the least like the sweet boy who was

holding Ye Qin's hand in the cinema last weekend.

Ye Qin returned to his seat and was about to tear the paper apart when Liao Yifang stepped up and stopped him. "Ye-tongxue, if you don't want it, can I borrow it for copying? A lot of our classmates…"

"Who told you that I don't want it?" Ye Qin interrupted his words angrily and slammed the paper on the desk. "And where are the notes on electrolytes from last time? Give them back to me. I need them now."

During the break before the night session started, Ye Qin went to the stationery store near the school gate and bought a file folder. He carefully collected the papers that Cheng Feichi had given him, including the crumpled notes on electrolytes that he didn't take seriously.

Time always flies when one is having fun, and this is also true when one is immersed in studying.

Before Ye Qin even realized it, the night session ended. He went to the bike-parking area and returned the exercise sheet to Cheng Feichi. After checking all the answers under the street lamp, Cheng Feichi raised his head and saw that Ye Qin pouted his lips, upset. He took a lollipop out of his pocket, opened the wrapper, and handed it to Ye Qin.

"Open your mouth."

Ye Qin didn't want to obey his rules now. He wanted to turn Cheng Feichi down by keeping his mouth shut, but Cheng Feichi just kept holding it. He was afraid that Cheng Feichi's arm might endure a long time in mid-air, so at last he opened his mouth and took it.

They were again the last two students leaving the school tonight. Ye Qin sat on Cheng Feichi's bike for a while, but soon demanded that they walk instead. He also took the sponge cushion that had been newly fixed down, saying that it made him feel unbearably hot. He would prefer walking to sitting on it all the way back home.

It was not yet June, yet the air in the capital was already getting stuffy and hot, like a badly ventilated house in the summer. All students started to wear the summer uniform overnight, and Cheng Feichi was no exception. The large uniform trousers were still a bit short for him, revealing some skin below the ankle. As for the short-sleeve shirt, he had left the first two buttons open, and the collar looked neat. Well, the only thing wrong about his clothing was probably the bottom hem of his shirt that got weirdly wrinkled with Ye Qin constantly clutching it when sitting on his bike.

Ye Qin's hand itched to pull the hem flat, and he did so. Then he tried to negotiate with Cheng Feichi about the daily learning tasks. "Emm...the English passage...can I recite it to you tomorrow? I've got too much Chemistry homework today, so I'm not familiar enough with it today."

Cheng Feichi looked at him. "No."

Ye Qin almost wanted to cry. On top of one exam paper each day, Cheng Feichi gave him another task: reciting a 400-word English passage every day. Apparently, Cheng Feichi believed that more reciting could get him familiarized with the flow of English writing, alongside memorizing more new words. As usual, Ye Qin was supposed to recite it in front of Cheng Feichi after school.

When it came to studying, Cheng Feichi was serious, stern and stubborn. No personal feelings could stand in his way of making sure that Ye Qin had finished the tasks. No matter how hard Ye Qin tried, he wouldn't let go off his principle of "never putting off till tomorrow what may be done today." He was strict with not only himself but also people around him—even his boyfriend couldn't slip through the net.

It happened to work in Ye Qin's case. Ye Qin tended to ignore the nice and kind advice, but usually gave in to the pressure from a real tough guy. Terrified by Cheng Feichi's serious, expressionless face, he continued to read the passage out loud over and over again.

Having stammered all the way to the end of the passage, he looked up and saw they had reached Ye Qin's home.

Much to Ye Qin's chagrin, he didn't get to actually talk with Cheng Feichi tonight. He took his backpack from Cheng Feichi, roughly pulled the zipper open, got out the folder and stuffed the piece of paper full of English words in it.

When he was about to put the folder back, Cheng Feichi pressed on his hand.

Cheng Feichi leafed through the exam papers and printed English passages, his eyes turning soft. "Are you feeling upset?"

Ye Qin avoided looking at him. "How dare I?"

Cheng Feichi sighed. "Didn't you say that you wanted to go to the same college as me?"

"Stop making fun of me." Ye Qin hung his head in disappointment and shame. "I know exactly what I'm capable of. If I'm going to the same college as you, there's only two ways out: either I install a new brain, or you don't show up for Math, Physics, and Chemistry exams."

Cheng Feichi laughed. "It's not that bad. As long as you listen to what I say, be a good boy and finish all these tasks, you can absolutely be accepted by great universities."

It sounded as if Cheng Feichi was trying to comfort Ye Qin, but Cheng Feichi wasn't telling lies.

He was used to making plans and schedules for the future. After Ye Qin had said that he wanted to enter the same university as him, he had already begun to regard improving Ye Qin's

academic performance as his responsibility. He was ready to get Ye Qin into a good university.

It was the same as when he decided to accept Ye Qin; he had already included Ye Qin into the future he had planned for himself, standing ready to make necessary concessions and sacrifices for their relationship, as long as they didn't go against his principles.

Ye Qin, comforted by Cheng Feichi's steadfastness yet brought to blushes when he heard "be a good boy," snatched the folder out of Cheng Feichi's hand and put it back into the bag. In the meantime, he demanded, "Since I've been following your orders for so many days, would Mr. Cheng grant me a reward?"

"A reward?"

Ye Qin made good use of the seconds when Cheng Feichi was lost in thought. He grabbed Cheng Feichi's collar and kissed on his lips. He was so excited that he nearly sucked Cheng Feichi's lips and made a loud noise when it was finished.

Ye Qin was on cloud nine because he finally acted before Cheng Feichi could move. He didn't feel ashamed at all. He dashed to the gate of the compound while waving to Cheng Feichi. "I've already got the reward! See you tomorrow, Mr. Cheng!"

With the best teacher as his boyfriend, Ye Qin reached a perfect balance between romance and studying. After some time, his academic performance was actually improving.

Partly, this was because Cheng Feichi had helped him review the important parts of the textbook and predicted some of the questions on the real exam papers. Ye Qin was lucky enough to get an "A" on the Chemistry exam and consequently his academic record for this semester got much better—his surpassed nearly ten students in the class rank. Mr. Sun, his head teacher, praised him for this major progress.

This made Ye Qin so proud that he invited half the class to a free dinner. Cheng Feichi was undoubtedly invited as well, but he hadn't realized there would be so many people until he reached the restaurant. It was already too late, and he could only stay. He kept a low profile and sat down in a corner, talking to Liao Yifang about the Physics and Chemistry Olympiads due to take place next term.

"Cheng, you're truly excellent. You've helped Ye-tongxue so much, but it didn't affect your grades at all. What impresses me more is that you still had time to prepare for the Olympiad!" Liao Yifang was never able to hold back his admiration whenever he met Cheng Feichi. "No wonder you're the new king of our school. It's no exaggeration."

Cheng Feichi was about to say something when Zhou Feng interrupted unpleasantly, "Save it. Being smart and being attractive is different, okay? We've got so many attractive boys, especially in our entourage. If I get dressed up, I can be the king of school as well."

Liao Yifang glanced at him, but was too bashful to retort.

Sun Yiran was the last one to arrive. When she entered the room, Ye Qin was drinking beer with some classmates, hanging on each other's shoulders. Seeing that Cheng Feichi was sitting in the corner, she was taken by surprise. When some girls ushered her to a chair, she was still examining Ye Qin and Cheng Feichi with doubt and suspicion.

"Darling, tell me that you've given up on Cheng Feichi?" a girl nearby asked worriedly.

Sun Yiran immediately assured her, "Of course...I'm just wondering why he's here. He's not one of us."

"He helped Ye-tongxue with his schoolwork," the girl answered. "Otherwise they wouldn't hang out together, don't you think?"

During the party, Ye Qin spent most of the time chatting and drinking with his classmates, so he didn't have much time for Cheng Feichi. After the party, he followed Cheng Feichi all the way to where he parked his bike, and insisted that Cheng Feichi sit in his own back seat.

"You couldn't possibly handle it." Cheng Feichi tried to persuade him, "It's hard to control the handlebar, and the brake doesn't work so well."

Ye Qin insisted. He was so drunk, snatching the back seat while continuing to make this unreasonable demand. "You're looking down on me! I don't care. I just want to take you home on it! I want to do it! Let me do it!"

Cheng Feichi couldn't talk him out of it. He conceded to Ye Qin and sat behind him.

"Get your feet off the ground!" Ye Qin turned his head and saw that Cheng Feichi was trying to steady the bike. He therefore grabbed Cheng Feichi's arms and put them around his own waist. "Hold tight! We're gonna fly!"

Well, flying was impossible. The bike, carrying the weight of two boys, advanced clumsily on the narrow bike lane. If Cheng Feichi had not stealthily kept the balance with his feet stepping on the ground, the two of them would have fallen onto the median strip along with the bike at the start.

However, the careless driver, so confident in his riding skills, knew nothing about it. He rode all the way to Yulin Compound, then was sent home by Cheng Feichi. When Ye Qin entered the house, he was unconsciously singing random songs. Luo Qiuling was amused.

"Just sent your little girlfriend back home?"

Ye Qin was taken off guard. His feet slipped, almost taking him down to the floor. Yet he soon recovered and started to pretend that no such thing happened. "What do you mean?"

The maid brought a bowl of soup to the table. Luo Qiuling got him seated by the table, and repeated what she had said to Ye Qin before, "You're my dear son. How could I not tell what's going on in your mind?"

She had long noticed that Ye Qin was behaving differently than usual. In the past, he never cared about school, but these days he seemed more interested in studying. Plus, he turned even more attentive to his clothes and hairstyle than before. He could spend more than ten minutes in front of the mirror, just to figure out whether the collar of a shirt would look better turned up than pulled down.

She had been there, too. What was even better: she followed her heart and her romantic fancy came true. Even though her "ideal" marriage did not end with a happily ever after, she could never forget the evanescent beauty of her love story with Ye Jinxiang, and she really cherished what she had now.

As a mother, she did her best to shield Ye Qin from the pain and challenges in real life, but the experiences in dealing with romantic relationships—Ye Qin had to learn them all by himself. Therefore, she wouldn't use herself as an example to stop Ye Qin from falling in love.

Ye Qin didn't know how to answer her question, so he buried his face in the bowl, drinking the soup. Then he heard his open-minded mother continuing, "It's totally okay if you don't wanna tell me who she is. I can respect your choice. But I'm just gonna give you one important piece of advice—don't have sex before you turn eighteen. It's for your and the young lady's own good."

Because of this exact piece of advice, when Ye Qin met Cheng Feichi on Saturday, his face turned red immediately.

He had too much fun yesterday, and therefore didn't finish his daily task. Now he was sitting in a KFC restaurant with Cheng

Feichi, the latter with a volume of *Olympiad Classics* in his hand, while Ye Qin focused on his exam papers, only glancing at Cheng Feichi from time to time. The noises around them seemed filtered out of the small corner where they sat. It was their private world.

They ordered a platter of snacks for lunch. Wu Rui, Cheng Feichi's co-worker at the restaurant, served the meal. Ye Qin had met her before, so now he greeted the girl with a big grin. "Hi, pretty jiejie!"

Wu Rui was so flattered that she couldn't stop smiling. "Well, considering that you used 'pretty' to describe me, I'm not gonna be angry at you for calling me jiejie." She put down the plate and said to Cheng Feichi, "Handsome, it seems that your didi got all the talent for being a sweetie from your parents, huh?"

Cheng Feichi smiled but didn't say anything. When Wu Rui left, he noticed that Ye Qin didn't seem very happy.

"You're tired?" He put down the book and placed it on the chair next to him, and then pushed the platter towards Ye Qin. "Let's eat something and rest for a while."

Ye Qin didn't answer him. Whenever someone referred to him as Cheng Feichi's "didi," he would feel upset—even though he knew that other people didn't mean to get it wrong.

He felt a bit better after eating two pieces of popcorn chicken and asked Cheng Feichi, "How old are you?"

According to the gossip, Cheng Feichi had a gap year before transferring to High School No. 6. That piece of intelligence, he still remembered. If Cheng Feichi was born in February, he must have turned eighteen by now.

"Nineteen," Cheng Feichi answered.

Ye Qin was surprised. How could he be nineteen? If so, Ye Jinxiang must have known Cheng Feichi's mother for a pretty darn long time!

"I attended primary school one year later than usual. Before I came here, I took a gap year. Otherwise, I should have been doing my sophomore year in the autumn."

Cheng Feichi didn't reveal any emotions when he made the explanation. It seemed that he didn't care about the time wasted at all. But Ye Qin felt bad about it. He could somehow deduce the reasons why Cheng Feichi attended school later than other kids and then took a gap year.

Not knowing how to comfort Cheng Feichi, he put another piece of popcorn chicken into his mouth and mumbled, "Why didn't you tell me about it when we were celebrating your eighteenth birthday in the hotel room?"

At that time, he used the candles in the shape of the numbers "1" and "8" to suggest Cheng Feichi's age, instead of "1" and "9."

Cheng Feichi's mood improved at the mention of that night. He put on a smile. "It doesn't matter. Eighteen's not so different from nineteen."

Ye Qin couldn't just ignore the difference. His own registered birthday was a year earlier than the real date. He thought that Cheng Feichi was just one year older than him, so they would appear as "of the same age" on their ID cards. But now Cheng Feichi was actually more than two years older than him... it made him feel weird. As if he really had become Cheng Feichi's didi now.

He didn't want Cheng Feichi to perceive what was on his mind, so he raised another question. "You're such an excellent student. Why didn't you skip a grade or two?"

After wiping his own hands clean, Cheng Feichi picked up a chicken nugget, dipped it in the sauce, and put it into Ye Qin's mouth. "If I did that, how could I ever meet you?"

Cheng Feichi was more sophisticated and sterner than he was supposed to be at this age. Therefore, when he was helping Ye Qin with his schoolwork, he became a serious teacher that

was hard to please. On the contrary, when he was again playing the role of Ye Qin's dear boyfriend, he spared no effort to give Ye Qin all his tenderness.

In the evening, they went to the cinema together. When the film was over, they were still sitting in the back row while the rest of the audience was long gone. Ye Qin, who didn't feel like moving away from the comfortable seat, not even a bit, was almost carried out by Cheng Feichi. Even when they finally got out, Ye Qin leaned on his shoulder, walking reluctantly with his guidance for a few hundred meters.

It got warmer each day, and there were more and more people waiting to have barbecue in the open air. The small restaurant near High School No. 6 where Cheng Feichi worked each night was packed with customers. Spotting the two boys, the restaurant owner took out a folding table for them himself. Sizzling grilled lamb skewers were served in less than ten minutes.

Ye Qin was sitting there with the air of a proud former employee. He was not a bit awkward about how he went so far to pursue Cheng Feichi by washing dishes in this restaurant. While eating the lamb, he kept looking at the kitchen and mumbling, "I'll order a washing machine for the owner." Then he turned around to ask Cheng Feichi, "Have you ever bought anything on that new online shopping platform? It's super convenient. Anything at your doorstep no matter how huge it is."

Cheng Feichi knew too well that whenever Ye Qin wanted to be nice to people, he did it by spending money on them. He didn't try to stop him. Instead, he put a skewer next to Ye Qin's mouth. "Eat something first."

Ye Qin opened his mouth and finished a few more kebabs that Cheng Feichi kept holding for him, but he soon wiped his mouth and waved his hand. "No, I must stop eating. I've gained so much weight lately."

"You're not overweight yet," Cheng Feichi said. "You need to eat more so you can grow taller."

One of the things that Ye Qin cared about the most was his height, so he had two more skewers of kababs.

It was only after he had arrived home that he gently pinched his chubby belly and felt quite confused. He sent a voice message to Cheng Feichi. "I'm not fat? For real?"

Cheng Feichi typed in response, "For real."

Ye Qin doubted it. "You've never seen my body."

Cheng Feichi answered, "I've touched it."

Ye Qin went over all the memories he had with Cheng Feichi to find the evidence. He was suddenly reminded that last Friday night, he had snatched Cheng Feichi's arm and ... did he put it around his own waist?

He started rolling on the bed a few times, and then the quilt bundled him like a cocoon, only revealing his bare feet and the top of his head. His toes were even curled up because of shyness and embarrassment.

Outside Luo Qiuling was knocking on the door, asking whether he wanted some soup, but now Ye Qin felt as if he'd become the same sort of pervert as Zhou Feng. Everything that was on his mind was rated R. When he heard his mother's voice, the idea of underage sex penetrated his mind, and it made him start rolling around on the bed again.

When his mother left, Ye Qin managed to get hold of his cellphone and opened the browser. He licked his lips and reassured himself that both Cheng Feichi and himself were officially above 18—at least their ID cards said so... So he was allowed to watch those things, right?

A few moments later, the pair of bare feet shrank back under the quilt. Then the top of the head disappeared too. The boy under the cover was like a mimosa that rapidly closed its

sleeves and drooped after being touched by someone. He hid himself completely.

When June started, the weather in the capital became more unpredictable and unbearable. It rained and shined alternatively, while the temperature never dropped amidst the intolerable humidity.

Summer vacation was around the corner. Compared to others who got anxious about the coming semester and the approaching College Entrance Examination, Ye Qin was worrying about something totally unimportant.

A few days after July began, Cheng Feichi was due to attend a training course for the Olympiad in a school far away from downtown. The course would last for a whole month, and accommodation was provided. Ye Qin grew nervous as soon as he had heard the news. How long had he and Cheng Feichi been in a relationship? Now Cheng Feichi was going to be away from him for a month. Would Cheng Feichi still be able to recognize him at the end of that course?

"I'm not going to jail; I can still use my cellphone." Cheng Feichi pulled a wry face, having heard his worries. "As long as you want to, we can do a video call every night."

Ye Qin was still pouting, looking rather upset. He remembered Zhou Feng's advice about how physical intimacy was the key to a successful romantic relationship. If he and Cheng Feichi could only meet each other online, how successful could that be?

He thought that their relationship was entering a plateau period. Everything seemed fine, but at the end of the day, he could sense that something was missing. Things seemed natural and normal between them—there was no chemistry, not like what the romantic novels depicted.

To put it plainly, they were not yet close enough.

Ye Qin was quick to act, especially when it came to Cheng Feichi. This evening, he put something into Cheng Feichi's pocket, feeling smug. "Jiayuan Compound, No. 10 Building, Room 1903."

Cheng Feichi took out a key, stared at it but still failed to see Ye Qin's point. "What?"

"That compound is very close to the school where you'll be training," Ye Qin said as if everything was supposed to go as he planned. "The accommodation they offer must be awful. This apartment belongs to my mother. You can stay there for the whole month."

Cheng Feichi returned the key to Ye Qin. "I'll just live in the school dorm."

Having predicted that Cheng Feichi would turn him down, Ye Qin was fully prepared. He took hold of Cheng Feichi's arm and gently shook it while trying to talk it through with him. "Stay there. It'll be great. I could go in the evenings …"

Cheng Feichi freed himself from Ye Qin's grip and stated bluntly, "No way."

Ye Qin was at once stunned by how forthright Cheng Feichi was. He had known that Cheng Feichi wouldn't accept it easily, but he didn't expect a completely cold shoulder with no leeway at all. He was about to say "and keep you company," but now there was no way that he could finish that sentence anymore.

Cheng Feichi had not expected himself to be so blunt either.

Ye Qin's behavior reminded him of some rumors about his mother and himself.

The rumors never died. Even now, he could still hear them from time to time. The rumors themselves were never updated, though. Some people said that Cheng Xin got pregnant before marriage and was therefore deserted by her own family, and the unknown father of Cheng Feichi never came for them. Another version was that Cheng Xin was the mistress of some rich guy, and that she had given birth to Cheng Feichi eyeing an inheritance. Someone even guessed that the house they lived in was a gift from the mysterious rich man. Otherwise, how could Cheng Xin, a woman of poor health, afford all the unnecessary expenditure?

He didn't like to be misunderstood. He only had a vague assumption about his mother's past, but he knew how they had pulled through all these years.

The moment he saw that key, the calmness and ease of which he had always been proud shattered. After all, he was not mature enough—he cared about how everyone viewed him and talked about him exceedingly. He was so tightly bound by his self-esteem that he could be provoked into outrage and lose control in such an easy manner.

But Ye Qin didn't think that far ahead. He just wanted to take care of me.

Therefore, Cheng Feichi concluded that Ye Qin had every reason to give him the silent treatment this time. He was supposed to pamper Ye Qin because he himself was the one to blame.

Because of this little incident, Cheng Feichi started to learn how to please others from ground zero. He sent Ye Qin loads of funny jokes and drew a red heart on the exam papers he prepared for this day.

During the break in the night's session, a classmate brought the papers back. Unfolding them, Cheng Feichi saw that Ye Qin draw a zigzag in the middle of the heart to suggest that the heart was already broken.

He was amused and, at the same time, relieved. Ye Qin wasn't really mad at him. Thank God.

After the night's session, Cheng Feichi stopped the boy hurrying out of the building. Ye Qin tried to dodge him and escape, but no matter how hard he tried, Cheng Feichi was always standing in his way. He was annoyed and shouted, "A good dog never gets in the way!"

Cheng Feichi expected Ye Qin to be still mad at him, so he didn't feel offended in the least. He stood in front of Ye Qin with open arms and said very honestly, "I'm sorry. I won't do that again."

Ye Qin was taken by surprise. But he soon recovered and dragged Cheng Feichi all the way to a staircase less frequented by students and continued shouting, "Why are you sorry? Do you know why you made me mad? If you aren't willing to live with me, just pretend that I didn't ask in the first place. Why are you bringing it up again..."

His voice was going lower and lower. He claimed that he didn't care about the whole thing, but the truth was that he still felt very much aggrieved. Growing up, he was surrounded by love and care. He may not be living like a prince, but he had everything he wanted. It was the first time that he tried so hard to care for someone in his entire life, only to be turned down on the spot; not once, but twice. What shame!

"Not willing to live with you?"

Cheng Feichi seized the most important piece of information in Ye Qin's accusation and felt perplexed. Wasn't Ye Qin lending the house to him? Why was it suddenly about them living together?

Ye Qin realized his slip of the tongue. He felt so ashamed of himself that he would rather bang his head against the wall and die at once. "No. Stop. I didn't mean it. Can't you just pretend that you didn't hear anything?"

"No way." Cheng Feichi maintained a very firm attitude.

Ever since this relationship started, Cheng Feichi had been going along with Ye Qin and taking care of him. It was rare that

Ye Qin would feel desperate. He kept his head low, trying to come up with an excuse to hide all the ugly and unspeakable plots and desires he had for Cheng Feichi.

At this very moment, Cheng Feichi held out his hand, turning his palm upward. "Give me the key."

Ye Qin stammered, as he was wont to do whenever feeling nervous. "Wh...why?"

Cheng Feichi answered, "Don't you want to live with me?"

Ye Qin got lucky and made a narrow escape again. Not knowing how it actually had happened, his plan for the first half of summer vacation was fixed.

Ye Qin hadn't just been so "kind" as to "forgive" Cheng Feichi; he also felt so much happier now. The rainstorm in his heart turned into warm and delightful sunshine.

He was the only student that had grown so excited when the final exam drew near. He spent most of his free time filling the empty house in the Jiayuan Compound with necessary items for everyday use: sheets, duvet covers, pillows, clothes, toothbrushes, towels, slippers and shampoo. Nothing would be missed.

Luo Qiuling, who thought her son was surely in love, noticed Ye Qin's unusual behavior recently. One day, she found that Ye Qin was packing his Legos and PS4, and was confused. "I thought your schoolmate's going to focus on studying. Wouldn't the game station be a huge distraction?"

Ye Qin didn't lie to his mother about why Cheng Feichi needed to stay in the house. Hearing that the boy was a straight-A student who helped Ye Qin a lot, Luo Qiuling immediately agreed and gave Ye Qin the key. This was why Ye Qin felt a bit guilty now.

"Well...He needs to relax from time to time. All work and no play makes jack a dull boy, right?"

When the empty house was all ready for Cheng Feichi to move in, the final exam also began as expected.

Ye Qin did a good job this time. For once, he ranked higher than 50% of his fellow students. Very proud of himself, he used his fingers to measure the distance between Cheng Feichi's name and his own name on the bulletin board. Now they were only a little more than one meter away from each other. *Very good, next time let's make it less than five spans...nope, maybe less than eight spans.*

The last school ceremony of the semester was held at the recreational yard. The dean on the stage was mightily excited, making a very hearty speech of encouragement, not least exhorting students in Grade 11 to cherish their youth and strive for a brighter future. Class No. 1 and Class No. 2 were standing next to each other. Ye Qin switched his position with the tallest boy in his class, so that he could stand at the end of the line, with Cheng Feichi right by his side, just off the stage having received an award for outstanding performance.

Last month, two students studying liberal arts were caught red handed when they were on a date in the small patch of woods. Since then, the dean of students had been doubling down his efforts to prohibit the existence of puppy love. When the regulations were strictest, a girl and a boy couldn't even walk side by side in the school without being penalized.

Now Ye Qin started to realize the good thing about falling in love with someone of the same sex. Even if he spent all the time in the world with Cheng Feichi in front of everyone, nobody would ever find it strange or weird, not even if they started wearing each other's clothes.

He felt so happy at this thought and pulled the bottom hem of Cheng Feichi's shirt, saying in a low voice, "Hey, how about going to Jia..."

Cheng Feichi seized his hand before he finished the sentence. Ye Qin was a bit flustered. "What are you..."

"Shh—" Cheng Feichi stopped him, looking completely calm. He was still looking forward and didn't even tilt his head, but his grip became even tighter.

A whole crowd of students was right in front of them, and up on the stage was a teacher still absorbed in his declamation.

Cheng Feichi's long and slender fingers were slowly gliding past Ye Qin's palm, into the space between his fingers. Two hollows of the palm, of different temperatures, slowly snuggled up against each other: the ultimate intimacy that could take place between two hands. Ye Qin pressed his lips together so hard; he didn't even dare to breathe. His face immediately and completely blushed as if being soaked in red.

CHAPTER 10

THOUGH they only planned to stay there for a month, Cheng Feichi still brought a lot of stuff to the apartment in the Jiayuan Compound.

...Well, at Ye Qin's request.

"You only packed two outfits? What if it just doesn't stop raining and the clothes won't dry? You should have two more pair of shoes too, so you won't need to go home when you need them...You only got one single towel for everything? Okay, you don't need to go back to picking more up. We'll buy another one at the supermarket."

Ye Qin was sitting in the car, helping Cheng Feichi sort everything out. Overwhelmed by his nagging, Cheng Feichi came upstairs twice more. In the end, his luggage was more than twice as large as before, nearly taking up all the room in the backseat.

It was only when they were driving on the road that a question struck Ye Qin. "Did your mom...ask you anything?"

Cheng Feichi smiled. "What are you afraid of? Of her asking me who I'm going to live with?"

Ye Qin couldn't help but stammer, "No, no, no...of course

not. I mean...you'll be living away from home, she's gonna worry about you, isn't she?"

Before he left the house this morning, he told Luo Qiuling that he wouldn't come back that evening because he needed to stay in the apartment with a schoolmate for two days. Luo Qiuling appeared to be quite agitated, calling the maid to make sure that utilities had all been sorted out, and the air conditioner functioned well. Then she reminded Ye Qin that he should not touch anything in the kitchen and that he should call her at once if anything happened.

Therefore, Ye Qin thought every mother in the world would be exactly like this; loving her son just as much as Luo Qiuling.

Cheng Feichi's smile became a bit stiff, but he managed to keep it so as to not frighten Ye Qin. "It's okay. She wouldn't be worried."

After they had put down the luggage in the house, the two boys went to a nearby supermarket.

The house was furnished with everything they needed, and Luo Qiuling even had the maid make sure that the refrigerator was full of beverages and fruits. They didn't really need to buy any more necessities. Ye Qin therefore spent a lot of money on snacks: an entire cart was not enough for him, and he bought two Want Want gift packs in addition and let Cheng Feichi carry them.

While they were waiting in the line near the cash register, Cheng Feichi inquired whether there was too much food for a single night. Ye Qin blinked his eyes and answered, "These are for you, too."

After a while, he turned back and stared at Cheng Feichi with sad eyes. "You only want me to stay here for one night?"

When they had returned to the apartment to unpack things, Ye Qin placed his towel right by the side of Cheng Feichi's. Their toothbrushes were placed side by side in perfect order as well, their bristles facing the same direction. Ye Qin felt quite satisfied and then left the bathroom to help Cheng Feichi with other things.

Cheng Feichi's luggage was mainly composed of books, where even an exercise book for Grade 11 students was included. Ye Qin was concerned that he might have taken it by mistake, yet Cheng Feichi said, "It wasn't a mistake. I took it here in order to made new exercise sheets for you."

Hearing this, Ye Qin rolled his eyes and dropped onto the bed.

Luo Qiuling bought this apartment because an old class-mate of hers, who was in the real estate industry, had told her some fake news. It was said that the local government would be headquartered in this block in a short time, and therefore the housing market in this neighborhood would soar.

However, two years passed, and the only function of the apartment was giving Ye Jinxiang more material for complaining. Whenever unsatisfied about some totally irrelevant things, he brought up this subject to demonstrate how oblivious a woman could be; stupid and ignorant about real life.

Ye Qin, on the other hand, found the place wonderful. The space was neither too large nor too small, ventilation was great, and the rooms were well lit up by sunlight during the day. Prob-ably because there were fewer cars and people here, the air in the district seemed to be much cooler and cleaner than that in the downtown, while the summer temperature was also lower.

—If only there could be fewer rooms! Ye Qin couldn't find a legitimate reason to sleep in the same room with Cheng Feichi. Having dined and bathed, Ye Qin moved very slowly towards the bedroom next to Cheng Feichi's room.

He kept looking back at Cheng Feichi along the way. "When are you supposed to go to that school tomorrow? Don't forget to wake me up."

"What for?"

"I want to have breakfast with you."

Cheng Feichi knew what a sleepy head he was. "Can you wake up so early?"

"Sure, why not?" Ye Qin instructed him, "If I don't, just put a piece of chocolate on my pillow. You know, the kind of chocolate that I bought yesterday. I'll wake up as soon as I smell it. It always works."

Cheng Feichi walked with Ye Qin to the latter's bedroom and said yes a thousand times before Ye Qin finally stopped nagging him and entered the room.

Cheng Feichi got back to his room too. He put the two empty luggage bags into the wardrobe, and then took out the glass jar which he had been trying to hide for the whole day. He didn't know why he didn't want Ye Qin to see it. Probably he was just a little shy.

Right at this moment, the door was suddenly pushed open and Ye Qin was looking in from the outside. "Right, don't forget to unpack the chocolate, otherwise I won't..."

It was too late. Cheng Feichi desperately tried to hide it behind him, but his efforts were in vain.

Ye Qin knew too well the things that he had made with his own hands. Even the fraction of a second was long enough to recognize what Cheng Feichi was trying to hide from him. The unfinished sentence was no longer important. He looked around, and the grin that could not be contained blossomed on his face.

"Well, now I've begun to realize, something's indeed missing here, isn't it?"

Ye Qin finally got what he wanted. The next morning, the two of them had breakfast together.

Yesterday they had bought convenient scallion pancake from the supermarket. Seeing that the kitchen was filled with all possible ingredients, Cheng Feichi stopped Ye Qin from putting the pancakes into the microwave oven. He poured some oil into the pan. When the oil was sufficiently heated, he put a pancake into the pan, chopped some Frankfurt sausages as well as tomatoes, and sprinkled them on the pancake. For the last step, he squeezed some salad dressing on it before flipping it in the pan. The finished pancake came out with perfectly crispy crust.

Ye Qin ate the pancake along with milk and felt extremely satisfied. All the drowsiness shaken off along the way, he felt spirited just as Popeye the Sailor after a can of spinach. He offered to wash the dishes and there was even energy left for two exam papers.

Cheng Feichi finished his own pancake and was ready to leave. Ye Qin followed him to the gate and asked him when he would return home at noon and when the classes would end in the afternoon.

"I'll just have the lunch in the school cafeteria," Cheng Feichi answered. "Put the finished papers on the desk, and then just follow your own agenda. I'll check your work in the evening."

What agenda would Ye Qin have for himself? In order to be with Cheng Feichi, he had given up the overseas field trip. Zhou Feng and the other boys were probably already on the plane now.

With the papers half finished, Ye Qin got up from the sofa and stretched. He went to the supermarket again.

He bought the instant noodles that Cheng Feichi forbade him to buy yesterday, and then he bought an egg pancake on the way home. He ate the pancake, lamenting that its flavor was far less satisfying than the one that Cheng Feichi had made for him.

When he got home, he was suddenly reminded of the two boxes of ice cream bought on the same trip to the supermarket. He took them out, disappointed to see that they had already melted. His only choice was to store them in the refrigerator, keeping telling himself that there would be no difference in flavor after it froze again.

Technically speaking, this was the first time that he ever lived away from home. Living with his friends didn't count, for they always had some people take care of them. Now he had to do a lot of things by himself; he needed some time to adjust.

He slept for a while in the afternoon and played the PS4 for some time. When he was bored, he went to Cheng Feichi's bedroom, collected the clothes he had worn yesterday and put them into the washing machine along with his own dirty clothes.

He studied the machine for a long time before he finally got it started. But when the program was finished, water was still dripping from the clothes, which were supposed to have been spin-dried. The fabrics felt slippery, as there was much washing powder left as well.

Too ashamed to bother his mother with such a trivial thing, Ye Qin called Sun Yiran, the only female friend he had. Hearing that Ye Qin was doing laundry on his own, Sun Yiran grew so astonished that she even proposed to film a documentary for him in order to record this moment forever.

Ye Qin was so annoyed that he hung up the phone. Then he took a photo of all the buttons on the control panel and sent it to Sun Yiran.

Finally, the girl began to offer him actual solutions, reminding him to rinse the clothes at least twice, and that he should choose the right length of time to spin them dry. Yet in the end, she was overcome with curiosity, asking, "Why are you suddenly doing your own laundry today?"

So annoyed by this damn washing machine, Ye Qin kicked it before typing the answer, "There's no laundry stores nearby."

Sun Yiran asked, "Where are you?"

"Jiayuan Compound."

Ten minutes later, the machine started working normally. This is when Sun Yiran continued, "That's very close to High School No. 13, isn't it?"

Ye Qin didn't see what the problem was. "Yeah."

Ye Qin saw from the top of the chat box that Sun Yiran was typing, but it was already past 5 o'clock in the afternoon! He immediately sent, "Gotta do my homework now. CUL8R" before tossing the cellphone aside and got back onto the sofa to continue to work on his exam paper.

Cheng Feichi returned at around 7 o'clock. The door opened for him before he could turn the key to open it.

Standing behind the door, Ye Qin was holding a strainer in his hand and a pair of chopsticks in his mouth while slurring his words, "Wait a moment. Dinner will be ready soon."

Then he returned to the kitchen. The stock pot was half full of instant noodles and water that had been boiled for god knows how many times and was still boiling. Ye Qin was trying to crack some eggs into the pot but was almost burned by the water splash.

Cheng Feichi turned off the stove for him and then let cold water run over his hand until he was sure that the scalding wouldn't leave a scar on Ye Qin's hand. He asked, "Didn't I tell you not to touch anything in the kitchen?"

That Ye Qin possessed no life skills wasn't a great piece of news.

Ye Qin himself, however, wasn't ashamed of the fact at all. He wiped his hands clean and stated proudly, "I'm making dinner."

Cheng Feichi took a look at the mess of noodles in the pot. He chose to answer honestly. "I've had dinner."

Before he moved in, he made an oral contract with Ye Qin about the rent. Ye Qin hadn't wanted to charge him anything. At Cheng Feichi's insistence, he asked for 50% of the normal rent in this neighborhood. He said that this discount was necessary, considering that Cheng Feichi was his boyfriend: any more rent would be the price held for ordinary schoolmates. This was how he finally made Cheng Feichi accept the offer.

Cheng Feichi had thought that Ye Qin was not serious about "living together." He thought that the best Ye Qin could do was to show up in this house once or twice, because the living condition here could be described as "horrible" for someone as well-protected and hard-to-please as Ye Qin. There was nothing for entertainment and no restaurant in this neighborhood. The only company Ye Qin could have was a bunch of exam papers. How could he ever bear a boring life like this? Therefore, he didn't plan to dine at home in the first place. He had been waiting in the classroom for a while, reading, until there were fewer people in the school cafeteria. There he had some noodles before returning home.

He didn't expect Ye Qin to be still at home. More surprisingly, he was even making dinner for him.

Ye Qin blinked. "You had dinner in the school cafeteria?"

Cheng Feichi nodded.

Ye Qin turned to look at the pot as well. He took the chopsticks from his mouth and put them down on the table. After a couple of seconds, he dragged out a response. "Oh..."

He seemed so sad, yet extremely lovely, with his head hanging low. Cheng Feichi suddenly felt sorry about it. He picked up the chopsticks and stirred the noodles in the pot. "But I'm still a bit hungry. I could really use an extra meal."

After they had finished the noodles together, Ye Qin led Cheng Feichi to the balcony to show him the clothes he had washed.

Cheng Feichi didn't say anything, silently adjusting the way a pair of trousers were hanged. When he saw two pairs of underpants fluttering in the night wind, he cleared his throat and said a bit awkwardly, "Emm...I'll wash my own clothes from now on."

"What's the big deal?" Ye Qin didn't understand why Cheng Feichi was embarrassed and pointed to the washing machine. "It did all the work. All I did was put our clothes in it and press some buttons. It's really nothing."

When he fetched the exam papers for Cheng Feichi, an idea suddenly crossed his mind. "Jeez...Are you annoyed because I didn't ask for permission before entering your bedroom?"

Cheng Feichi was about to deny it when Ye Qin held up his hands and yelled, "I promise that I just collected your dirty clothes. I didn't touch anything else!"

Cheng Feichi didn't know how to reply. He was the one that was defeated by Ye Qin's innocence.

For two boys with totally different family backgrounds and daily habits, living together wasn't easy. Nearly every hour there could be some sort of conflict escalating.

Most of these unpleasant squabbles could be solved pretty fast as long as they both tried to stand in the other person's shoes and deduce the reasons behind the other person's behavior. A few other embarrassing things, however, didn't have such an easy way out. Neither of them had the courage to bring them up or even to ask. They could only keep guessing, wondering, and suffering.

A typical example was that Cheng Feichi couldn't figure out why Ye Qin was unwilling to return to his own bedroom again. The latter would rather struggle to recite another English passage

than go to his own bed. While trying to memorize the sentences, Ye Qin kept picking at his hangnails until they became a disaster as well—yet he just didn't want to leave.

The hour hand pointed to the number 11, and Ye Qin was already so drowsy that he could hardly sit up straight; his head knocked the desk multiple times, his forehead reddening consequently. Not knowing what to do with such a stubborn kid, Cheng Feichi could only lift him up under his armpits like a baby and take him to the other bedroom.

Once Ye Qin lay on the bed, his eyelids became so heavy that he could hardly open them, but his hands were still clutching Cheng Feichi's collar. He didn't want him to leave.

Cheng Feichi thought for a while and then leaned down to give Ye Qin a very soft, gentle kiss on his lips.

Ye Qin's bright, dark eyes immediately opened and widened. He bit his lips, and the outer corners of his eyes reddened. Angry out of embarrassment, he pushed Cheng Feichi's face away. "Who told you that I want a goodnight kiss?"

So this was called "goodnight kiss." Cheng Feichi made a mental note.

From now on, Cheng Feichi had another "research project" to work on—that is, to understand Ye Qin as much as possible so that he wouldn't be pouting in a sulky way all the time.

He found that all the simple and rational equations that he was used to, all the rules that had told him one's devotion equaled his harvest, didn't work here. Because this wonderful boy deserved to be treated in the best and most careful way.

After two days' research, Cheng Feichi reaffirmed his conclusion: formulations didn't work in romantic relationships.

He was ready to experiment on the new term more frequently, only to find that Ye Qin had driven home already and wouldn't return anytime soon.

On Friday evening, Ye Qin came back, but he still seemed quite annoyed. After a shower, he shut himself in his own bedroom, the sound effects of his video games piercing.

Cheng Feichi had finished two more math problems, without reaching the reason why Ye Qin was so angry at him. All he knew was that Ye Qin wasn't completely disappointed with him, for at least he was willing to come back to this house.

He knocked on Ye Qin's door. "I made some warm milk for you. Drink it and don't stay up too late, would you?"

The noises from Ye Qin's room became even crazier. Cheng Feichi could almost feel the floor shaking.

He put the glass of milk down on the dresser next to Ye Qin's door and sent him a WeChat message as a reminder.

When he had just returned to his own bedroom, the lights suddenly went out. The whole house was in complete darkness.

The game noises suddenly stopped. Cheng Feichi heard a series of rattling sounds, and then Ye Qin's door opened. Immediately afterwards there was a crisp, crunching sound of glass hitting the floor, scaring Ye Qin into wailing, "Ahhh! What happened?"

Cheng Feichi held on to the wall and walked towards Ye Qin. "Did you break the glass?"

Ye Qin gasped. "Eww! Why is the floor wet?"

Cheng Feichi knew that his guess was right. He approached Ye Qin, while his eyes gradually adjusted to the darkness. He managed to take Ye Qin's by his arm and took him to the sofa in the living room.

"Sit here. I'll go check the fuse."

Ye Qin didn't even know that people were supposed to check such things when there was a blackout, so he sat there quietly. He took out the cellphone to light up the room. Seeing Cheng Feichi's

earlier message, he could not sit anymore. Carefully he stood up, one hand resting on the handle of the sofa. Following the sounds Cheng Feichi was making, he walked towards the kitchen.

Using the flashlight on his phone, he glanced at the other buildings through the window, and found complete darkness outside as well. He directed the light at Cheng Feichi's hands and said worriedly, "It seems we're having a general blackout. There's no lighting outside...Why is this happening so often?"

Cheng Feichi tried to turn the breaker, but his efforts were in vain. He closed the switch box and started walking toward outside. "You stay here. Let me clean the shards up first."

Ye Qin quickly snatched the hem of Cheng Feichi's shirt, saying in a tiny voice, "I'll go with you."

When Cheng Feichi was picking up the glass shards, the sharp corners of the glass reflected a blinding light. Startled, Ye Qin tugged at Cheng Feichi's sleeves, not daring to look.

"Leave them be. You can do it after the power's back on."

Cheng Feichi patted the back of Ye Qin's hands as a gesture of comfort. "It's okay. It's almost done."

After the shards were cleared, Cheng Feichi swept the floor again to make sure that no shattered glass was still on it. Ye Qin held the flashlight for him. It was not until now that Ye Qin realized why Cheng Feichi was so anxious.

They sat back on the sofa. Cheng Feichi bent down to check Ye Qin's feet. "Let me see."

Ye Qin was not hurt. The milk wasn't boiling hot, and Ye Qin didn't wear socks. The milk that had spilled on his feet had already disappeared into the warm summer night. The only thing that needed to be taken care of was Ye Qin's slippers, which had gotten wet because of the milk.

Cheng Feichi touched Ye Qin's instep. Ye Qin shrank back with a tremor. "Stop! That tickles..."

There were no more slippers available. Cheng Feichi washed a towel and fetched a pair of sneakers. He squatted down by Ye Qin's feet and wiped his feet very carefully before helping him put on the sneakers.

The feeling of having his feet held was weird to Ye Qin. He moved his toes and felt his ankles and knees somehow stiff.

"Still ticklish?" Cheng Feichi raised his head to ask, hurrying up on the task at hand.

Ye Qin shook his head and stretched his neck to look at his shoes. "Why did you choose those? Shoelaces are such a headache."

Cheng Feichi smiled. A streak of light cast a shadow over his face, which slightly rose and fell as he breathed. "It's okay. I got you."

He then made a beautiful bow-knot with a deft motion of his nimble fingers.

At this time of this year, an air-conditioned house was indispensable for survival. Half an hour after the blackout, the temperature inside was already unbearable.

Complaining about the heat, Ye Qin kept drinking iced beverages from the fridge, one bottle after another. Cheng Feichi, afraid that he might have diarrhea afterwards, forced the refrigerator door closed to prevent Ye Qin from getting another bottle of drink.

Ye Qin puffed his cheeks out, crying, "It's so damn hot, and you don't even let me have a drink! I want it! I gotta have it!"

"Sit still and you'll be just fine." Cheng Feichi was acting very much like a stern parent right now; one who would not let Ye Qin rebel against his order.

How on earth could Ye Qin sit still? The room was completely dark. The television wasn't working. His cellphone's bat-

tery was dying. The heat was drowning and suffocating him like invisible hands. He could no longer breathe; he was about to die from a shortage of oxygen.

Seeing that Cheng Feichi didn't allow him any more cold drinks, Ye Qin begged Cheng Feichi to go outside with him. Cheng Feichi was amused by—but also slightly annoyed by—his sudden change of attitude. "You're not angry now?"

Ye Qin suddenly didn't know how to respond. He'd forgotten why he was even angry.

...Why was he angry just now?

Walking on their way to the parking lot, Ye Qin was still bothered by the question. Maybe he was becoming dumb because of Luo Qiuling's constant nagging. Anyway, there was no way that he was going to tell her about the blackout.

After making a great effort to walk down through all the stairs from the 19th floor to the 1st floor, Ye Qin was exhausted and gasping. He drifted towards the parking lot; the whole place was completely in darkness as well. Ye Qin turned around to look for his own car, but in vain. A security guy in a patrol car approached them from afar, telling them to leave right away, since it was dangerous to move his car during a blackout.

It was devastating for Ye Qin. Walking out of the underground parking lot, he raised his head to look at where the 19th floor was, unable to imagine how he could climb all the stairs back there if the power just wouldn't come back tonight.

A lot of residents were enjoying the coolness in the yard. A few middle-aged men and women were even doing public square dancing under an overly bright LED light. Ye Qin sat there and watched them for a while. Suddenly he was not so annoyed at the heat, so he pushed Cheng Feichi's hands away, which had been waving a book to fan him.

"I don't feel hot now. Fan yourself."

A madame in a floral dress sitting next to them asked, "You two are brothers? Which building do you live in? Your faces don't look familiar."

Ye Qin barely managed not to roll his eyes hearing the word "brothers," while Cheng Feichi answered very politely, "The 10th building. We're new here."

The madame smiled. "I knew it! The residents here are all seniors. I hardly ever see anyone as young as you. You're still students, huh?"

"Yes. We'll soon be in the last year of high school."

"You two are the same age? So not biological brothers?"

"No."

The madame examined the two and finally rested her gaze upon Ye Qin. "Oh, you look so young. I thought your friend was quite some years older than you."

Sitting in the same place soon bored them, so they left for a walk. Yet the madame's words were still lingering in Ye Qin's mind.

"Do I really look that young? She said that I didn't seem to be in the 12th grade. Was she suggesting that I look like a junior high student?"

His question very much amused Cheng Feichi. The latter soon regained his calmness and put on a straight face. "It's not that you're too young. It's me, I look much older than my real age. Therefore, you look young when I'm with you."

"Who told you that you look old?" Ye Qin's eyes bulged. "A tall guy just has to be older than everyone? Nonsense! I can also say that they're short because they clearly have a poor diet! Tell me who said that. I need to sort things out with them."

Having succeeded in distracting Ye Qin's attention from the madame's meaningless comment, Cheng Feichi held Ye Qin's clutched hand. "It's okay as long as you don't think it's a problem."

Under the cover of an unlit night, they had the privilege of holding hands in public. It took less than fifteen minutes for Ye Qin to turn from bashful to bold. Even when a building attendant approached them, he didn't let go of Cheng Feichi's hand. Confident that their holding hands won't be seen, he even shook their arms while asking when the power would be back on.

"Very soon. Go home now. It's not safe to walk in the dark." The attendant glanced at his own cellphone. "The electric company said 9 p.m."

So, they went back home, hand in hand. Since the buildings looked very similar in the dark, they got on the wrong track twice. When they finally reached the 10th building, the residents were already queueing up in front of the elevator door.

Ye Qin waited for a while, but soon he had enough. It occurred to him that the ice cream he had bought last time was still in the refrigerator, so he proposed on a whim, "How about climbing the stairs?"

When it came to trivial things as such, Cheng Feichi never minded following Ye Qin's orders. This was why he let Ye Qin drag him to the staircase, even though the idea sounded not realistic at all.

The existence of staircases in high-rise buildings is hardly ever acknowledged, for they are hardly ever used. The stairs were covered with dust, without any windows or other equipment for ventilation. Walking here from a well-lit hall was like sneaking into a secret passage where the lowest sound would be greatly magnified—footsteps turned into thunder and breaths sounded like blowing storm.

Ye Qin found it very exciting. No longer bothered by the heat, he climbed the stairs very fast as if he were a wild monkey and kept urging Cheng Feichi to go faster.

Afraid that Ye Qin might trip over his own feet, Cheng Feichi turned on the flashlight in his cellphone. Yet Ye Qin turned around and pressed a finger to the camera. "Turn it off! Let's just walk in the dark. This is super fun!"

Unable to talk him out of it, Cheng Feichi walked behind, neither too far nor too close, in case anything should happen.

Between every two floors there were 21 steps. Nineteen levels are equal to 399 steps. Just as Cheng Feichi had predicted, Ye Qin wanted to quit before finishing a quarter of the steps.

He was panting, his hands resting on his waist. "How could this be more demanding than going downstairs?"

Cheng Feichi answered, "Because gravity pulls you downward. When you go downstairs, you are going along with gravity; when you go upstairs, you do negative work. This is why climbing up is more difficult than descending the stairs."

Ye Qin put one foot on the next step, but he could no longer climb it. He rolled his eyes and complained, still out of breath, "Now I...I want...my...boyfriend, not...not a...a teacher."

Having rested for five minutes, they resumed climbing for thirty seconds. Ye Qin thought they were near the end of the journey and refused to believe it when Cheng Feichi said it was only the 9th floor. Skeptical, he looked out of the enclosed stairway to check the floor number on the elevator door, hand still resting on the wall, only to admit that Cheng Feichi was right.

"How about we go out and wait for the elevator?" Cheng Feichi suggested.

Devoid of any strength, Ye Qin only felt dizzy. He waved his hand wearily. "A better idea would be, you go downstairs. When the power's on, call 120 and have them send an emergency stretcher here to carry me upstairs."

Cheng Feichi didn't say yes. Instead, he squatted down in

front of Ye Qin. "Come on."

Ye Qin was taken aback. "Why?"

"Your boyfriend's carrying you."

Ye Qin had always used the word "boyfriend," but when it came from Cheng Feichi, it felt like a sudden clap of thunder.

"No." Despite his naivety, Ye Qin knew how hard it was to climb stairs with a heavy burden. He clenched his teeth. "Just let me sit for a while, then I can go on."

"I can handle your weight." Cheng Feichi didn't change his position, slightly tilting his head. "Just consider me a stretcher."

Ye Qin didn't ever remember being carried in his life.

Luo Qiuling wasn't strong enough to do it. After Ye Qin was enrolled in elementary school, she could no longer hold him up. The only thing she could do was bend down to give the little one a hug when he returned home from school. Ye Jinxiang, on the other hand, was busy with his business all the time. He was hardly home and when he was, he always gave Ye Qin a long face, especially after reading Ye Qin's transcript. How would he ever have the patience to be nice?

Thus Ye Qin felt a bit nervous on Cheng Feichi's back, not knowing where to put his hands. He loosely held Cheng Feichi's shoulders, but the warmth of Cheng Feichi's body—even under the cover of a T-shirt—was unbearable.

Cheng Feichi seemed to have sensed his anxiety, his hands holding Ye Qin's thighs, lifting him up just a little bit higher. "Hold me tight. Don't let go."

Ye Qin immediately circled his arms around Cheng Feichi's neck and clamped his legs tightly, looking like a koala afraid of falling from a tree.

They climbed two floors. Cheng Feichi's steady footsteps pacified Ye Qin, who finally caught his breath and began to talk normally. He wanted to know whether Cheng Feichi was tired and needed a rest, but when he opened his mouth, he heard himself ask, "Why are you so good at carrying people? Have you done this for many others?"

Ye Qin still couldn't forget that Cheng Feichi had been Prince Charming to so many people. A deep sense of insecurity loomed in his heart.

Cheng Feichi walked at a very steady pace and breathed evenly. He looked more than ready for the task. He answered while walking, "Other than my mom, I also carried the elderly man living downstairs. There were a few days when he had difficulties moving around, and no one in his family was here. So, I helped him out."

He gave a very clear and flawless explanation, leaving no room for Ye Qin to find fault. Ye Qin pursed his lips, mumbling, "Well then...thank you for helping me out."

"You don't need to say thank you to me," Cheng Feichi answered, "for this is what I should do for you. It's not about helping you."

It took Ye Qin a long while to realize that by saying this, Cheng Feichi was regarding him as a family member as important as his own mother. It stirred quite mixed feelings in his heart—he thought it was sweet, but at the same time, he felt somehow sad.

He still didn't understand why he was sad. He just knew that he wanted to give Cheng Feichi something; no matter what that was, he couldn't wait.

Ye Qin kicked his leg. "Hey, you still didn't tell me what you want me to call you."

"Anything other than 'hey' is fine."

"What is fine, exactly?" Ye Qin gave another kick. "You didn't like to be called by your name or 'Mr. Cheng.' You really think I didn't notice?"

Indeed, I didn't realize that you were so perceptive. Cheng Feichi smiled and gave a rather indirect answer. "I think...what that madame said just now was great."

Ye Qin climbed the last five floors himself. Ten floors amounted to such a long height that he was afraid that Cheng Feichi would get hurt for carrying him for too long. If so, he would have no one to help him out if the same thing happened again next time.

When they finally reached home and opened the door, the lights inside and outside of their home suddenly lit up. They looked at each other and grinned simultaneously, their foreheads covered with sweat.

After a bath, Ye Qin lay on his stomach on Cheng Feichi's bed, dealing with the exam papers made for him. Though absent for the past two and a half days, Cheng Feichi wouldn't let him skip the assignment. The number of exercises saved was even larger than usual. Ye Qin kept scratching his head and moving around to activate his brain as the problems proved too difficult for him—he even went to the kitchen to grab a box of ice cream.

Although the ice cream didn't look good as good as before it melted, Ye Qin ate it with a spoon. A few moments later he started to feed Cheng Feichi: a spoonful for Cheng Feichi, a spoonful for himself.

Mr. Cheng could be a serious tutor, but he did care about his student. Given that Ye Qin was really exhausted today, he agreed that the second half of the paper could be left for tomorrow.

Ye Qin jumped from the bed, thinking that he had succeeded in "bribing" Cheng Feichi with the ice cream. He ran to the kitchen to heat up a glass of milk for Cheng Feichi and brought it to him. He explained that since the only other one was broken, they had to drink from the same cup.

Not knowing anything about Ye Qin's tricks, Cheng Feichi finished his share and urged Ye Qin to go to bed. Ye Qin didn't want to leave, but he just couldn't say his real need out loud. He stomped his feet, and then hurried to his own bedroom. He returned with his pillow and put it on Cheng Feichi's bed, before jumping on it and lying down.

He had a very good excuse, too. "I'm afraid of the dark. What it the power's cut off again?"

Cheng Feichi didn't realize what Ye Qin meant to do until he lay down next to Ye Qin. *He thinks that we can't be counted as "living together" if we've never slept in the same bed?*

It had been years since Ye Qin shared a bed with someone. Naturally, he was too excited to fall asleep. He also felt weirdly nervous. Having tossed and turned for a while, he turned aside and poked Cheng Feichi at his shoulder, asking in drawn out voice, "Are—you—still—awake?"

Cheng Feichi was used to sleeping on his right shoulder. Feeling Ye Qin's prodding, he tried to turn his head back, but Ye Qin immediately stopped him, his finger point pressing Cheng Feichi's lower back. "Don't move."

Cheng Feichi stopped moving.

Ye Qin licked his lips and opened his mouth. Then he closed it. He repeated it a few times but couldn't say anything. For the past seventeen years he had never faced such a dilemma. He had been preparing himself for it when they were still climbing the stairs, but now several hours had passed and he still couldn't say it.

Cheng Feichi asked without turning around, "What?"

Ye Qin covered the lower half of his face with the blanket and mumbled a few words. Cheng Feichi didn't catch it clearly, so he asked, "What is it?"

This is it. Ye Qin thought to himself and made the decision. He flipped over the blanket and said it very quickly, "Good night, gege."

Then he covered his head with the blanket, pretending that he was going to sleep, but Cheng Feichi turned around even faster. Before Ye Qin could hide himself altogether, Cheng Feichi seized his hands.

Ye Qin could not hide from it anymore. Seeing that Cheng Feichi was staring at him, his face burned so hot that he couldn't take it anymore. He closed his eyes in embarrassment. "I'm gonna sleep now. What are you—"

The rest of the sentence was muted by a sudden kiss.

Cheng Feichi's kisses were all long and soft, like a gentle breeze or a thin drizzle. He always stopped after reaching Ye Qin's teeth and never invaded the world behind them. It seemed that he was being a gentleman, good at controlling his own desires, but only Ye Qin knew what power these kisses could truly command.

After a long kiss, Ye Qin was basically a drowning man. He couldn't breathe normally even by using his mouth and nose at the same time. He leaned against Cheng Feichi's chest, panting, feeling even more exhausted than he had after climbing nineteen floors.

Since Ye Qin was afraid of the dark, the bedside lamp was still on. Cheng Feichi could see his reddened face and his watery eyes clearly. His eyelashes were slightly shaking as he breathed, decorated by tiny water drops.

It again reminded Cheng Feichi of a cat. When Ye Qin was annoyed, he acted like an angry cat, yet when he behaved himself, he was as cute as a cat too.

He ruffled Ye Qin's soft and fluffy hair. "Good night, Xiao-Ruan."

In the past, summer vacation equaled "staycation" to Ye Qin.

If he was not at home all day long, he must be staying in a hotel room inside a holiday village, or he stayed in the Liu family's club. When he was out for entertainment, he visited places like malls or cinemas only. To sum up, it was nearly impossible to get him moving. Zhou Feng had always said that his pale skin was a result of staying indoors all the time.

The only thing different this summer vacation was that he spent the staycation elsewhere. For each week, he spent two days at home and the rest of it in the apartment in Jiayuan Compound.

He seldom left the house, but when he did, even just for the nearby supermarket, he complained about the sunshine. But he was not willing to use a UV umbrella or apply some sunscreen. There was one afternoon when he didn't want to have snacks and went out to buy a pancake instead. It took him twenty minutes in the queue. His belly full, his thoughts started wandering: he wanted to get an internet plan for the apartment. He asked for directions and walked many streets under this sun, before finally reaching his destination.

In the end, Wi-Fi became available in the apartment, but Ye Qin got sunburned as well. Appalling reddish rashes appeared on all skin that was exposed to the sun. In the evening, the burned skin got itchy and painful, which prevented him from falling asleep. Cheng Feichi wiped his skin with a cool and moist towel several times before the suffering turned bearable. Even asleep, he was still holding Cheng Feichi's arm and mumbling in pain.

Since then, Cheng Feichi wouldn't let Ye Qin leave the apartment to hunt for lunch anymore. As long as Ye Qin stayed in the apartment, Cheng Feichi would get enough groceries after school. After dinner, he cooked Ye Qing's lunch for the coming day, leaving instructions about how each dish should be heated up. At lunchtime he would check whether Ye Qin had followed his orders, asking him to send pictures, one of the dished heated up before the meal, one after.

Now Ye Qin really regretted forcing Cheng Feichi to buy a

new cellphone and asking him to install WeChat. How could he know that it would be used "against" him like this?

But it was not bad to have a decent meal for lunch instead of random snacks. Freshly prepared meals tasted certainly so much better than puffed food. Ye Qin, who was used to being taken good care of by everyone, was more than willing to have someone cook for him wherever he was.

Even though the price he had to pay was completing some exam papers.

To prepare for the Olympiad training here, Cheng Feichi had stopped doing part-time jobs other than tutoring. He was already an expert at time management; now that he had more spare time than before, he took greater efforts in making sure that Ye Qin studied every day.

Sometimes they would play games together, too.

Ye Qin had an axe to grind: sure, Cheng Feichi was a straight-A student, but that didn't mean he was gifted at playing games as well, did it? *I've been a strong player for so many years, how can he be as experienced as me? I would be a fool not trying to take advantage of him under the circumstances.*

Just as he expected, for the first a few rounds, Cheng Feichi was far from as good as him. Ye Qin won many bags of chips, gummies, and boxes of ice cream. He tore the packages open and stacked them on the table, picking them up as he wished, showing off in front of Cheng Feichi.

But as they went for more rounds, things became different. Having familiarized himself with the handling of the controller, Cheng Feichi transformed himself into a super player, achieving higher and higher scores in each round. The boss in the "hard" mode was just another piece of cake. Every minute he was breaking Ye Qin's records, which knocked Ye Qin for a loop.

He thought Cheng Feichi was just getting lucky, so he tried for a few more rounds, only to owe more and more English passages to recite—and having to call Cheng Feichi "gege" numerous times.

As a result, when Zhou Feng, currently in the U.S., called him and asked about his lunch, Ye Qin answered without thinking, "My gege made lunch for me."

Zhou Feng remained silent for a while before replying, "I didn't know that a straight-A student would be so kinky."

Ye Qin was so angry that he hung up on the spot.

In less than an hour, he redialed Zhou Feng's number to show off the Lego combination machine that Cheng Feichi had made for him. He introduced proudly to Zhou Feng the linkage, the crank-rocker mechanism, the pulleys and gears, as well as how a simple push could make the whole thing function magically.

Zhou Feng was stunned. He had started playing with Lego at age four, yet making a Gundam with the help of a design drawing was still the best he could do. When Ye Qin started to look at his face, however, he turned up his nose and said that Yuanyuan could make the same thing as well.

The next moment he woke up Liao Yifang, who had already been asleep for a while, and showed him the video from Ye Qin. "Yuanyuan, I wanna make this."

Liao Yifang groped for his glasses in bewilderment and stared at the cellphone screen for a while, before giving an answer with hesitation, "Well...shall we start from middle school physics?"

Ye Qin burst out laughing and could barely hold his cellphone. Zhou Feng refused to admit it. "Cheng Feichi is using this to teach you something, not to let you show it off. You're no better than me."

Ye Qin shrugged. He didn't care even if Cheng Feichi was

really trying to teach him middle school physics in this way. It was so much better than crawling through middle school physics textbooks.

A life dotted with a moderate number of little surprises was so much more comfortable than a decadent life without any purpose.

Before Ye Qin could realize it, he was already getting accustomed to receiving new exam papers every Monday, Wednesday and Friday, eating the slightly spicy food coming from Cheng Feichi, waking up every morning with Cheng Feichi by his side, and hearing the sweet "good night" Cheng Feichi said to him each night.

He didn't know that he was already drowning in this game. At the end of July, he spent half of the afternoon working out a draft in his mind, trying to force Cheng Feichi to agree to continue living here for the next month, so that the affection between them could grow to a high level as soon as possible, described by Liu Yangfan as the level where "the sky itself will fall when you break up."

Yet Cheng Feichi called him in the afternoon. "My mom fell ill. I had to go to the hospital. Start dinner without me."

Ye Qin made a bowl of instant noodles for himself and sent the picture to Cheng Feichi, feeling dispirited. Half an hour later, he received no reply. Beginning to get worried, he got changed and was ready to leave the apartment.

When he reached the front door, he couldn't justify his own behavior. *Cheng Feichi's mother is sick—why should I go there? To cause more trouble?*

What's worse, that woman is Ye Jinxiang's mistress.

Ye Qin got rid of his sneakers and returned to his bedroom. He lay down on the bed after taking a shower, suddenly finding the king-size bed so empty. Tossing and turning for a long time, he didn't fall asleep until after midnight.

Half an hour past one, Cheng Feichi had finally helped his mother settle down in the hospital. He then checked his cellphone and saw the picture Ye Qin sent him.

He enlarged the photo and immediately frowned at what he was looking at. Recently Ye Qin had taken up the habit of adding a cute sticker to every photo that he took. This time the sticker was an arrogant cartoon figure making faces, as if parading in Cheng Feichi's face, reminding him that he could do nothing when Ye Qin had instant noodles at hand.

Yes, indeed, there was nothing he could do. He knew that his strength was limited; he was not capable enough to get most things under control. He couldn't even take good care of the people surrounding him, let alone take control of his own life.

Cheng Xin was found by the neighbors on the stairway. She collapsed when she returned from the supermarket. The neighbors said that she was lucky to fall down on the landing. If she had fallen down the steps, she would be much more seriously hurt.

On his way to the hospital, Cheng Feichi withdrew some money from his account. With that money, he paid the neighbors back for the medical charges, but the rest of the money was merely enough to cover the various checkups and hospitalization expenses. Cheng Xin had postpartum bleeding when she was giving birth to Cheng Feichi and had been suffering from Sheehan syndrome ever since. She took various kinds of expensive hormonal extracts, which was the main reason they had been living from paycheck to paycheck.

The syndrome wasn't something that she could easily get rid of, and it was a major factor that caused this incident. Cheng Feichi counted the money left on him and decided to withdraw the fixed term deposit before its time was due. After all, the money was saved for unexpected needs.

Only the emergency room was open at night, so the more thorough medical examinations would have to wait until tomorrow. Mrs. Feng left just after midnight, but hearing that Cheng Feichi had to attend classes tomorrow, she promised to come back early in the morning.

Cheng Feichi didn't want to trouble others, but now he had no alternatives. The courses for the last few days were especially important, and he had to attend the mock test too. He needed this test to know exactly how good he was. When it came to his future, he could never take it seriously enough.

The hospital wouldn't be in silence even deep into the night. Patients and their families freshly arriving at the emergency room made considerable noise. A drunk young man who had fallen from the stairs and consequently broken his leg was lying on a makeshift bed in the hallway. He had been howling in agony for over an hour, making it impossible for people in the room to sleep—except Cheng Xin, who was in a coma.

Cheng Feichi had come here straight from school. Now that he had nothing better to do, he took out textbooks and started studying. Midway through reading, he checked Cheng Xin's body temperature twice and moisturized her dry lips with drinking water.

Lying in the bed next to Cheng Xin was an elderly lady with diabetes. She looked at Cheng Feichi, full of contentment. "Good boy. Your mom's in the hospital, but why are you the only one here?"

Cheng Feichi did not like sharing his family issues with outsiders. "Tomorrow my aunt will be here."

The elderly woman didn't mind his coolness. She handed a clean apple to him, smiling. "It'll be a long night. An apple will perk you up."

The next morning, Mrs. Feng returned. Cheng Feichi told her all the dos and don'ts, and then hurried to High School No. 13.

When he arrived, he came to Jiayuan Compound first. The door of the main bedroom was still closed. Ye Qin was still sleeping. Cheng Feichi only had the time to heat up baozi and milk. Breakfast in the kitchen, he crept over to the bedroom without any noise, slightly pulled the blanket so as to reveal Ye Qin's head, and kissed him gently on the forehead.

In the middle of the day, Cheng Feichi, unsurprised, received a long trail of messages from Ye Qin, filled with angry emojis of a wide variety, as well as exclamation marks. He was questioning why Cheng Feichi didn't wake him up.

Cheng Feichi called Mrs. Feng, making sure that Cheng Xin had woken up, was fully conscious, and done all the necessary checkups before he went to the dining hall. He replied to Ye Qin on the way, "I want you to get more sleep. Don't have snacks and instant noodles for lunch. I'll make dinner for you tonight."

Ye Qin sent a sad message back, "I won't eat anything until you're back."

Cheng Feichi sighed. "Don't starve yourself. Just be a good boy and have lunch without me, okay?"

Ye Qin didn't challenge him again this time. He replied with "okay" and asked about his mother.

Cheng Feichi didn't lie to him. He told Ye Qin that the results had not come back yet and that he would check again this afternoon. Ye Qin replied with an emoji showing apprehension and said, "Why don't you...just go straight to the hospital after class? You don't need to come back."

Such sacrifice was nothing small for the self-centered

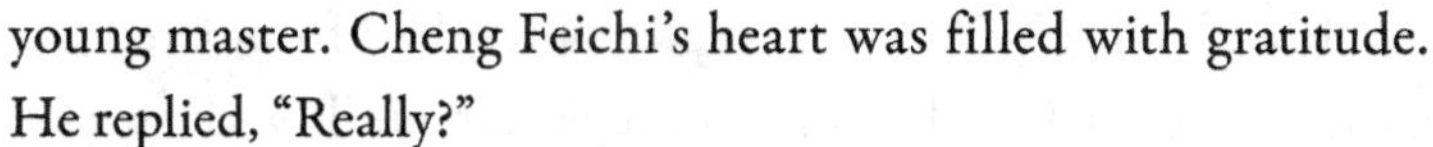

young master. Cheng Feichi's heart was filled with gratitude. He replied, "Really?"

Ye Qin sent him a "yeah" along with a sad little face, lips pursed.

Cheng Feichi gave out a little laugh and promised, "Whenever I have the time, I'll always cook for you."

After classes, Cheng Feichi returned to the Jiayuan Compound to make dinner for Ye Qin.

With time limited, all the dishes were quick and stir-fried. Ye Qin helped Cheng Feichi prepare the vegetables too, though Cheng Feichi had to do the work again by himself after that— at least Ye Qin proved that he cared for Cheng Feichi and was willing to try.

When he was seeing Cheng Feichi off by the front door, Ye Qin said, "If you need anything, just tell me. We're... Y'know, after all. There's no need for courtesy."

"What are we?" Cheng Feichi couldn't help making fun of him. "Brothers?"

Ye Qin was still embarrassed by the many "gege"s that had come from his own mouth. He glared at Cheng Feichi and yelled, "Teacher and student!"

Consequently, Mr. Cheng refused Ye Qin's proposal of driving him to the hospital, instructing him to stay home and finish the homework.

On the way to the hospital, Cheng Feichi received a picture of a huge bucket of ice cream. He knew that Ye Qin was trying to tease him, but still, he tried for persuasion. "Don't have too much ice cream. You'll catch a cold."

Ye Qin replied with a sticker named "humph."

Cheng Feichi thought that after the training, he'd better spend more time cooking for Ye Qin. The stomach trouble that had been haunting Ye Qin completely resulted from irregular meal timings and the bad habit of replacing meals with snacks. Hearing that soup was supplied every day when Ye Qin was at home, Cheng Feichi also planned to learn how to cook soup.

Deliberating, Cheng Feichi walked into the sick room and bumped into a guy that looked quite familiar.

Knowing that Cheng Feichi would take over, Mrs. Feng had already left.

A pile of medical reports lay on the bedside table. Cheng Feichi was skimming through all of them when he heard Cheng Xin saying, "This is Mr. Ye. You can regard him as your uncle. Say hello."

Cheng Feichi greeted the man with a polite "good evening" and resumed reading the reports.

"Mr. Ye" was dressed in a nice suit. A look told Cheng Feichi that he was accustomed to sitting high up on the social ladder, to being a member of the so-called elite. Embarrassed by the cool greeting, he left the room at the excuse of needing a cigarette.

Cheng Xin leaned against the headboard and said very slowly, "He's my friend. Be polite."

Cheng Feichi thought he had been polite enough. The man could be a representative of *that* man, could be one of *those* people with whom Cheng Xin should lose touch as soon as possible, according to her father.

The moment he entered the room, he had recognized the man as the person standing on Cheng Xin's right side in the photo featuring three fresh college graduates. Given that he had arrived so promptly, Cheng Feichi could tell that Cheng Xin and this man had been in contact.

"Your friend? Yet another guy from college?" Cheng Feichi retorted bluntly. "You can ask him to leave. One person is

enough for taking very good care of you."

Cheng Xin was silenced for a long time. Finally, she stopped talking in a condescending way and said in a manner of pleading, "He's helped me with a lot of things. Just do me a favor and be nice to him."

When Ye Jinxiang finished smoking and returned, he could sense that the atmosphere in the sickroom was more relaxed.

Cheng Feichi got a chair for him. Having been seated for a short while, he couldn't resist making comments on the hospital facilities, as if he was in charge of the place. He claimed that he would ask some friends to transfer Cheng Xin to a single room.

He was strutting about and giving himself airs, as if trying to impress them.

This went against Cheng Feichi's assumption about him. If he had not known that Cheng Xin was so crazy in love with *that* man, he would also have doubts about the relationship between these two, just like his grandparents had.

Unsurprisingly, Cheng Xin turned him down, saying that everything was fine here. She would be discharged a few days later, so there was no need for moving around.

Before departure, Ye Jinxiang demanded a word with Cheng Feichi, giving off the airs of an elder. "Your mother has gone through a lot bringing you up. Try to be obedient to her. Do not upset her."

Cheng Feichi was not sure how much this man knew about his family, but a nod would not be amiss.

Ye Jinxiang seemed to be satisfied with Cheng Feichi's good manners and even praised him for it. "If my son could be half as considerate as you, I would be the most grateful man in the world."

In the end, Cheng Feichi kept Ye Jinxiang's business card

and promised that he would call him if necessary. But when he returned the room, he put the card aside and basically forgot about it.

Cheng Xin had taken medication and was taking a snooze by the headboard. Cheng Feichi adjusted the bed to make it more comfortable for her to lie on. When he walked up to the bedside table, reaching for the flask, he heard Cheng Xin saying in a hoarse voice, "Prepare for studying abroad when you have the time. It's a much easier compared to winning first prize in the Olympiad."

Cheng Feichi stopped what he was doing and answered without looking at Cheng Xin, "I'll wait until you are discharged from the hospital."

Cheng Xin did not say anything more. She turned her head to the other side and closed her eyes.

People would unexpectedly reveal their vulnerabilities when they fell sick, and Cheng Xin was no exception. Cheng Feichi couldn't recall how long it had been since his mother was so nice to him. Perhaps she was taking advantage of her vulnerability, knowing that Cheng Feichi could hardly reject her demands at this point. He was indeed unwilling to ruin the hard-earned peace between them.

Before he attended the training, Cheng Feichi had a quarrel with Cheng Xin.

They were still fighting over whether Cheng Feichi should study abroad. Cheng Xin took his ID card and applied for an interview with the admissions officers of a foreign university behind his back. He only found out about it when an officer called him. This was the first time he failed to control his temper. He couldn't understand why Cheng Xin was so determined to send him away.

Cheng Xin was quite calm at the time. "I'm doing this for

you. I can't understand why you don't want it."

At that point, Cheng Feichi was finally convinced that he was never going to be a person who could stir his mother's emotions. He had never been the one that Cheng Xin cared the most about.

He'd come to understand this little by little while he was growing up. This quarrel between them was no more than a final check of the truth; an opportunity to tear apart all the pretension and wishful thinking.

The realization brought him more bewilderment than sadness. When he was a child, he already knew that Cheng Xin was sick because of his birth. This was why he strived to take good care of her, trying to secure a better future for her. This had become the biggest impetus and purpose in his life. He never, even for a small moment, dared to leave it behind.

But Cheng Xin didn't want it. All the efforts he made were in vain.

Even though Cheng Xin had stressed for a thousand times that she was doing everything for his own good.

Ye Qin sent Cheng Feichi a drowsy emoji just after ten o'clock, and then he sent a voice message. "Mr. Cheng, I don't have to recite the short passage tonight, right?"

Hearing Ye Qin's cute little voice, Cheng Feichi finally saw some light in his dark world. He typed, "Of course you do. Send a recording to me."

Ye Qin sighed sadly. "Fine..."

The short text was no more than 400 words, but Ye Qin couldn't recite it fluently in one go. He stumbled through six messages and then sent the recordings to Cheng Feichi, who was patient enough to listen through them all twice. After that, Cheng Feichi asked Ye Qin, "Were you reading the passage?"

As if suffering a great injustice, Ye Qin replied with a voice message shorter than one minute. In it he read through the whole passage at the fastest speed and said, "Can you hear the difference? When I'm reading it, I read like this!"

Cheng Feichi couldn't help but smile. He entered the hallway and sent Ye Qin a voice message. "I heard it. You did a very good job."

"I know." Ye Qin was not humble at all. "How are you gonna reward me?"

Cheng Feichi thought about it and answered, "I'll make a very delicious meal for you tomorrow."

Ye Qin went further by demanding a "goodnight," and then went to bed feeling content.

Cheng Feichi returned to the room and focused on the Olympiad exercise book again. Ye Qin had been so hard-working; he had to make full use of every minute too.

Not to mention that they also shared the dream of going to the same college.

Such a short conversation was somehow enough to pacify Cheng Feichi. He felt that while something was silently slipping away from his mind, he was also gaining new energy before he knew it. The bewilderment and confusion that had been haunting him for days gradually lost its weight.

If he had to give some meaning to his fighting and striving, he would call that meaning Ye Qin.

CHAPTER 11

SOMETIMES, Ye Qin thought of himself as an introvert. When he felt like that, he didn't want to be disturbed by anyone at all. But other times he turned back into a very gregarious person, eager to have the whole world revolving around him.

On the last day of his training program, Cheng Feichi only came back to cook a meal for him. Before he left, he told Ye Qin that he would be staying in the hospital for the next few days; therefore, he'd better go home. He looked exhausted, as if he hadn't slept for days. Ye Qin suddenly felt sorry for him, so he didn't say that he wanted Cheng Feichi to stay.

He didn't see it coming that they would be separated for a whole week.

In the beginning, everything went well. Ye Qin enjoyed good sleep and delicious snacks, and no one around was good enough to beat him in video games. But he soon grew bored. With only four walls as his company, a "small" house of 108 square meters brought infinite loneliness.

So, Ye Qin went home. The maid, seeing him entering, rejoiced that he had gained some weight. She then went upstairs and asked Luo Qiuling to take a look. Pleased to see him, Luo

Qiuling bade the maid to buy more groceries; as Ye Jinxiang was coming home today as well, some fancy dishes should be prepared.

Hearing that his father would be home soon, Ye Qin immediately wanted to escape, yet Luo Qiuling grabbed his arm and forced him to stay. "You returned at a very good time. Your dad said that he brought something for you. It's so hot out there. Just stay at home."

Ye Qin kept his long face plastered on, and sent Cheng Feichi a sulky emoji. Cheng Feichi didn't reply until noon.

"Another difficult problem?"

Screw the problems! Cross, Ye Qin blamed Cheng Feichi for all the awkwardness and anxiety that he was feeling right now. Ye Jinxiang's lecturing, on the other hand, just made him drowsy. When it was finally over, Ye Qin went back to his bedroom with everything Ye Jinxiang had given him. After getting some sleep, he got up and delved into the bags, only to find they were filled with vitamins: DHA Algae Oil Capsules and other health products, all from People's Hospital No. 3.

The bags were normal hospital plastic bags. The simplicity appeared quite abnormal, considering Ye Jinxiang's addiction to luxuries. After all, the cheapest things he had ever given Ye Qin were clothes and watches from famous brands.

Ye Qin didn't know why, and he didn't even care to know the reasons. The next day when he was standing in front of the door, ready to leave, he returned to his room on second thought and took the bags with him. He didn't need these supplements, but Cheng Feichi might find them helpful.

In the morning, Ye Qin went to the airport to pick Zhou Feng up.

After his study tour, Zhou Feng stayed in the States for

another two weeks. He even made Liao Yifang stay with him, posting pictures of fancy food and the fun they had there in his WeChat Moments from time to time.

Once, he posted a photo of a sunset in California. Liao Yifang was unwittingly present in the picture, still reading books on the beach, his feet bare. Looking at the photo, Ye Qin felt as if he was seeing a loving couple.

The flight arrived on time. Seeing the two people walking next to each other, Ye Qin was sure that he wasn't being oversensitive: the two of them had indeed been together.

Liao Yifang, who was obviously tanned, got into Ye Qin's car and was very pleasantly surprised. "Ye-tongxue, you came to pick us up even though you're so busy with your studies. Thank you."

Ye Qin looked at him in the rearview mirror. "Who said I was busy studying?"

"Cheng-tongxue did. I asked him on WeChat one day when I had a question, and he said that he was preparing an exam paper for you."

Ye Qin was speechless. Now everyone knew that he hadn't been having fun this summer, but was doing his homework pliantly at home instead.

Ye Qin drove the two to the apartment in Jiayuan Compound. Zhou Feng looked around and was surprised at how domestic everything in the apartment looked—two pairs of slippers, two teacups, two face towels, and two pillows side by side on the same bed. Even the toothbrushes were identical to each other except for their colors: one was red, and the other blue.

"Hey." Zhou Feng dragged Ye Qin to the corner. "You and the straight-A student, you guys did *that*?"

Ye Qin didn't understand. "Did what?"

"What people usually do in the same bed."

"...Sleep?"

Zhou Feng elbowed him. "Don't blow me off like that."

Ye Qin was reminded of countless goodnight kisses, and looked away, his eyes rolling. "Who...who said that you have to do *those* things if you lie on the same bed with someone?"

Zhou Feng looked at him as if Ye Qin was an alien. "What could you possibly do in bed together, apart from *those* things?"

When Liao Yifang saw Cheng Feichi's books on the desk, he looked as if he'd found a treasure. He took out the small book he had with him and started copying notes, not caring to stop even when Zhou Feng asked him to leave the room and have fun with them.

After playing a few games together with Ye Qin, Zhou Feng, who was still feeling jet lagged, went into the room and flirted with Liao Yifang. He came out with a satisfied face, stretching his back while asking, "Where is the straight-A student? Is he that irresponsible? After gobbling you up, he just ran away like this?"

Ye Qin jumped up to muffle his voice, as if he wanted to kill him so that he could be silenced once and for all.

Fortunately, Liao Yifang did not hear the comment clearly. He peeked out with his face still red. "What do we have for lunch?"

Ye Qin recalled what Cheng Feichi had told him and felt unhappy. *Didn't he say that it was nothing serious, and that his mother will be discharged from the hospital soon? How come he hasn't called me today?*

After lunch, he called Cheng Feichi, and it took almost a minute to get through.

"Where are you?" Trying to show how much influence he could exert on Cheng Feichi in front of his friends, Ye Qin put on a bossy tone.

Cheng Feichi's call had a lot of background noise; he was obviously in a public place. He left the ward and found a place that was as quiet as possible. "In the hospital."

Ye Qin asked, "Your mom still hasn't been discharged?"

Cheng Feichi held the phone between his ear and shoulder, unfolding the bill that had just been printed and started skimming. "Hmm. She'll be discharged this afternoon."

"That's great!"

Ye Qin was more excited to hear that Cheng Xin was going to be discharged than he was to hear that Ye Jinxiang was going on a business trip. There was still half a month of summer vacation left; he could ask Cheng Feichi to come and spend time with him again.

Cherishing this thought, Ye Qin could not help but ask, "So tonight, you..."

Halfway through the conversation, Ye Qin heard a middle-aged man's voice coming from the phone.

"Xiao-Chi, why are you hiding here? I've been looking for you."

The footsteps were getting closer. When the speaker was finally standing in front of Cheng Feichi, his voice was clear enough for Ye Qin to hear.

The man was overly polite. "I told you to let Uncle Ye take care of this. Listen to me, just go in and help your mother pack her things."

Cheng Feichi's response was naturally to excuse himself, saying that he wouldn't bother the man. His attitude sounded polite and detached, as if he was talking to a stranger.

Ye Qin, however, could not bear another word. His hand slowly squeezed tight around his cellphone, his knuckles turning faintly blue.

He couldn't possibly have heard it wrong. That voice—if it wasn't Ye Jinxiang, who else could it be? He could even see Ye Jinxiang's attentive face when he spoke.

Ye Qin sneered.

No wonder Ye Jinxiang had brought him those supplements. He went to the hospital for a family reunion, not for Ye Qin.

At the payment office on the first floor of People's Hospital No. 3, Cheng Feichi managed to get rid of Ye Jinxiang. Looking back at his phone, he found that Ye Qin had already hung up.

He joined the queue to pay the fee, and decided that if nothing else was expecting him when he returned the ward, he would go to Jiayuan Compound. He still had things left there. If Ye Qin hadn't left yet, he could have a meal with him. The market there didn't have a great variety of daily products, and they weren't fresh enough. He could buy some vegetables downtown and cook them at the apartment.

Thinking in this way, Cheng Feichi's footsteps became lighter.

Cheng Xin's condition was not serious. The doctor said that it'd been too long since she'd last been to the hospital. The hormones her body needed now were different, and she needed new medication. She should take what she lacked, instead of taking whatever medications she herself decided she needed.

Because of the new prescriptions, the total cost of medication rose sharply; far exceeding Cheng Xin's previous monthly budget. Cheng Feichi was worried that he would not be able to afford the medicine soon. Under the recommendation of the father of a student whom he tutored every Saturday morning, he took on a short-term tutoring job in an educational institution. The tutoring course lasted for 20 days. Meanwhile, he resumed work at the breakfast shop and promised the boss to stay until the end of the year. This way, he could earn over 3,000 yuan in what was left of that month.

Although his salary was but a drop in the bucket, it could always make up for a little bit of the household income, so that

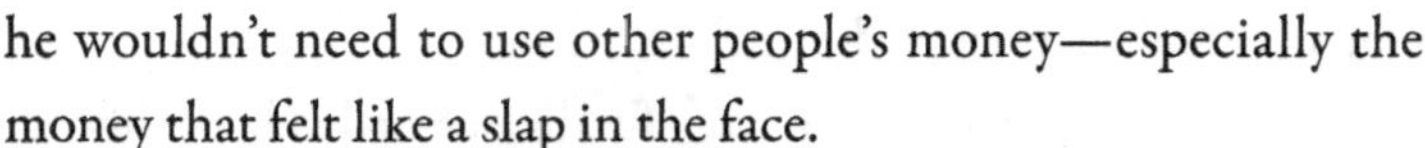

he wouldn't need to use other people's money—especially the money that felt like a slap in the face.

No sooner had he gotten out of the elevator on the second floor of the inpatient ward, than did Cheng Feichi meet Mrs. Feng, who was walking in a hurry.

"Xiao-Chi, come on, your grandpa and grandma are here."

Before reaching the door of the ward, Cheng Feichi heard them quarreling inside.

His grandpa was furiously looking for weapons with which to beat Ye Jinxiang. "I already warned you to leave Xinxin alone so many years ago now. Look at her! Such a good kid, and she was ruined by your gang!"

Ye Jinxiang was terribly scared, but too embarrassed to leave, so he answered cautiously, "Sir, calm down. Things aren't like what you think. I just came by to see how Xin's doing..."

Grandpa yelled, "Why didn't you come earlier? When she went her own way, none of you stopped her. Maybe you were even by her side, fanning the flames! Well, well, she's now been called a mistress for the past twenty years. Her health was ruined too, just for giving birth to a child who didn't even have a father. If she died earlier than us, we'd have to prepare our own daughter's funeral!"

Cheng Feichi stopped at the doorstep. Sitting on the edge of the bed, Cheng Xin, her face pale, saw him first and gave him a little wave. She was telling him to leave.

"I tried to persuade her then, but she just wouldn't listen..."

Ye Jinxiang was still trying to defend himself. Grandma took Cheng Feichi outside, walking until they could no longer hear the quarrel. After careful consideration, she began, "Your grandfather can't control his words when he's angry. He said some nasty things, but don't take it personally."

Still thinking about what his grandpa had said just now,

Cheng Feichi gave a low "hmm."

Grandma sighed. After having finally persuaded her husband to come and see their daughter, she didn't expect the situation to deteriorate again like this. Heavens knew how much the old man loved his daughter and wanted to see his grandson, but he had been conservative for all his life; regarding his reputation as the most important thing on earth. In addition, he had a firecracker temper. Seeing Ye Jinxiang in the hospital had instantly made him furious. No one could stop him from letting it out.

Growing up at her parents' side, Cheng Xin was accustomed to her father's temper. But Cheng Feichi was still young, and children who had suffered were more likely to grow sensitive and paranoid. Worried that he might have been hurt, his grandma tried to explain things to him.

"Don't listen to your grandfather talking nonsense. He's in a bad mood, so he tends to say inappropriate things to whoever happens to be around. Your Uncle Ye was a student whom we both taught. After going to college, he wooed your mother and even came to our house for her. Your grandfather asked your mother, 'Do you like this young man, Xinxin?' Your mother was also very honest and gave a direct, 'I don't.' As a result, your grandfather chased after Xiao-Ye and hit him. The whole thing didn't come to an end until they'd ran for a few blocks."

Grandma was saying this to cheer Cheng Feichi up, but as she went along, she grew sentimental. "I didn't expect them to get back in touch after so many years. Even if she'd married Xiao-Ye, things would be so much better than they are now."

Cheng Feichi thought differently.

He knew that his character was mostly influenced by his mother, though he hadn't really compared himself with her. Cheng Xin's stubbornness was carved into her bones. As long as she was convinced of something, even if everyone around her said it was wrong, she could stand the pressure and go ahead, fighting them all with silence.

Before leaving, Grandma quietly put a wad of money on the bedside table. Cheng Xin found out about it and chased her down, money in hand, followed by Ye Jinxiang and Mrs. Feng.

Cheng Feichi stayed in the ward to pack things up. Having acquainted herself with the mother and son, the old lady in the next bed got up to help him. She comforted Cheng Feichi, "Parents always love their children, no matter what. In fact, the fiercer their scolding is, the sadder they actually feel. When a kid is beaten by his mother, the mother is the one that truly hurts."

The old woman was very keen-eyed and clear-headed. Cheng Feichi knew that she'd said this for the same reason his grandmother did. She played down the harm caused by the words "a child who didn't even have a father" by saying that Grandpa was speaking without thinking.

But he couldn't even hold a grudge against Grandpa for it.

He didn't have a father—that was true. If it wasn't because he still had some value, perhaps he would have been discarded long ago.

After sending Cheng Xin home and helping her settle down, Cheng Feichi arrived at Jiayuan Compound. It was already 6 p.m.

Cheng Feichi made sweet and sour short ribs and cashew nut shrimp. Since the bottom of the pot was still oily, he stir-fried some bamboo shoot slices. It was a perfect dish for hot summer days. To accommodate Ye Qin's sweet tooth, he tried to get rid of his own previous habit of adding dried chilies to every dish and instead added a few spoons of sugar.

After cooking, he checked his cellphone. Still, no messages came. He thought that Ye Qin might not be looking at his phone and was having fun with his friends.

He covered the vegetables with plastic wrap and placed them on the table. It was getting dark, so he called Ye Qin.

The first time he called, Ye Qin didn't answer; the second time, he waited until the busy signal was about to sound. Ye Qin finally answered the call, and lazily said "Hello" as if he'd just woken up.

There was music and noisy human voices in the background. Cheng Feichi asked him where he was several times before Ye Qin could hear him clearly. Ye Qin answered, dragging out his voice, "Have a guess."

Cheng Feichi heard someone yelling to Ye Qin, "Qin-ge's boyfriend is calling him? Why don't you invite him to come over?"

It seemed that Ye Qin was with his friends. Broken sentences were coming through, and Cheng Feichi thought that perhaps there was a problem with the cellphone signal. He walked to the balcony.

"Should I come to pick you up?"

"Come on, bro! Hurry up, we're all waiting for you!" Zhou Feng's voice sounded. "We're at the clubhouse that you went to last time. Just enter the hall, tell the waiter that you know me, and go directly to the third floor."

Cheng Feichi was silent for a moment and then said, "Let Ye Qin speak."

Someone was laughing. "He only takes orders from A-Qin. Stop making a fool of yourself."

Cheng Feichi heard a rustling sound. It was Ye Qin approaching the microphone. "Come here. Today is my friend's birthday."

Cheng Feichi turned his head and glanced at all the dishes on the table. He only hesitated for two seconds before answering, "Okay."

On the other side, in a box inside the South Manor, Liu

Yangfan was sitting with his legs crossed. He raised his eyebrows and said, "This time, you promised that you'll let us do whatever we want with him. Don't chicken out again."

Ye Qin threw the cellphone onto the tea table, his face turning gloomy. "If I chicken out, I'll change my last name to yours."

An hour later, the reception downstairs notified them that Cheng Feichi had arrived.

Zhao Yue took out a wide-mouth glass, poured half a glass of wine into it, opened a bottle of Sprite to fill the rest, and then threw a few ice cubes into it. The bubbling liquid overflowed from the mouth of the glass, leaving a pool of foam on the tea table. Liu Yangfan called the waiter to open two more bottles and bring them in.

Liao Yifang, who was sitting in the corner, sensed that something was wrong. He asked cautiously, "Is Cheng-tongxue already here?"

Zhou Feng leaned on the sofa with one arm around him, slanting his eyes as he answered, "Yeah, are you happy about that?"

Liao Yifang shook his head and turned to look at Ye Qin, who did not look happy at all.

When Cheng Feichi was brought in by the waiter, he was "welcomed" by everyone except Ye Qin.

"Look, look, I told you our straight-A student will show respect for your feelings. He came! You guys didn't believe me. Do you not have faith in my judgment, or the charms of our lovely Qin-ge?" Zhou Feng took Cheng Feichi into the room and pushed him closer to Ye Qin, who was having a doze, his head tilted aside. "Qin-ge, wake up. He's here."

Ye Qin turned his eyes to the right and glanced at Cheng Feichi. He didn't even bother to greet him. Instead, he closed his eyes and continued to sleep.

The temperature in the room was low because of the air conditioner. Cheng Feichi saw that Ye Qin was only wearing a short-sleeved shirt and was afraid that he would catch a cold. He touched Ye Qin's arm and said, "Don't sleep here. If you feel sleepy, let's go home."

Somehow these words very much amused the rich boys in the room. Liu Yangfan grinned. "It's a rare event that you can come around here. Don't think about leaving so soon."

Zhao Yue was also smiling mischievously, holding a glass of wine while approaching Cheng Feichi. "Indeed. All of us and Cheng…Cheng what? As the common saying goes; out of blows, friendship grows. Let's finish this glass of wine first. Just have a good laugh and forget all about the past."

Cheng Feichi glanced at the boys, indifference in his eyes, then stood up politely, took the wine and gulped it straight down.

Brandy mixed with carbonated drinks. The alcohol was largely diluted, but the bubbles still burned Cheng Feichi's throat and esophagus. He took a few deep breaths to get rid of dizziness and nausea, then put the empty cup firmly down on the tea table.

Liu Yangfan gave a careless round of applause. "The straight-A student is really something. But you shouldn't drink good wine like *that*. You have to savor it. If you gulp it down, then…what's the saying? You guys must know it… A reckless…"

Zhou Feng interjected. "Are you thinking of 'a reckless waste of nature's gifts'?"

"Hmm, yes," Liu Yangfan commented with the airs of an experienced gourmet. "Next time, no matter where you go, never drink like that again. After all, you've visited our South Manor. If you don't behave like a pro, people will definitely be talking behind your back. They'll say that I'm not being a good host if I don't teach you everything."

It was only when everyone had been properly seated that Zhao Yue started to ask everyone to introduce themselves.

Cheng Feichi told them his name. Liu Yangfan asked, "Feichi... Does that mean 'something that shall never be limited to a small pond'?"

Cheng Feichi didn't answer, yet Zhao Yue slapped his thigh and said, "That's for sure. The straight-A student's name has to be different from us ordinary people. There's a lot of expectation and idealism condensed in that name."

At first it might've sounded like a compliment, but in fact, anyone could tell that Cheng Feichi was being teased. It was just like that when they were teaching Cheng Feichi how to drink wine—even the most foolish could see that they were mocking Cheng Feichi for being poor and ignorant.

Liao Yifang couldn't figure out why everyone suddenly had become so bitter and mean. He tried in his own way to lift Cheng Feichi out of this trap. "Cheng-tongxue is excellent in every aspect. In a few years, he'll become an awesome person; worthy of his name."

His serious face made everyone laugh. Zhao Yue also gave him a glass of wine and asked Zhou Feng, "Where did you find such a funny boy? Can I take him home and have some fun with him?"

Liao Yifang's shoulders trembled, and he shrank back nervously. Fortunately, Zhou Feng was not so playful that he'd agree to this ridiculous proposal. He held Liao Yifang even closer. "Piss off. Yuanyuan is mine. Don't even think about it— I mean all of you."

Soft music playing in their private box, Cheng Feichi took the blanket from Liao Yifang and put it on Ye Qin, tucking his wayward arm under the blanket. Ye Qin's eyelashes trembled slightly. His upper eyelids wrinkled because he was trying hard to not open his eyes.

After the initial provocation, the boys gradually lost interest in Cheng Feichi in face of the latter's calm response. They poured themselves some liquor and started drinking and chatting casually.

"By the way, is Yuanyuan his real name? If so, it's a weird name for a guy," Liu Yangfan said.

Before Liao Yifang was about to explain, Zhou Feng answered, "How are you allowed to call him Yuanyuan? Change it up."

Zhao Yue smiled and said, "Then we'll call him A-Yuan. Once he came here, he became one of us." Then he turned to Cheng Feichi. "Speaking of which, you may not know that Master Liu's from G Province. When he just came here, he loved to add an 'A' in front of anyone's name. When he called Ye Qin 'Xiao-A-Qin' for the first time, he got slapped in the face."

"Ha ha ha ha, I remember that," Zhou Feng said. "Qin-ge always thought that his name sounds like a girl's, and he hates being called 'Xiao-Qin' or 'Qin-Qin.' Only his mom can do that."

Cheng Feichi turned his head to look at Ye Qin, who was twisting his neck, still pretending to be asleep. He recalled how Ye Qin's cheeks reddened when he was first called "Ye Xiaoruan," yet he later insisted to be called by that. A smile unknowingly came to his eyes, which had been calm to a fault ever since he had entered the box.

Having sat for a while, Liu Yangfan took out some poker cards and invited Cheng Feichi to play along. Cheng Feichi said that he didn't know how, so Zhou Feng came to be his tutor, bubbling over with enthusiasm. The rules of Texas Hold'em were simple, and he remembered all the basic card types at once.

The chips were also given to him by Zhou Feng. After all, he didn't take Cheng Feichi seriously. Surprisingly, Liu Yangfan and Zhao Yue both looked very cautious. No longer reckless as usual, they hesitated again and again over the course of the game, as if they really wanted to beat Cheng Feichi.

However, in the next few rounds, Cheng Feichi, who had gradually taken the rules and skills into his heart, won several rounds in a row. His chips accumulated, and the faces of the two who had wished to humiliate him became uglier. Cheng Feichi, who was playing this game for the first time, remained very calm. Liu Yangfan and Zhao Yue, who were accustomed to judging the strength of the opponent's cards from expressions and movements, couldn't figure out what Cheng Feichi had in his hands. As a result, they grew agitated and made mistakes frequently.

They started another round and this time, again, the rich boys lost the whole game. Zhao Yue dropped the cards and snapped, "I'm out."

Liu Yangfan was more composed than him. "Hey, it's no big deal. Have a drink. It'll cool your head." Then he also put down the cards and said to Cheng Feichi with a fake smile, "We're not as good as you. We admit that."

Cheng Feichi didn't understand the conventions at the poker table. He thought they were just playing a game. When he won, he thought he was lucky—he hadn't expected that they would be so annoyed. Putting the cards in his hands neatly together, Cheng Feichi stood up and was about to leave the table when Liu Yangfan stopped him. Liu Yangfan waved to the croupier next to them.

"Come, count how much Mr. Cheng has won today."

Cheng Feichi was taken aback for a moment. He didn't know that this was really about money. No one had told him about that at the beginning.

Fortunately, he was on the winning side. When he was going to say that there was no need since he didn't intend to take the money, the experienced croupier had already counted the number of chips and reported a number that was neither too big nor too small—just exceeding 10,000 yuan.

Liu Yangfan was holding a chip in his hand. He knocked it on the table and raised his chin at Zhou Feng. "If I remember correctly, it was you who lent Mr. Cheng the chips at the beginning?"

Zhou Feng was confused, but answered, "Yes."

Liu Yangfan looked downwards, slowly pushing away the neatly stacked chips in front of him and messing up the table. He then picked up a few chips, rubbing them with his palm while saying, "One must follow the rules at the gaming table. Since your chips were borrowed to begin with, you should pay back the money. Unfortunately, I have no cash here; only checks, and they're all round numbers, which means no small change for you. I'll need you to repay the borrowed chips so we can sort this whole thing out."

Even though Cheng Feichi had already sensed that these people were trying to trap him, he didn't expect that the trick would be right here waiting for him.

The atmosphere froze for a while. Zhou Feng couldn't stand it anymore, so he intervened.

"Hey, forget it. It's just a few thousand. I don't really need it."

"Just as the saying goes, even among brothers, accounts should be settled without ambiguity. It's indeed just a few thousand yuan." Liu Yangfan rested his right elbow on the table and eyed Cheng Feichi with surprise. "Of course our straight-A student has the money, right? Or are you actually worrying that I'll welch on our agreement after you give me the cash?"

Most people would panic or get angry out of embarrassment, facing such undisguised contempt. Cheng Feichi, however, remained calm, looking straight back. There was no panic nor embarrassment in his eyes.

He curled his lips and said, "I don't have so much money on

me. Can I go home and grab it?"

Zhao Yue, who was angry now, burst out laughing. "A few thousand yuan is 'so much' for you? The glass of wine you just drank is worth more than that."

Liao Yifang, who had witnessed the whole thing, couldn't bear it anymore. It was obvious that they had made an alliance to bully Cheng Feichi. Even though he himself was a bit scared, he really couldn't continue to pretend that he didn't know what was going on. He stood up and stammered, "H...how much do... do you want? I'll pay it for him."

Liu Yangfan waved his hand and continued speaking to Cheng Feichi. "Master Cheng may not have known this: gambling debts must always be settled on the spot. There's no such a thing as leaving before paying up. I think you can figure out why." Then he rested his chin on his palm, pretending to be thinking. "Well...I remember that A-Qin said you can cook? We happen to be in need of a cook who's good at making Chinese food. Why don't you condescend to take a post here and work for a few days—"

Suddenly, everyone heard a loud bang. A chair near the sofa fell to the ground. Ye Qin, who had been lying on the sofa for several hours, had knocked the chair over, sat up straight, and thrown the blanket on the ground.

He shouted furiously, "Enough! If you still don't think it's time to stop, I'll leave."

Jiayuan Compound, eleven o'clock in the evening.

Ye Qin walked ahead, and Cheng Feichi followed, not far away from him. The elevator doors opened, and Ye Qin went in first, desperately pressing the close button before indicating which floor he intended to go. When Cheng Feichi was about to enter, he was caught right in the middle by the closing doors.

Even when Ye Qin took out the key to open the door, Cheng Feichi, who was standing behind him, still didn't utter a word. It seemed that he would talk only if Ye Qin started the conversation.

Disturbing thoughts crowded Ye Qin's mind. He was filled with mixed emotions, and only irritation could be most clearly perceived. What irritated him the most was Ye Jinxiang's shamelessness. How many times had he wronged Luo Qiuling; having another family out of the public eye, while pretending sanctimoniously to be a good husband and a good father?

He was also angry because Cheng Feichi was so dumb to have been fooled by Liu Yangfan and the other rich boys. Wasn't Cheng Feichi a straight-A student, excelling more than everyone else at everything? Wasn't he the popular guy, Ye Jinxiang's favorite son? Why did he just stand there and let them humiliate him, without saying a word?

Ye Qin completely forgot that it was him who had told Cheng Feichi to come.

Pushing the door open, he entered the room, hearing footsteps behind him. The anger in his heart suddenly reached a critical level. He turned around and pushed Cheng Feichi very hard.

"Why are you following me?"

Cheng Feichi was caught off guard and staggered because of Ye Qin's push. He stepped back to stabilize himself, raised his head, and gave Ye Qin a weighty glance.

At this moment, Ye Qin felt extremely uncomfortable. He couldn't bear to be looked in that way; as if Cheng Feichi was able to dig deep into his heart and see all the unspeakable things there. He lifted his foot and kicked off a slipper that he had just put on.

"This is my house. What are you doing here?" Seeing that Cheng Feichi didn't move, Ye Qin raised his hand and pointed at the door. "Fuck off!"

The door closed at his command, and the room became quieter.

Ye Qin stood there until he'd caught his breath and the buzzing sound in his ears stopped. Then he kicked off the other slipper and returned to his room barefoot.

As soon as he entered, he found that the blanket which he'd used two days ago had been neatly stacked at the end of the bed. The books he had opened and the pens without caps were also reorganized. Apparently, someone had come in and cleaned them up.

Not wanting to look at this, Ye Qin walked quickly towards the balcony. He lowered his head accidentally, only to see that the money plant on the ground had been moved away from sunshine. The soil was still moist, as if someone had just watered it.

He had bought that back on the day he went to a nearby supermarket and saw someone selling potted plants by the curbside. He bought one on the way, thinking that the house could use some greenery. After placing it on the balcony, he forgot all about it. The responsibility of watering and taking care of it fell totally on Cheng Feichi. He made sure that it was watered properly every day, even though he was already so busy with studying and working.

Ye Qin raised his hand and ruffled his own hair. The annoying feelings were drowning him. Why was Cheng Feichi's presence everywhere?

At this moment, his cellphone rang.

It was Zhou Feng, who asked the moment he picked up the call, "Is he okay? You two didn't have a fight, did you?"

Ye Qin replied, "It's none of my business if he's okay or not. So what if we had a fight?"

Zhou Feng commented, "...It seems that you did. Well, it's reasonable for him to be angry. Qin-ge, just try your best to comfort him."

Ye Qin rolled his eyes. "I'm the one who's angry!"

"Why? You weren't the one humiliated in public."

Ye Qin didn't want to share his family secrets, so he made up something. "I'm angry that he's so stupid. He jumped right into the trap, and even dared to win money from them."

Zhou Feng was silent for a few seconds before answering, "He didn't know that money was involved at first..."

Ye Qin snapped, "Whose side are you on? Why are you still speaking up for him?"

"Easy, easy. I'm just calling because they have something to tell you. Liu Yangfan said that he didn't expect that you'd be so angry. If he'd known, he wouldn't have gone that far. Qin-ge, you're not completely in the right, either. If you didn't want to see him being bullied, why bother asking him to come?"

Zhou Feng knew that Ye Qin couldn't beat him up right now, so he dared to say everything.

Ye Qin' had just calmed down, not without difficulty, but now his mood was full of ripples again. Fuming with rage, he was about to hang up the phone right away when Zhou Feng tried to persuade him one last time.

"He bit the bullet because of you. Anyway, if I were him, I would've flipped the table and left on the spot... Qin-ge, don't be so hard on him."

Ending the call, Ye Qin, who was no longer so irritated, again stood there for a long time.

When someone isn't preoccupied, many of the less noticeable things in their life will come to mind.

Ye Qin still remembered the first time he saw Cheng Feichi. That seemingly mild, but in fact indifferent, aura seemed to have drawn a circle around him, blocking everyone else from intrusion. Cheng Feichi's eyes were especially cold, sharp, and alert.

And he wasn't sweet-tempered—it only took a punctured tire for him to grab Ye Qin's wrist with such strength that he dropped the knife. Then he dragged him along for several miles towards the police station, almost making Ye Qin cry.

He was no coward.

So why did he stay in the club without saying anything? No one was forbidding him from leaving.

Ye Qin thought about it and started to feel upset again. He gave the money plant another kick before turning around to grab a drink from the refrigerator.

When he walked past the living room, he inevitably saw the three dishes on the table sealed with plastic film. Cheng Feichi had made meat and shrimp for him—his favorite dishes. Bamboo shoots were also one of the few vegetables he was willing to eat a few bites of. When he entered the kitchen, the rice cooker's light was on, suggesting it was in heat preservation mode. There were two empty bowls next to it, with two pairs of chopsticks on the bowls. Everything was obviously ready for a meal.

It reminded Ye Qin of the WeChat messages he had received in the afternoon, but did not reply to. And the message he had received at the same time, asking what he wanted to eat.

Ye Qin straightened his back, inhaled deeply through his nose, and then exhaled with a lot of force.

At this point, he had to admit it, though he felt so guilty and was therefore unwilling to face the truth—Cheng Feichi had changed a lot after being with him.

Cheng Feichi took care of him all the time. As long as he was there, Ye Qin only needed to sit down at the table and open his mouth. He would hand over his own coat, already warm with his own temperature, before Ye Qin ever felt cold. He would squat down when Ye Qin was tired, offering to carry him on his back. He was so poor, but he'd arrange everything so well when they were on a date, never letting Ye Qin spend a penny.

He tolerated all his unreasonable emotions, tolerated his deep-rooted bad temper, and stood in the rain for two hours. Even when his clothes were soaked, he didn't complain. When he couldn't figure out why Ye Qin was angry, he would still try his best to make him happy.

The light still on, Ye Qin turned his head and saw the jar of stars that had been openly displayed on the bedside table since it had first been spotted.

Ye Qin couldn't help recollecting the many ways in which Cheng Feichi treated him so nicely and carefully. Just a few hours ago, in face of ridicule and mockery from a whole house of people, Cheng Feichi's first reaction was neither to be angry nor to leave, but to sit down next to him and put a warm blanket on his body.

If only Cheng Feichi wasn't Ye Jinxiang's son!

These unrealistic thoughts made Ye Qin's heart swell with soreness, as if being cruelly pulled down towards the earth by some heavy object. However, among these messy and overloaded emotions, he groped and unexpectedly reached a bright exit.

What did any of that have to do with Cheng Feichi? It wasn't as if he himself actually wanted to be Ye Jinxiang's bastard.

Ye Qin's heartbeat suddenly accelerated, sending forth deafening pounding in his chest, as if a piece of thick, solid ice was finally falling apart in front of his eyes. The shattering ice gave off crisp sounds. All the uncomfortable feelings found their explanations and directions, flooding away through the big hole.

Taking three steps at a time, Ye Qin ran to the door and put on his shoes, thinking about where to look for Cheng Feichi — or maybe he should call him first?

Will he pick up the phone? What should I do if he doesn't answer?

The more eager Ye Qin became, the more panicked he was. Wearing only one slipper, he jumped around the house looking for the key. He couldn't find it anywhere, but he couldn't wait any longer. *Forget about the key. Cheng Feichi had it. I won't come back here if I can't find him.*

In just one minute, he had done all the mental preparations—ready for having to sleep on the street, ready for the possibility that Cheng Feichi wouldn't answer any of his calls. He didn't even have the patience to check if he had put on his shoes properly. A sneaker on the right foot, a slipper on the left, he opened the door, only to find the man who he'd kicked out was still standing right on the doorstep.

Cheng Feichi had been leaning against the wall. Seeing that the door was open, he straightened his back and released his folded arms.

Ye Qin saw Cheng Feichi still holding the slipper that had been kicked off by him.

On the stairway, the two boys looked at each other in the dim light for a long time. They were both waiting for the other to start talking.

In the end, Cheng Feichi made the first move. He took two steps ahead, and squatted down. Holding Ye Qin's slender ankle, he took off the untied sneaker, and put the slipper on Ye Qin's left foot—the slipper that had been in his hand for more than half an hour.

Ye Qin looked down at the top of Cheng Feichi's head, his mouth moving in silence. He wanted to say something, but he didn't know where to start.

Growing into adulthood, he had never fetched water for his mother to wash her feet as a gesture of filial piety, even at the request of the elementary school teacher. Therefore, he was unable to figure out how Cheng Feichi could stay so calm and natural when carrying out such a service, as if it was a common occurrence. In the traditional context, it was demeaning; a man lost face by doing this.

Now he suddenly understood that Cheng Feichi had never cared about so-called "face" in front of him. When Cheng Feichi agreed to be his boyfriend, he said that he would be responsible. He really kept that promise in his heart. He expressed care and affection with day-to-day actions, in every minute and every second, rather than with cheap, cheesy words.

It was almost midnight. The stairway was filled with silence, and the voice-activated delay lights went out. There was only some light coming through the windows, barely enough for Ye Qin to distinguish the outline of the person in front of him.

Cheng Feichi stood up and said in the darkness, "Let's go inside."

The moment when he turned around, Ye Qin dashed forward without even thinking about it and hugged Cheng Feichi's waist from behind.

Cheng Feichi staggered. The light above his head turned on automatically. Ye Qin's hot breath was imprinted on his back through a thin layer of fabric, and he could clearly hear Ye Qin's sobbing. Cheng Feichi couldn't move, as if he had been nailed in the place by thousands of small hooks.

"I was wrong; I know I was wrong." Ye Qin spent all his strength hugging Cheng Feichi, for fear of him leaving forever.

After losing all his face and making an overdue apology, Ye Qin found that Cheng Feichi showed no signs of turning around. Ye Qin was both afraid and aggrieved. He sniffed a few times and said in a hoarse voice, "Please don't be mad at me...gege."

When the bell chimed midnight, the microwave oven

timer rang.

Ye Qin hurried to take out the hot dishes and accidentally burned his hands. He gasped.

"Let me." Cheng Feichi got in front of him and brought the food straight to the table.

Having seated himself, Ye Qin painstakingly raised his fingers and blew on them, which finally attracted Cheng Feichi's attention. He took Ye Qin's hand and looked at it. "You're okay. Let's eat."

Knowing that Cheng Feichi wouldn't become a meticulous boyfriend in a single day, Ye Qin picked up his chopsticks and had a mouthful of rice.

The two boys hadn't had any food that evening; by now, they should've been hungry. But when Ye Qin refilled his bowl, he noticed that Cheng Feichi's bowl was still full—he had barely taken a bite.

Having taken a close examination of Cheng Feichi's face, Ye Qin finally realized that he didn't look good at all. He was unnaturally pale.

"What kind of wine did they have you drink? Why didn't you tell me that you feel bad?" Ye Qin threw down his chopsticks and started ransacking the house for medicine.

Before they moved here, Luo Qiuling asked the housekeeper to stock the house with some common drugs, but Ye Qin wasn't paying attention at the time and forgot exactly which cabinet the medicine was in.

"I don't know what it is," Cheng Feichi answered. "I'm fine, just in need of a good night's sleep. Don't bother looking for medicine."

Ye Qin still got the medical kit out. Since he himself often suffered from stomach problems, there were as many as seven or eight kinds of stomach medicine in it. He was too anxious to read the instructions word by word, picking up the phone so as to ask Liu Yangfan what kind of stupid wine he had offered. How could it make such a healthy guy fall sick all of a sudden?

Cheng Feichi stopped him.

"It's really nothing," Cheng Feichi said resignedly. "It'd be better to go to sleep or read a book if you have so much time on your hands. When the term begins, it'll be our final year."

Ye Qin couldn't fall asleep or read a book. He glanced at Cheng Feichi each time he turned a page, making sure that he was only uncomfortable for the time being and a few cups of warm water would be enough for him to recover. Still worried, Ye Qin got out of the bed and sat in front of Cheng Feichi, holding his own face in his hands as he read so that he was able to look at Cheng Feichi whenever he lifted his head.

It was okay at first, but after a while, Cheng Feichi felt as if he hadn't been kicked out just now, but had instead escaped—and now, he'd been recaptured by Ye Qin and put under his careful watch.

Cheng Feichi knocked on the table with his pen cap. "Time to sleep."

"Aren't you still awake?" Ye Qin defended himself.

Cheng Feichi said, "I have class tomorrow, and the teaching plan isn't finished yet."

It was for his tutoring class. Cheng Feichi had planned to finish the material last night, but when his plans had been disrupted, he had no choice but to stay up and get it done before dawn.

Ye Qin began to feel guilty again. He slumped his shoulders and let out a low "Oh" sound.

After a while, he changed his position and rested on his stomach. His chin pressed against the back of his hands and his mouth was puckered. He mumbled, "So you...you're not angry at me?"

Despite everything, Ye Qin was still worrying about what

had happened a few hours ago.

Cheng Feichi sighed. He didn't know how to explain to him that he didn't care about whatever angry statements slipped out of Ye Qin's mouth without thinking. Even though he felt like his heart had been stabbed in the moment, the only thing he could remember in the end was the happiness Ye Qin had given him.

He was not stupid. He was fully aware of what Ye Qin was thinking behind all these behaviors. He had also thought about whether he should teach this naughty little boy a lesson. But Ye Qin was always able to shrink into a ball and roll to his feet when he wanted to be cruel, like a lovely little hedgehog—whining and poking so precisely and so perfectly into the softest place in his heart.

Therefore, he thought that it wasn't a bad thing if someone got uppity when they felt loved and supported. As long as he could bear it, that little boy could always be just a boy.

Speaking of which, even Cheng Feichi himself couldn't believe it—in less than a year, he'd become totally enchanted by Ye Qin's raw innocence and immodesty, even though he knew they were totally different when it came to personality and family background. Even though he knew he could occasionally be hurt by Ye Qin's fangs and claws, he was still reluctant to kick him out of his heart, or to make Ye Qin feel sad.

However, Ye Qin didn't know Cheng Feichi so well yet. He became even more panicked when he heard him sigh. He grabbed Cheng Feichi's hand and swung it towards his face. "Hit me. Blame me for talking nonsense. Hurt me and I'll never dare do it again."

Whether Ye Qin was actually letting Cheng Feichi hit him was still a matter of doubt. But at least they both knew that Cheng Feichi could not use force to solve the problem.

So, when Cheng Feichi freed his hand to squeeze Ye Qin's

chin, Ye Qin was so scared that his face turned pale, afraid that Cheng Fei would really beat him. He closed his eyes and got ready to duck a punch when warm fingers gently brushed his cheeks.

"Stopped crying?" Cheng Feichi asked softly.

Ye Qin, who couldn't help crying in the staircase, blushed. He turned his head and stood up, then quickly climbed back to the bed and wrapped himself with the blanket. He had his back to Cheng Feichi and pressed his knees against his chest, curling himself up like a lump of dough.

Before two minutes had passed, he remembered that despite having wronged Cheng Feichi, he hadn't made Cheng Feichi forgive him yet, so he slowly poked his head out.

"Come...sleep with me."

Cheng Feichi said, "Not now."

"Let's sleep together...gege."

Cheng Feichi felt weird and looked back at Ye Qin, who only revealed half of his head.

Ye Qin was uncomfortable under his scrutinizing eyes. Suddenly, he forgot all about taking it slow and being gentle and patient. He wanted to just send the helve after the hatchet in a very cool way, yet he found no momentum for the performance.

He mumbled like a tiny cat, "Do you want to sleep with me or not? I'll let you be on the top, just for the first time. I won't wait for you forever!"

CHAPTER 12

WHEN Cheng Feichi really closed his book, turned off the lamp, and walked towards the bed, Ye Qin flinched again.

But he couldn't eat his own words. He wanted to take the lead in this relationship in the future. Right now he could only stay in Cheng Feichi's arms and close his eyes, as if he was about to die for some sacred undertaking.

Cheng Feichi moved closer and asked, "Who taught you to say that?"

Ye Qin opened his eyes slightly. Seeing Cheng Feichi's handsome face not an inch away from him, he hurriedly closed his eyes again. He shook his head and said, "No one taught me. I said that all on my own."

The fact is that, indeed, no one had taught him. That night when he was staying at home, he did all the necessary online research. After that, he didn't sleep well the whole night—a huge fire had been kindled in his body, and the heat did not subside for a long time.

Now things were even more serious. Cheng Feichi's warm breath ghosted all over his face, and every cell in Ye Qin's body seemed to have been activated. It made Ye Qin feel dizzy and unable to breathe.

But in the end, Cheng Feichi merely leaned forward and gave him a quick kiss, before letting him go. Cheng Feichi lay down on his right side.

"Sleep now. Good night."

During the day, while doing his homework, Ye Qin was tangled in deep thought about why yesterday's "seduction" had failed.

He even called Cheng Feichi "gege"—usually any time Cheng Feichi heard that, he got quite excited; he'd kiss Ye Qin so fiercely that he wouldn't be able to keep his feet on the ground. But what about last night? Was it because Cheng Feichi was tired and therefore couldn't be turned on, or was Qin-ge losing his appeal?

Ye Qin threw down the pen and dashed to the bathroom for the mirror. He found in the mirror a pretty boy with a high-bridged nose, big eyes, and smooth skin that wasn't at all affected by his late night.

Ye Qin scratched his head. Nothing seemed to have gone wrong.

...So it must be Cheng Feichi's problem.

Cheng Feichi had gone to the educational institution where he was working, and would not return until evening. So, Ye Qin called Zhou Feng, who was also idling around.

Zhou Feng was so busy having fun last time. This time, seeing a straight-A student's summertime homework, his eyes lit up and started copying it as soon as he sat down. Not satisfied with just copying it himself, he urged Ye Qin to join him. "If you don't copy it, it'll be a waste of such a good opportunity. If you only count on yourself, when would you be able to finish so many sheets?"

After painful struggling, Ye Qin's conscience and self-es-

teem prevailed after all. Thinking of Cheng Feichi who, himself already occupied, was so busy preparing test papers for him, walking him through problems that were hard to tackle, he pushed back Cheng Feichi's amazing exercise books and stated with staunch righteousness, "I won't copy them!"

Biting his pen, Ye Qin had difficulty in finishing even the first two questions when he suddenly recalled something. He asked Zhou Feng, "Didn't the class monitor give you lessons? Why are you still copying other people's homework?"

Zhou Feng said indifferently, "He doesn't know that I'm doing this, anyway. So long as I finish my homework, he'll have to reward me."

Wanting to get some learned experience, Ye Qin asked curiously, "What reward?"

Zhou Feng laughed. "The same reward that you gave Cheng Feichi, of course."

In the blink of an eye, the two-month-long summer vacation came to an end with Ye Qin furiously trying to catch up with his homework.

On the first day, the school auditorium was appropriated for the freshman class's opening ceremony. All the senior students once again gathered on the recreational yard. This was very annoying for Ye Qin, who had studied late into the night yesterday and now looked like hell. The teacher on the stage was shouting campaign slogans until his voice was hoarse, his hand pointing to the huge words "College Entrance Examination Countdown: 310 Days" on the wall. But Ye Qin couldn't hear a thing. He was standing in the recreational yard, dozing off.

When he tilted his head, Cheng Feichi, who was standing nearby at the end of the line, caught him with his shoulder. He gave his waist a push to help Ye Qin stand straight and whispered by his ear, "It'll be over soon. Try not to fall asleep here."

Ye Qin leaned on Cheng Feichi instead and closed his eyes to continue dozing. Anyway, Cheng Feichi wouldn't let him fall.

It was universally acknowledged that staying at home was immensely better than going to school. However, what Ye Qin never expected was that the intense study wasn't the most annoying thing, nor the distance between him and Cheng Feichi. It was instead the hundreds of newcomers in the school—thousands of adolescent girls.

Since the beginning of the semester, Cheng Feichi had never had a minute's peace. Those who sent him love letters in public, flirted with him in secret, confessed to him in person, peeked at him from the back window...had been flocking to Class No. 1 nonstop.

If it was just the freshman high school girls, that would be tolerable. But the naïve girls from the junior high school also joined the flock. As soon as Cheng Feichi walked through the school gate, they gathered at the windows, shouting his name in a very cheesy way. They even dared to say that it was sweet to have an age gap between lovers, and beseeched Cheng Feichi to wait for them to grow up.

Bearing witness to such a scene, Ye Qin sighed that public morals were indeed declining—today's girls were a far cry from being ladies. He himself, on the other hand, became more of a frequent visitor than anyone else, always rushing out of his classroom and running to Class No. 1 as soon as the bell rang.

Later, the Office of Academic Affairs intervened. During the students' gathering on Monday, the dean seriously criticized students who failed to abide by school rules and regulations and dared to undermine the learning atmosphere of the senior students. It was now forbidden for students from other years to even go near the teaching building in which the senior students

resided. Penalties would be imposed if anyone dared to flaunt these rules.

The students in the audience knew what the dean was talking about. As soon as the students were dismissed, the campus forum began to discuss the juicy piece of news very enthusiastically.

The post was even transferred to Baidu Bars, and students from other schools in the neighborhood heard of the "collective premature love" incident that had been brought to the Office of Academic Affairs. Cheng Feichi's photos were everywhere. There was news that talent scouts had tried to get him signed as an idol—it was so plausible that Ye Qin almost believed it when he saw it.

Despite the ban, there were still girls who wouldn't be deterred. Today, there was another love letter that Cheng Feichi's classmate was helping smuggle to him before it got intercepted by Ye Qin.

"You are the most beautiful scenery in my eyes..." Ye Qin squinted at Cheng Feichi as he read the letter. Seeing that Cheng Feichi was immersed in reading and gave no response, Ye Qin lost interest, stuffing the letter back into the envelope.

Ye Qin plonked himself down on the chair and leaned closer to Cheng Feichi, examining his face. "Let me see if you could really be a star."

Cheng Feichi never browsed the campus forums. Hearing this, he raised his head and asked, "What star?"

"Those actors in idol dramas on TV." Ye Qin got goose bumps when he thought of the Korean dramas that Sun Yiran had recently been watching on her mobile phone, the screen smeared by her tears. He warned Cheng Feichi seriously, "If there's a talent scout trying to recruit you—I mean, hypothetically—you are not allowed to be an idol."

Cheng Feichi asked, "Why?"

Ye Qin lied through gritted teeth. "Why? It's not the right job for you. You look so intimidating when you're stern, you'd scare the audience."

"When have I ever looked stern in front of you?"

"Last year when you took me to the police station. It was so scary."

Cheng Feichi curled his lips and smiled, thinking that Ye Qin might never be able to forget that in his lifetime.

Ye Qin pretended to be dissatisfied and gave a snort. He leaned back on the table to continue reading the posts in the campus forum.

Of course he would never tell Cheng Feichi that it was because he was afraid that he would be seen and noticed by more people, and that he would have to flirt with the pretty actresses.

Of course he would not tell Cheng Feichi that when he looked stern, he didn't look intimidating at all; his smile, on the other hand, was unimaginably enchanting.

Of course, Ye Qin's worries were unnecessary. Before becoming a lady killer, Cheng Feichi was first a straight-A student.

The cool September breeze blew away the last traces of summer heat, and autumn quietly arrived. Not long after the National Day holiday, the results of the two competitions that Cheng Feichi had participated in at the beginning of the semester were made public.

The school gate was decked with red lanterns and streamers, and happy tidings were printed on red paper and posted on every bulletin board, from the school gate to the corridors of the teaching building. Cheng Feichi's name could be seen even when one was on the way to the toilet.

The physics and chemistry competitions were only half a day apart, and yet Cheng Feichi had won the first prizes in both.

This unusual achievement was enough for the principal to show off at numerous school opening ceremonies in the future.

Ye Qin felt himself sharing the honor. He ordered pricey takeaway and invited all the students in Classes No. 1 and No. 2 to enjoy bubble tea. Someone asked him why he was even happier than Cheng Feichi himself. Ye Qin proudly waggled his head and said, "He's my teacher. Shouldn't I be this happy for my teacher after he won such a big prize?"

Well, normally it would be the student who should make his teacher proud. But when it came to Ye Qin, it was the other way round and nobody thought there was anything wrong about it.

After the night sessions, Ye Qin jogged out from the back door with his hands in his pockets. Cheng Feichi had been waiting in the parking area for a while.

"Guess what I just did?" Ye Qin asked mysteriously.

Cheng Feichi thought for a while. "You were detained by the teacher again?"

Ye Qin was upset. "How's that even possible? I am now a positive example that Mr. Sun uses to encourage my classmates. I'm chock full of positive energy."

Because Mr. Cheng didn't give up on helping Ye Qin with his schoolwork even during summer vacation, Ye Qin got unprecedentedly good grades in the first monthly exam. He was completely out of the Backward Students League.

"Guess again," Ye Qin urged him, not willing to give up.

Cheng Feichi couldn't come up with an answer, so he shook his head.

An uncontrollable smile spread across Ye Qin's face. He blinked his eyes a few times and said with some mystique, "You'll know tomorrow."

The next day, Cheng Feichi was dragged to the school gate by his deskmate, and saw that a heart, hand drawn with a marker, had been added to his name on the bulletin, circling two letters: YR.

Cheng Feichi immediately recognized the person behind this chubby heart. However, other students were still in the dark. They seized onto these two letters, bringing up all the girls whose name had a "Y" and "R" on campus forums and checking them out one by one. A formal police investigation couldn't have been more thorough.

That made Ye Qin terribly sore. He had come up with a way to secretly show his affection for Cheng Feichi—not without difficulty—only to be mistaken for someone else. It turned out that no one thought he was the one who did it.

In late October, Classes No. 1 and No. 2 were taking a physical test together. When the teacher was absent, someone took the opportunity to ask whether that "YR" was referring to Sun Yiran. Sun Yiran blushed and said no, while Zhou Feng also supported that statement to help her out. But people wouldn't buy it. After all, when Cheng Feichi had just been transferred to this school, she was pursuing him with much enthusiasm. That fact was known by all.

In the end, Cheng Feichi had to stand up for her. "It's not her. I know who it is."

One stone stirred up millions of waves. The students, driven crazy by the intense curricula, finally seized upon an opportunity to see how the most popular gossip unveiled itself. None of them would let Cheng Feichi get out of it easily. With great eagerness, they demanded him to reveal the person's real name.

"Me, it's me!" Ye Qin couldn't bear to see Cheng Feichi bombarded with questions, so he admitted it. "When I wrote it, it was too dark, so I miswrote the second letter. It should be a 'Q.'"

The crowd was silent for a few seconds, and then all burst into laughter.

Ye Qin was mystified. Why didn't they believe that he and Cheng Feichi were together? Didn't they seem to be a wonderful fit?

No wonder his seduction had yielded no results.

Somehow, this made Ye Qin feel insecure. He stayed listless for the whole day. Cheng Feichi, who was very sensitive, noticed it and dispelled his worries with action: after the night sessions, he held Ye Qin at the corner of the empty staircase and gave him a long kiss.

After the kiss, he continued holding Ye Qin tightly. Ye Qin's whole body was immersed in warmth. Then he felt the hands around his waist slowly moving down, and gently stop a bit below his waist—not going far enough to reach his round bottom.

Cheng Feichi whispered, "I missed something last time. It's soft here, too."

If it was someone else saying this, Ye Qin would probably take offense. But when these words came out of Cheng Feichi's mouth in such a low voice, all Ye Qin could feel was unbearable dizziness.

Ye Qin could sense the underlying meaning of what he said: *I want you, but I want to cherish you more.*

Normally, Ye Qin absolutely detested physical contact, but he didn't hate the intimacy between him and Cheng Feichi—he even felt happy about it, and wanted him to be even closer. He guessed it might have something to do with the blood shared between them. Thinking about it in this way, he didn't feel so bad about their relationship.

Secretly, he felt somehow fortunate that at least the blood bond between them was undeniable; it could not be cut. Even if one day Cheng Feichi accidentally found out that his motivation for pursuing him in the first place was impure, he wouldn't be so cold-hearted to not forgive him eventually.

Having thought this, Ye Qin let out a sigh of relief, then

raised his hand and gave Cheng Feichi a soft punch. "*Your* butt isn't soft?"

Cheng Feichi was tall, while Ye Qin was a little more than 5'6". Ye Qin could perfectly fit in the space between his arms. As Cheng Feichi hugged him for longer time, him felt even more comfortable. He lowered his head and rubbed Ye Qin's fleshy earlobes with his thoroughly kissed lips.

"Mine isn't as soft as yours... Ye Xiaoruan."

Ye Qin was utterly abashed when he heard that nickname. He tried to shrink out of Cheng Feichi's embrace, who took the hint and released his arms to let him escape.

Suddenly, a strange sound came from behind. Cheng Feichi turned around and saw Ye Qin frozen just two steps away from him.

Less than three meters away, Sun Yiran stood on the last step leading to the corridor. Her hands were covering her mouth, and her wide eyes were fixed on them blankly.

On the small road stretching from the back gate of Middle School No. 6, the three of them walked side by side.

Cheng Feichi wheeled the bike forward, walking close to the driving lane. Ye Qin, who was walking near the curb, raised his hand to calm down his right eyelid which had been twitching like crazy since the afternoon. He thought to himself that bad luck could indeed only ever be late; never absent.

Sun Yiran, who was caught in the middle, turned out to be the calmest one. She had already been on the way home after the evening sessions, when she suddenly recalled that she had left her exercise book in the classroom. Having asked Mr. Sun for the key, she rushed back, only to bump into the two boys making out at the corner of the staircase under cover of darkness. Once the initial surprise passed, all the clues gathered from the past

suddenly reappeared in her mind. After the sudden realization, she accepted it as fact.

Seeing Ye Qin with his head still hanging low, looking as embarrassed as if they'd been caught *in flagrante delicto*, Sun Yiran patted him on the shoulder. "Qin-ge, there is absolutely no need to worry. I promised that I'll never tell anyone. I won't go back on my word."

Just now in the staircase, Cheng Feichi had stood in front of Ye Qin, whose mind had already gone black, and pleaded with Sun Yiran to not spill the beans. The two boys seemed like Romeo and Juliet at the eve of parting. Sun Yiran sympathized with them, and therefore agreed right away.

Ye Qin wasn't worried that she would tell anyone, but couldn't shake off the embarrassment of being caught "red-handed." He and Cheng Feichi had kissed for such a long time and said so many intimate words, thinking that no one was around. Only God knew if she had heard them. Even worse, Sun Yiran had once pursued Cheng Feichi. It just added embarrassment to this situation.

Ye Qin was about to have a mental breakdown whenever he thought about the accident. How could he ever raise his head and feel normal and comfortable among his classmates in the future? So many things were weighing him down, yet he had to feign calmness.

"A good heart accompanies your good looks. Of course I know you won't."

Sun Yiran rejoiced at the compliment, yet soon started to complain. "You should have told me! You've kept it from me for so long. Fortunately, I have sharp eyes; I already spotted something going on between the two of you."

Ye Qin's heart suddenly thumped. "Is...is it so obvious?"

"Well, not really." Sun Yiran stroked her chin. "Maybe I'm

just meticulous enough to notice it."

Having escorted Sun Yiran back to the faculty residential area not far from the school, the two boys continued walking. As soon as Cheng Feichi held out his hand, Ye Qin distanced himself over three meters away and hid his own hand behind his back.

Having failed to grab Ye Qin's hand, Cheng Feichi said resignedly, "No one would see it here."

Ye Qin rolled his eyes, and sneakily pointed to the surveillance camera above his head. "It's watching!"

Seeing him as panicked as a frightened bird, Cheng Feichi couldn't say anything anymore. He grew obedient and kept a distance between them, walking slowly behind Ye Qin, neither too far nor too close.

No one likes to be a thief in love; always on the alert and easily frightened.

At the gate of the compound, Ye Qin kept his head low in dismay, looking like a frosted eggplant, feeling even more upset than before. Cheng Feichi wanted to ruffle his hair, but his hand froze in the air and paused for a while. Finally, he put it down.

When he turned around and was about to leave, Ye Qin grabbed the back seat of his bicycle and whispered, "Don't be angry."

Cheng Feichi suddenly let out a sigh of relief. He turned and said, "That's what I should say to you. I'm sorry for scaring you."

Ye Qin pulled his hair with frustration. "You didn't scare me. I did this to myself." He organized his words and tried to make himself sound calm. "You finally got that prize. Everything will be ruined if the news blows up at this point. No school would ever accept you."

Cheng Feichi was stunned. He hadn't expect that Ye Qin was being nervous for his sake; for his future.

His efforts to contain his emotions failed, and he raised his

hand again and ruffled Ye Qin's hair. His hand finally stopped at the back of Ye Qin's neck, with his palm pressed against Ye Qin's protruding cervical vertebra. He forced Ye Qin to look up.

"Others won't find out," Cheng Feichi tried to comfort him. "Even if they do, what can they do to us?"

Ye Qin said anxiously, "It would be detrimental! Didn't you transfer to our school because..."

Realizing that he'd just blurted it out, Ye Qin stopped in the middle of the sentence, attempting to cover his mouth. He looked at Cheng Feichi with big innocent eyes, trying to pretend that he didn't say anything just now.

Cheng Feichi quickly realized that Ye Qin had probably heard about the reasons behind his transfer. After all, the first time they met was when Zhou Feng caused him trouble. Maybe Ye Qin and his friends had already inspected everything about his background.

Ye Qin waited for a long time, but the questioning he had expected did not come.

Cheng Feichi was still smiling. He softly squeezed the nape of Ye Qin's neck, and was still comforting him. "It's not that serious, I promise." Then he added, as if he was afraid that Ye Qin would not believe it, "I didn't transfer to this school because of the reasons you heard. The rumors aren't true."

Over the next few days, Ye Qin felt a bit overwhelmed.

Liu Yangfan and Zhao Yue were going abroad for study next week, so they organized a send-off party for close friends. Ye Qin could be absent-minded even with darts in his hands, and when he was alone, his brain would automatically revolve Cheng Feichi.

The rumors weren't true? Cheng Feichi isn't gay? Then how did he end up in this relationship with me?

The dart hissed past and almost hit Zhou Feng. Zhou Feng wailed and threw himself at Sun Yiran, but Sun Yiran kicked him away.

"You're murdering your husband!" Zhou Feng howled even louder.

"Husband? Are you A-Qin's husband?" Liu Yangfan laughed. "Be careful, Straight-A Cheng will come for ya."

Zhou Feng got up from the ground and continued moving towards Sun Yiran with a flattering smile. "I'm Yiran's husband, that's for sure. Besides, we don't know about things between Qin-ge and Cheng Feichi. Maybe Qin-ge is the 'husband'?"

Such words made Ye Qin very happy. He put down the darts in his hand, and sat back on the sofa in search of some snacks.

"By the way, why didn't Cheng Feichi come today?" Zhao Yue asked Zhou Feng, "And your Yuan..."

This sentence was interrupted by Zhou Feng's cough.

Ye Qin held up a glass of iced drink. "He needs to work today." Then he took a big gulp.

If Cheng Feichi was here, he wouldn't dare to drink like this.

"Didn't he get the first prize in that contest? Doesn't it come with a reward?" Zhao Yue asked.

Ye Qin scoffed as if in disgust, taking Zhao Yue for a materialist. "He didn't participate in that competition for money. Throughout the country, he's the only one who can win the first prizes in both physics and chemistry."

There was pride in his tone, which he himself hadn't noticed.

Since he was going abroad in a few days, Liu Yangfan was a bit depressed tonight. After taking a few sips, he became even quieter and reminded Ye Qin as if he was leaving his last words, "I think that straight-A student isn't an easy nut to crack. A-Qin, don't wind up trapped in your own game."

"Of course I won't!" Ye Qin hated being questioned about

his abilities in dealing with romantic relationships. He immediately retorted, "It was him who got trapped, not me."

"Really?"

Ye Qin held up his chin and said, "He loves me like crazy. I can end this relationship at any time. It's my call."

Sun Yiran was a little bit confused. "End it? Why would you want to break up with him? You're getting along so well."

Zhao Yue laughed right after hearing that. "You are innocent indeed. After hearing that two boys are in love, you accepted it faster than anyone else."

Zhou Feng was afraid that he would start saying inappropriate things again, so he dragged Zhao Yue away to play billiards. Liu Yangfan followed.

Sun Yiran was stunned for a long time, feeling confused. She sat down next to Ye Qin and asked carefully, "You and Cheng Feichi...are not actually in a relationship?"

Ye Qin didn't want to lose face in front of friends; indeed, there was no reason to change what he had just said in front of so many people. So, he managed to answer with a piece of truth that didn't hurt so much. "I'm not gay."

"You're just playing him?"

"Yup."

"Why?"

Ye Qin randomly picked a reason. "He annoys me."

Sun Yiran sucked in a breath, appearing more shaken than when she saw the two kissing in the staircase. "How can you..."

"What?" Ye Qin answered very quickly, with feigned frankness. "He'd wind up tricked either by me or by other people. He's poor, that's his mistake. He's destined to be pranked. He's lucky enough to be in love with me. If it'd been someone else, things might be even worse now. You've got to have something to offer when you're in a relationship. Yet what does he have? I might be the only one who can tease some fun out of him."

He explained himself in a few words. Now that they were already in a relationship, whether Cheng Feichi was gay or not was not important. He himself was not gay, but hadn't he won Cheng Feichi's heart despite that? Now that he felt good being together with him, wasn't it natural to let things remain as they were? In fact, there wasn't much to think about. Cheng Feichi wouldn't leave him anyway.

Ye Qin was always complacent about how Cheng Feichi tolerated and cherished him.

Sun Yiran couldn't accept that he could play with other people's feelings with such indifference. She stood up and glared at Ye Qin. "I didn't expect that you were this kind of person."

And she walked away angrily.

Knowing that she wouldn't go out and tell anyone about this, Ye Qin picked up the phone and frowned.

He had just paraded his importance to Cheng Feichi. Now Cheng Feichi wasn't replying to his messages?

Cheng Feichi didn't do that intentionally. He was too busy tonight.

After class, he was first called to the office by the head teacher, who gave him several self-admission application forms from well-known universities. And then he listened to the head teacher comparing different institutions and majors, drawing up a school list for him.

When he left the office, the sun had already set. Riding his bike, Cheng Fei thought, *Fortunately, I told Ye Qin that I'm going to work tonight, and that he does not need to wait.*

Then he rushed to the fast-food restaurant and kept himself busy until late at night. Having finished today's work, he changed clothes and picked up his mobile phone. Only then did

he see the two messages from Ye Qin. One was "Do you still have time to come over?" and the other was "I don't care whether you come or not. I'll sleep here tonight. Bye, good night."

Cheng Feichi smiled. Between the lines, he could see very clearly Ye Qin's dissatisfaction.

After work, he walked for a while with his co-workers. Wu Rui had recently begun preparing for the postgraduate entrance examination. When she heard that he had won two first prizes in the national competitions, her jaw dropped. She asked him why he still continued to go to school and work. Even only one first prize was enough to guarantee admission to a very good school.

"If I were you, I would choose a school now and then sleep at home until next year, when the time for enrollment comes," Wu Rui said enviously.

Cheng Feichi smiled, but didn't give any comment.

It was not that he hadn't thought about temporarily taking a break from school, so that he could focus on making money while taking care of his mother. The application forms were already a form of guarantee for him. Whether he took the college entrance examination or not didn't matter anymore. Even the head teacher asked him if he needed a rest and offered to grant him a few days off.

But Ye Qin still had half of his senior year to finish. Cheng Feichi had to help him make progress in his studies, so that he might qualify for ideal universities. In the afternoon, he hadn't decided where he was going, for he still needed time to see how much progress Ye Qin could make. When the semester was over, he could roughly figure out what level of school Ye Qin could be admitted to, and then he could submit his own application. It wouldn't be too late.

If that didn't work, he could just take the college entrance examination with Ye Qin. It may be difficult for Ye Qin to catch up with him in merely six months, but it was still easy for him to sign up for the universities that Ye Qin could reach.

Cheng Feichi did not share these thoughts with the head teacher, nor did he plan to tell his mother. He also convinced himself early on that, although top universities and ordinary universities seemed to have different starting points, whether one could learn a lot was still depended on the efforts one made. For him, there was no difference between the university's affiliated high school and High School No. 6. The reasoning was similar.

The only thing that needed to be considered was whether something was worthy or not. He believed that he had the right to make this decision for himself.

It was an early autumn night. The breeze was cool, and the mist obscured the light of the street lamps.

Carrying the bicycle into the quiet corridor, Cheng Feichi heard a crunching sound and saw the door on the second floor open. Mr. Li stood at the door and gave him a wave, a coat covering his shoulders.

"You got some visitors at home. They came in the afternoon and haven't left yet," Mr. Li said worriedly. "I thought about going up and knocking on the door, but I was afraid of interrupting anything important. I heard footsteps upstairs just now, so your mom should be fine."

According to Mr. Li's description, Cheng Feichi thought *that* man was here again. Standing at the door, he was still hesitating about whether to go in or not when the door suddenly opened from inside.

The one who came out was a middle-aged woman. She was about the same height as Cheng Xin, wearing a luxurious women's suit. She wore a updo. Her high heels made muffled noises as they stepped through the corridor.

When she saw Cheng Feichi, she was taken aback for a moment, then she lifted the corner of her mouth and smiled. She turned her head, saying towards someone in the apartment, "Oh, so this is your son? Didn't you say that he won't be back today?"

After that, she turned back and examined Cheng Feichi from head to toe, as if she was appraising some product.

Cheng Feichi gazed back, seeing her clenched hands and trembling jaw.

In the end, the woman cared more about her face. Self-respect forbade her to appear unimposing, so she sneered. "You've been hidden away for so many years. She dared not let me meet you. But now...obviously my expectations were too high."

She didn't need to say the rest. Cheng Feichi already understood what she meant.

The woman did not lose her demeanor. Even when she left, she looked graceful and proud, strutting about holding herself tall. During that exchange, Cheng Xin sat inside and said nothing.

Cheng Feichi closed the door to keep the noises out. Then he went to the kitchen and put the kettle on.

A thin layer of mist formed on the window, and the tea on the table was already cold. Maybe Cheng Xin had been sitting here from the very minute the woman came.

The autumn night was already too cold for Cheng Xin to sustain. When Cheng Feichi poured her a cup of hot tea and was about to put a blanket on her, she finally moved.

Her lips moved stiffly. "She will come again."

Cheng Feichi's hands froze, but he soon resumed his movements and wrapped the blanket around her as if he hadn't heard anything.

Cheng Xin's thin body suddenly trembled. She gave Cheng Feichi's hand a hard press. "Just go abroad, will you?"

Her withered hands were shaking, and so was her voice. "Go abroad, your mom is begging you."

Cheng Xin rarely referred to herself as his "mom." This heavy word prevented Cheng Feichi from turning back and leaving.

With a glimmer of hope, he asked, "Go abroad, and then do what?"

Cheng Xin thought he was finally persuaded, and she held his hand tightly again. "Get into a good school, and then he will take you back..."

"Who is 'he,' and where would he take me?"

"He is your dad." Cheng Xin faintly smiled, her eyes full of radiance, as if she was thinking of something pleasant. "Go back where you should be. That's your home."

Cheng Feichi's lips moved, but it took a long time for him to finally say, "I don't have a father."

"But you do. You do have one." Cheng Xin was a little anxious. "He came here during the Spring Festival. You met him. Didn't he go to your school and give a speech last semester?"

Cheng Feichi thought it was funny, but he couldn't laugh. It had been twenty years, and the man had only showed up a precious handful of times, but he was always able to win and keep his mother's heart and loyalty.

He wanted to ask Cheng Xin if she had lost her mind, if she was crazy, but he knew that his grandpa and grandma had asked those questions countless times. What difference could he make?

Cheng Xin went crazy twenty years ago, and there was no cure. The normal state she had remained in all these years had simply been her disguise, and now she had finally torn off the mask, revealing her true self.

"Two years, just wait another two years, and everything will be fine. He promised that he'll take us home. Then you'll be the only heir in his family, and no one can drive us away again."

Cheng Xin spoke faster and faster. Her breath quickened and her words became incoherent. "You go abroad first. Listen to what your mom says, okay? Go abroad now, the sooner the better."

The arrival of that woman had obviously upset her, forcing her to say things that were hard to say before. Although Cheng Feichi had some assumptions about his mother's secrets, he couldn't stop trembling inside when he heard her confirming them one by one.

"Go abroad, and continue to live underground like ants?"

Cheng Xin froze. She probably hadn't expected that Cheng Feichi would sum up their life with such an ugly metaphor; in such a straightforward and cruel manner. She immediately wanted to refute, but could not find a single valid reason.

She could only hold Cheng Feichi's hand tightly, like a drowning man grabbing a lone piece of driftwood. "Listen to mom, could you? When you come back from abroad, we don't have to live like this anymore."

The wind blew. The windows kept banging. Cheng Feichi felt as if the cold wind had blown into the depth of his heart, freezing everything inside.

All the efforts he made, over so many years, were for the sake of banishing the shadows that had haunted him. And despite his wishes, his mother was desperately dragging him back into the darkness.

On Sunday, Ye Qin was working on his homework at the apartment in the Jiayuan Compound. Cheng Feichi came later than expected, thus receiving complaints when he entered the house.

"Did you get another part-time job without telling me? No wonder why you wouldn't let me pick you up."

Following the start of the term, the two had fewer opportunities to be together, and this apartment became the best place for them to meet once a week. But for Cheng Feichi's tutor work on Saturday, Ye Qin would have him stay with him for the whole weekend.

"No," Cheng Fei said while changing his shoes. "All my part-time jobs are at night."

Ye Qin asked nonchalantly, "Then why are you here so late?"

Cheng Feichi let the question pass lightly. "Something's up at home."

While helping Ye Qin with his homework, he received another call from a study abroad agency. He was told that the relevant procedures had been gone through, and was asked to take some time completing the visa procedures. Cheng Feichi said straightforwardly over the phone that the application had not been submitted by him, and that he did not need their service. The person at the other side seemed at a loss, telling him that since most of the fees had been paid, he needed to go there in person.

After hanging up, Cheng Feichi wanted to call his mother, but finally gave up after a quick consideration. Cheng Xin's attitude was clear, and he couldn't change her mind by his own efforts. Yet he had decided to stay in the country to pursue further studies. Now one of them had to compromise.

"You haven't finished the call yet?"

Hearing the voice from behind, Cheng Feichi turned his head and saw Ye Qin craning his neck. He poked his head out, his cheeks bulging like an unhappy kid whose toy was stolen.

Cheng Feichi went back to the room and resumed "class." Ye Qin became lazy again, and he began talking nonsense. Failing to catch Cheng Feichi's attention with "what shall we eat tonight," he tried to talk about study. He yawned and asked, "If I keep working like this, what kind of school can I get into?"

Cheng Feichi said, "It depends on your performance."

Ye Qin let out a sigh and bent over the desk.

"But I can promise," Cheng Feichi continued, "that you will definitely be admitted to the same university as me."

Ye Qin rolled his eyes and said he didn't believe it. Cheng Feichi smiled, but did not explain further.

He would not forget any promises he had made. Even if Cheng Xin pleaded with tears, even if he was heartbroken for her, he would not change his mind.

This was what he had promised to Ye Qin. This was also the first decision he had made following his heart's desire, after so many years' unwanted arrangements and deprived choices.

Naturally, Ye Qin knew nothing about it. He was still living his life in a muddle-headed manner.

He studied hard when Cheng Feichi was around, and slacked off when he was away. He was not stupid, yet he was the sort of student who refused to work hard even though he could learn well. Even by studying in such a laid-back manner, his grades were steadily going up.

On the day they saw Liu Yangfan and Zhao Yue off, Zhou Feng cried so hard it was as if he was sending his blood brothers to the execution ground. Ye Qin thought the scene was quite embarrassing, so he left the terminal immediately after the two boys departed, walking in front of Zhou Feng. It wasn't until they got back to the car that Zhou Feng finally stopped crying and dragged Ye Qin to the store so that he could choose a birthday present for Sun Yiran.

They visited boutiques one by one. Several items caught Zhou Feng's eye, but he couldn't make a decision. One moment he felt that a bag was so good that Yiran would definitely like it, while the next he felt that a necklace was also perfect because it matched Yiran's skin color.

"Just buy them all," Ye Qin said.

"Of course I can't do that! A birthday only comes once a year. You have to be very careful choosing birthday presents. If you send all the best things at once, then it's a wrap. What's the point in risking that?"

Ye Qin found it strange. "You're paying so much attention to Yiran's birthday. Aren't you afraid that the class monitor will be jealous?"

"Why would he be jealous?" Zhou Feng couldn't figure out what he was talking about.

"Aren't you two in a relationship?"

"Who told you that? He telling you stories again?" Zhou Feng laughed. He knocked on the counter and asked the salesperson to take out a men's wallet. Holding it in his hand for a moment, he said, "Well, if that's the case, I'll buy him something too."

Ye Qin didn't like how Zhou Feng was enjoying meals from a bowl while longing for something else in the pot, but he was not in a position to interfere in Zhou Feng's own business. So he simply ignored it and went to the next counter, so that he might examine a ring that had caught his eye just now.

He usually wore casual clothes and had no interest in jewelry. However, this ring was designed in a unique way. Several geometric patterns were evenly distributed on the plain metal ring, tiny diamonds interspersed between them. Together, they glimmered with an inconspicuous but gentle light under the lamp.

He had wanted to ask the salesperson to take it out in order to take a better look, but he soon noticed that the ring belonged to the "Love" series—it was one of a pair. He immediately felt numbness in his head, so he gave up on making the request.

After looking around in the boutique, Ye Qin didn't see any other things that attracted him. Unwilling to take a defeat, he took out his cellphone and took a photo of the ring, and then posted it on WeChat Moments with a few casual words: "Looks pretty."

On Sun Yiran's birthday, she invited everyone to eat out at a restaurant. Ye Qin didn't go, but asked Zhou Feng to pass on his presents and good wishes.

But Zhou Feng returned the unopened presents soon enough. He said resignedly, "I tried to talk sense into her, but she wouldn't listen. She said that she'll only talk to you after you've told Cheng Feichi the truth."

Ye Qin sneered at Sun Yiran's righteousness. After the evening sessions, he tossed the bracelet he bought for Sun Yiran to Cheng Feichi, asking him deal with it in whatever way he wanted. He didn't care about it anymore.

He seemed to be angry and fierce, but Cheng Feichi could sense that he was upset.

He knew that Ye Qin was two-faced. He said he didn't care, yet in fact, he cared most about his friends. So, he stood up and said, "I'll give it to her."

"Don't." Ye Qin wasn't willing to let him do it. He held Cheng Feichi's arms, afraid that Sun Yiran would somehow tell Cheng Feichi all about it. He played the spoiled kid. "It's fine that she didn't want it. I'll just wear it myself. The design isn't just for girls."

The temperature had dropped sharply tonight, and a cold front warning was constantly broadcast on TV. After the evening session, the two went to a food stall and sat there for a while. Ye Qin's hands and feet were cold, and he was still shivering after putting on Cheng Feichi's coat. Cheng Feichi wanted to keep Ye Qin's hands warm in his own sweater, but Ye Qin's head shook like a rattle. He seemed extremely reluctant to let him do that.

"I have a T-shirt underneath the sweater," Cheng Feichi said. "You wouldn't actually be touching me."

Ye Qin's face went brilliantly red. He couldn't tell whether it was out of shame or the coldness.

When the soup with chopped mutton intestine was served, Ye Qin warmed his hands with the bowl while drinking the soup. Finally feeling more comfortable, he sniffed and said, "I'll be celebrating my birthday soon."

Cheng Feichi made a noise. "Hmm."

Seeing that he didn't say anything, Ye Qin couldn't help but ask, "Are you free that day?"

"It's the Winter Solstice. I should be free."

The ambiguous answer made Ye Qin worry. "Then have you...have you decided what kind of present you'll give me? Don't get too many things for me. Just one thing will be enough."

He still remembered what Zhou Feng had said about the meaning of birthday gifts. It was rare for him to be superstitious, but he was afraid that Cheng Feichi would give him too many things at once, and then their relationship would come to an end.

Cheng Feichi was amused by how he took the fact he'd be receiving gifts for granted. He reached for his schoolbag and took out a brand-new set of exercise books: *Five Years of College Entrance Exam, Three Years of Mock Exam.* Putting them on the table, he gave them a pat.

"Here, your present."

Knowing that he was making a joke, Ye Qin still pretended to be angry. He fiercely pulled out the answer book tucked in the exercise books and put it in his pocket. "Okay, I'll take it!"

Ye Qin firmly believed that Cheng Feichi would get a birthday present for him. He was anxious, however, because his birthday was not on the Winter Solstice in December, but instead at the end of November. Now there were less than two weeks left.

He wanted to tell Cheng Feichi the truth, but he didn't have the courage. He was afraid that Cheng Feichi would be suspicious and realize that his motive of entering this relationship was not simple. It was said that one lie needed another ten thousand lies for cover. Ye Qin had learned that firsthand.

So, these days, whenever he had free time, he would ponder what excuses he could find to make Cheng Feichi give up working on November 29th and spend the day with him.

His birthday was getting closer and closer, yet before he could come up with a perfect excuse, Cheng Feichi sent a message and asked him to return to his own home in the next few days.

Ye Qin asked for the reason, and Cheng Feichi replied, "My mom's in the hospital."

This time, Cheng Xin had fainted after a cardiac arrest. After being sent to the hospital for emergency treatment, she relied on an oxygen tank for a long time. In the afternoon, she was finally out of critical condition.

It was Ye Jinxiang who came first, and Cheng Feichi worked together with him to take care of Cheng Xin.

Later, Cheng Feichi's grandma arrived as well, saying that she had kept the news from her husband. She held her daughter's scrawny hand while sobbing quietly. After wiping away the tears with a handkerchief, she asked Cheng Feichi, "What happened? Last time when we visited, she seemed just fine, didn't she?"

There was no need to hide secrets from his own family, so Cheng Feichi told his grandmother about that woman's visits; one of which was the stimulation that had triggered Cheng Xin's current state.

Grandma was shocked at first, then she covered her face and started weeping again. "God forbid...Why is this happening to my girl?"

At dusk, Cheng Feichi saw his grandma off by taxi. Then he walked alone on the yellow-leafed path in front of the hospital. His footsteps became slower and slower. Looking up at the stars in the sky, he couldn't find any peace in his heart.

That woman's harsh words still echoed in his ears. Over the years, he had heard a lot of slanderous rumors and vicious comments. He thought that he already had a bullet-proof body and soul, but he still felt demolished when that woman said he was only worthy of staying with his mother in this shabby place forever.

When he got upstairs, he stood by the window at the end of the corridor and took a few deep breaths in the cool night air. Taking out his mobile phone, he replied to Ye Qin's messages, and then entered the ward feeling that he had calmed down a bit.

He had the dinner in the ward with Ye Jinxiang, who offered him the chicken thigh in his own lunch box. "You're still growing, so you need to eat more. I have another social engagement later. I'll have another meal there."

Although Cheng Feichi didn't like the condescending attitude he gave off occasionally, he had to admit that this man at least really cared about Cheng Xin, so he answered politely, "Thank you, Mr. Ye."

Ye Jinxiang could sense Cheng Feichi's attitude had softened, so he talked more, "By the way, you're in the third year of high school, just like my son. Which school are you in?"

"High School No. 6," Cheng Feichi replied.

Ye Jinxiang was a little surprised. He thought Cheng Feichi would at least be in a key high school, such as the university's affiliated high school. He asked him which class he was in, and when he heard that he was in Class No. 1, he showed a knowing look.

"Your mom told me that you were an excellent student. I

knew you must be at the top of your class."

Cheng Feichi couldn't imagine under what circumstances Cheng Xin would praise him for being excellent. He suspected that it was just something she had said in order to avoid embarrassment. For a moment he didn't know how to respond.

Ye Jinxiang seemed to be very interested in this topic. He continued, saying, "My son is also in your school, but he's not in your class. You probably don't know him."

The classrooms of Class No. 1 Class and Class No. 2 were in two separate buildings, separated by a long corridor. Usually students from the two classes met only during daily exercise time. Indeed, there were not many opportunities for communication.

But Cheng Feichi did know many of the students from Class No. 2, and the last name of one of them happened to be Ye. What a coincidence! He thought for a while and asked, "Mr. Ye, what is your son's name? Maybe I know him."

Ye Jinxiang was only too eager for his son to befriend students with good grades and strong motivation, so that he could learn from them, and Cheng Feichi was the son of *that* man. There would be absolutely no harm for Ye Qin to make his acquaintance. So, he answered right away.

"His name is Ye Qin. Qin as in the word 'Qin Pei.'"

Worrying that Cheng Feichi might not realize right away which character it was, he stretched out his index finger and wrote the character in the palm of his hand. After that, he realized that the action was superfluous. Smiling in slight embarrassment, he said, "You're such an excellent student. How could you not recognize this character? That was unnecessary."

CHAPTER 13

WITH only one day left until November 29th, Ye Qin felt that communication via WeChat was too inefficient, so he called Cheng Feichi instead.

Pretending to be the considerate little boyfriend, he asked when the call went through, "How's your mother?"

Cheng Feichi told him that Cheng Xin's condition was stable for now, then Ye Qin immediately changed the subject. "Then how about coming to Jiayuan tonight? I have something to show you."

"What is it?" Cheng Feichi asked.

Ye Qin didn't want to spoil the surprise. "You'll find out when you come."

After a moment of consideration, Cheng Feichi rejected him. "Not today. I have to go to work tonight."

Ye Qin suddenly fell from cloud nine. "Is work more important to you than me? How much money can you make one night? I can give you that money, okay?"

Yes, those ugly words were said hot-headedly. But tomorrow was his eighteenth birthday. How could he not be angry when this blockhead was only thinking of working and money?

After waiting for a long time, he only got a "sorry" from Cheng Feichi. Ye Qin could hardly breathe for a moment, so he hung up without saying a word.

At the other end of the line, Cheng Feichi sighed helplessly, hearing the rapid "beep" sound coming from the receiver.

These days, he stayed with his mother in the hospital in the morning, worked in the fast-food restaurant in the afternoon, and came back to his mother in the evening so that Mrs. Feng could go home. He hardly had any time to spare. He did want to be at Ye Qin's side, but he had more important things to do before the Winter Solstice came.

He went downstairs again to pay the hospital expenses. He had little money with him after that. Cheng Feichi decided that he would not touch the money which his grandma had given him for now. Even if it was used, it would be spent on Cheng Xin. He felt it was not his place to divert it for other purposes.

The meals provided by the hospital were not cheap. Cheng Feichi didn't have dinner at all. Before leaving home, he drank a lot of water and thought that it should be enough to get him through the night.

At midnight when he was finally wrapping up, he felt a subtle stomachache. He rubbed his stomach and had a cup of warm water to ease the pain. Then he used his mobile phone to read his WeChat Moments. Ye Qin had posted a picture of a round table full of delicious dishes, with the caption "East or West, home is the best."

Cheng Feichi knew that the intended audience for this post was no one else but himself. A wry smile appeared on his face, which was pale because of hunger. This little guy was such an expert at targeting his weaknesses.

Zooming in on the photo, Cheng Feichi noticed that there was a man sitting directly on the opposite side. Cheng Feichi could only see his hand holding chopsticks. It was impossible to tell who exactly he was. But since he was at Ye Qin's home, it should be his father, Ye Jinxiang.

When Cheng Feichi had first heard that Ye Qin was Ye Jinxiang's son, he was naturally surprised by such a coincidence.

Then, he thought about it and analyzed it objectively. As far as he could tell, Ye Qin's father didn't know about the relationship between him and Ye Qin. Moreover, whether in past or now, the relationship between Ye Jinxiang and Cheng Xin always looked suspicious and tended to stir people's imaginations and cause them to make assumptions. If Ye Qin knew about it, he might misunderstand something.

So, Cheng Feichi had told Ye Jinxiang that Ye Qin's name "sounded familiar."

Now it seemed that Ye Qin really didn't know about things between Ye Jinxiang and Cheng Xin. Cheng Feichi was relieved for now, but at the same time, he began to ponder what he should do if Ye Qin found out. After a while, he felt that he was being unreasonably worried. What did their parents' relationship have to do with them?

No matter what happened, he would protect Ye Qin and cherish this relationship.

Without Cheng Feichi's face-to-face supervision, Ye Qin's grade ranking dropped as if it was taking a ride on a slide in the monthly examination at the end of November. And just like him, the class monitor Liao Yifang was also on the list of "Good Students Who Should Work Harder."

This time, Ye Qin hadn't paid much attention to the exam. He was taking the opportunity to show his anger towards Cheng Feichi, who did not celebrate Ye Qin's real birthday with him, so he didn't care about the exam results at all. But Liao Yifang was different; he was not as composed as Ye Qin was. Haven received several mild remarks from the teacher, such as "those were points you should've kept" and "this mistake could've been avoided," he was so ashamed he looked as if he'd rather jump off the top of the school building to end this life for good. He didn't feel like having lunch; instead, he sat in the classroom to seize time to learn more.

Ye Qin didn't go home for lunch at noon that day. He came back from a restaurant outside the school and brought Liao Yifang a boxed meal, but Liao Yifang refused to eat.

Ye Qin knocked on his desk and said, "What's up? You only lost some points, why are you taking it more seriously than losing your virginity?"

Unexpectedly, Liao Yifang's mouth flattened, and a teardrop fell from his eye, as if saying "Congratulations, bingo!"

Ye Qin was absolutely shocked and asked about the whole story. Liao Yifang was normally a reserved guy who wasn't accustomed to talking about his personal life, so it was hard for him to tell the story fluently.

Ye Qin managed to grasp the general idea, and got the two key points: "he asked me do it" and "we did it several times." He felt veins standing out on his temples, thinking that Zhou Feng had gone too far. Ye Qin rolled up his sleeves and was ready to go reason with him, only to be stopped by Liao Yifang.

"My grades dropping is my own fault. I should've figured out a balance between maintaining this relationship and studying. Don't blame him for it," Liao Yifang said while wiping his tears. He suddenly felt a bit shy, his cheeks turning red. "Also, he wasn't the only one who wanted it. I wanted it, too."

Ye Qin looked up to the sky and rolled his eyes. Seeing that Liao Yifang was drowning in love and happiness, he tried very hard to forbid himself from telling Liao Yifang about how Zhou

Feng was still pursuing Sun Yiran.

Then he went directly to Zhou Feng, trying to talk sense into him and persuade him to stop playing with Liao Yifang's feelings. He urged Zhou Feng to make a choice between Liao Yifang and Sun Yiran as quickly as possible.

Zhou Feng didn't even give it a thought. "Only kids make choices. Adults want them all."

It was obvious that he was joking about the fact that Ye Qin was still a few days from turning 18.

Ye Qin couldn't speak out loud during the class hour, so he lowered his voice and said, "You're so shameless. Well, in fact, I don't think you should choose. Just stay with the class monitor. After all, you guys have done *that* already."

Zhou Feng was always sleepy in English class. He hid behind the book and yawned. "What already? He really tells you everything. Are you my buddy or his?"

Ye Qin said very seriously, "I'm on the side of justice."

Zhou Feng let out a noisy laugh, his shoulders trembling violently. He only managed to keep his voice down a little bit after the teacher on the stage warned him.

Seeing that Ye Qin was pretending to be listening to the class carefully, he poked him with his elbow. "Don't pretend as if I'm the only one doing wrong things here. When will you get serious with Cheng Feichi? Maybe then I could make do with Yuanyuan."

Ye Qin didn't have time to think about whether he was serious or not. He just wanted to know when Cheng Feichi would go back to school and when he could continue to send him home with that broken bicycle.

This year, winter came earlier than usual. A week before the Winter Solstice, the first snowflakes fluttered to the ground.

It snowed on and off. One day it snowed, the next day flakes stopped falling. Yet the snow never fully stopped. The school was concerned about the potential dangers students would face on the way to and from school, thus they cancelled the morning reading class and evening sessions during this period.

Ye Qin woke up early on his own today, which he seldom did. He brushed his teeth, washed his face, put on clothes and shoes, and didn't realize that he didn't have to go to school so early until he reached the door and saw the big piles of snow. After standing there for more than two minutes, he slowly returned to his bedroom.

A school day without a chance of seeing Cheng Feichi. He couldn't get excited, even when he didn't have to get up early.

After a while, Ye Qin, armed with a down jacket, a hat, and a scarf, pushed open the door again. Holding a spatula in his hand, he found an open space under the eaves with snow that was not yet deep, and squatted down to make a snowman.

A fat snowman was piled up. It was about the size of his palm, because the day was cold and the spatula was not easy to use. During the stacking process, Luo Qiuling was worried that he would catch a cold and came out several times to urge him to go back into the house. In the end, Ye Qin didn't even have the time to make a nose for the snowman. He hurriedly took a picture and followed his mother into the house to warm himself with the heating.

He had wanted to send this photo to Cheng Feichi, had already selected the picture in the dialog box, but before actually sending it, he exited the application in anger.

That guy hasn't taken the initiative to send a message to me. And it's been sixteen hours since we last talked. Why should I still be thinking of him? Ye Qin switched to the Moments page.

By the end of school in the afternoon, even Liao Yifang,

who was always focused on studying, had liked his post, but Cheng Feichi was still quiet.

While Ye Qin was angry, he couldn't help but feel worried for Cheng Feichi. Was his mother's health not good again? Why didn't he get her transferred to a better hospital? *If you don't have money, you can always tell me. An IOU would work if you don't like receiving money from me. Is it wise to care so much about self-esteem now?*

If Luo Qiuling didn't ask him to come back early before he went to school today, he would have already taken a taxi to People's Hospital No. 3 by now. *It would make sense for me to visit his mom as a schoolmate, right?*

Ye Qin was so immersed in his thoughts that when he got home, he lay on the sofa and fiddled with his mobile phone, waiting for dinner to be served. He did not notice that something was wrong at home.

Until he heard the sound of heavy objects hitting the floor from upstairs.

This time, it was Luo Qiuling who got angry first.

Ye Qin hurried upstairs. The door of the master bedroom was open. A mess of papers were scattered on the floor. There was also a black mobile phone.

When Ye Jinxiang was about to pick them up, Luo Qiuling grabbed his arm. "Take good care of our business right now. Don't aim too high. Let's do it step by step, okay?"

Ye Jinxiang shook her off and went to pick up the things on the ground while saying snappishly, "The Chinese herbal medicine market is down. If you don't start planning for something else soon, it'll be too late."

"Planning? So, your plan is to go gambling with that woman?"

"What could you possibly know about it?" Ye Jinxiang was

furious and said very stubbornly, "I'm investing. If I hadn't been out working to expand the business for all these years, how could you and your son stay at home and idle around all day?"

Ye Qin often saw Ye Jinxiang yelling at home, but he had never seen Luo Qiuling being so aggressive in front of him.

She gritted her teeth and resisted her tears, her delicate face turning hideous. "Then how do you explain those text messages? I have tolerated you again and again for the sake of this family, but it doesn't mean I know nothing about it."

"How many times have I told you that I'm just putting on a show when it's useful? You just have to make a scene. You probably have too much free time." Ye Jinxiang probably wanted to boost the credibility of this statement by seeming morally upright. Picking up the mobile phone on the floor, he threw it on the table. "I'll let you handle this cellphone. Is that enough?"

Because of this fight, supper was not served until eight in the evening.

Ye Jinxiang said that he still had a dinner party with his clients and left directly after the quarrel. Ye Qin picked up something as a weapon and was about to follow him, but Luo Qiuling spotted him and stopped him in time. Right now she was wiping tears as she ate, and she choked a few times. Ye Qin regretted not having followed Ye Jinxiang outside and smashing his stupid head in.

"Last time, I found lipstick marks on his collar. This time, it was the mobile phone he uses to contact that woman. I knew that he hadn't broken up with her." Knowing that Ye Qin had witnessed their fight, Luo Qiuling stopped hiding the truth from her son. "I'm only trying to warn him, because I'm afraid that he'll be led astray by her. My only wish is that we can live our own lives. We three, together, as a family. I'm quite satisfied. I don't want to be super rich. I just don't want him to risk what we already have."

She was usually gentle, soft, without definite views of her own, but she was stubborn in this regard. Ye Qin understood that she couldn't let go of the relationship between her and Ye Jinxiang after so many years.

This was why Ye Qin thought that he could never persuade his mother to get a divorce. The only solution was to get Ye Jinxiang to back down.

But something was a bit strange. Lipstick marks on a collar? Ye Qin thought about it, and couldn't picture Cheng Feichi's mother as someone who could do that kind of thing. The impression he got from Cheng Xin was that of a sick woman in bed who usually stayed at home. Now she was even hospitalized. How would she be physically capable of provoking Luo Qiuling with lipstick marks on his father's shirt, or other such bad taste methods?

When he went upstairs after the meal, Ye Qin resorted to a clever trick. While his mother was still downstairs, he sneaked into the master bedroom swiftly, picking up the mobile phone that was lying by the door to look at it. Its design looked familiar—the same model was also being used by Cheng Feichi.

Ye Qin returned to his bedroom, totally overwhelmed. He overthrew the previous beliefs in his mind and re-analyzed the whole story from where his inferences could've gone wrong. After letting go of all those associations and speculations with insufficient evidence, the only thing that he could be certain about was that Cheng Feichi's mobile phone had not been given to him by Ye Jinxiang.

Ye Qin's head was empty for a long time when he came to this conclusion. The first thing that came to mind was that he had done things he shouldn't have due to the anger incited by this misunderstanding.

Then he remembered that Cheng Feichi wouldn't even accept things from him—how could he possibly want Ye Jinxiang's mobile phone? He clearly had bought a new mobile phone because Ye Qin demanded it. He didn't know how to add new friends on WeChat, and Ye Qin had to teach him.

Now Ye Qin realized how stupid he had been at the time. He hadn't realized such obvious things until now. Without even thinking twice about it, he had vented all his anger on Cheng Feichi. Not only did he ignore Cheng Feichi for several days, he also made him go to the clubhouse and wait for two hours in the rain.

At this very moment, the phone in his pocket rang. Ye Qin took it out and saw that Cheng Feichi had sent a photo of a snowman to him. It was only slightly larger than the one Ye Qin had posted on Moments, with a round face and two branches inserted in its body. On each side, there was a glove hanging from the branch. The character "Ruan," which resembled "Qin," was written on the bulging belly of the snowman.

Looking at this snowman, which gave off a charming air of naivety, Ye Qin opened his mouth but couldn't really laugh. After gazing at it for a long time, he only typed one word as a response. "Me?"

Cheng Feichi's hands was probably busy, giving him no time to type. He replied with a voice message, "Uh-huh, is it cute?"

Ye Qin was trying to stop his tears from falling. *I'm far from cute. The only thing I ever did was constantly bully you. Only you'd be foolish enough to think that I'm cute.*

After a while, Cheng Feichi sent another voice message, "There wasn't much time. This snowman is a little small. Next time, I'll make one as tall as you."

Cheng Feichi, who was turning twenty years old after the Spring Festival, rarely sounded this childish. It should have been so sweet for Ye Qin, but at this moment it filled his heart with sourness, as if he had taken a bite of a green strawberry. The unbearable sourness made him want to cry, but still, he couldn't help but want to take another bite.

Ye Qin, who had just had his eighteenth birthday, said with earnest feelings that were also rarely seen, "I don't want another snowman. I want you."

The day before the Winter Solstice was a Friday. Ye Qin was restless all day long, and finally, he gritted his teeth and mustered all his courage. When Liao Yifang went to the bathroom during the break, he dragged him to the corner at the end of the corridor. "Class monitor, I have something to ask you."

Liao Yifang waited and waited, but only saw Ye Qin scratching his cheek, and not a word came out. He thought Ye Qin was going to borrow his homework and immediately made a cross with his hands, signaling refusal. "No way, Ye-tongxue. Another exam is coming next week. You should prove yourself with your hard work. Don't let yourself be so depraved."

Ye Qin was embarrassed by the word "depraved." Yet considering that he had already dragged Liao Yifang all the way here, he thought he had better fire his question after all. Therefore, he finally managed to recite the words he had prepared for asking about this particular topic by telling Liao Yifang why he wanted to do it.

Liao Yifang was a little surprised, and then he blushed. "That's a good idea, but Ye-tongxue...are you eighteen now?"

Ye Qin had expected this question, so he took out his ID card and showed it to him. Liao Yifang adjusted his glasses and looked at it carefully. After hesitating for a moment, he said, "Well, fine. But this is all my personal experience. You should know that there are individual differences. I'm not sure if it will work for you."

After school, the two boys went shopping at a supermarket a little farther away from the school.

At checkout, Ye Qin was so embarrassed that he pushed Liao Yifang toward the cash register, hiding behind Liao Yifang with his head shrunk away. Liao Yifang, however, refused to move forward either because of embarrassment.

Ye Qin lowered his voice and asked, "Haven't you guys done it several times by now? Why are you still so shy?"

Liao Yifang hummed like a mosquito and replied, "He... he's the one who buys everything. I just need to lie down."

Ye Qin was thirsty for knowledge. "You just need to lie down? Don't you need to move?"

"Ah, um...sometimes you have to lie on your stomach. If you want to move...you can do that if you want..."

After buying the necessary stuff, Ye Qin gave the money to Liao Yifang, watching him carefully take out the wallet Zhou Feng had given him, put the money in, and put it in a separate compartment of his schoolbag as if it was a sort of treasure. Ye Qin couldn't stand it, and tried to persuade him, "Class monitor, don't do whatever he asks. He's a terrible person. The more you obey him, the more demanding he will be."

"No, he treats me very well."

Liao Yifang's eyes narrowed as he smiled very happily. The dullness that always ruled his face magically disappeared. Even Ye Qin was able to appreciate his prettiness, lit by that gentle smile.

He counted on his fingers. "There are six billion people in the world, and the average lifetime is 29,200 days; if we assume that each one of us could live for 80 years. Even if you could meet 1,000 different people every day, you can only meet 29.2 million people throughout your life. Divide that number by 6 billion. The chance of two particular people meeting in their lives is less than 0.05%."

Having finished the calculation, Liao Yifang adjusted his glasses and realized that Ye Qin hadn't really seen the point. He concluded while smiling, "It's even more difficult for two people to fall for each other. The future is unpredictable. With that in mind, I just want to be nice to him and make every day he spends with me a happy one."

Ye Qin hadn't expected that the class monitor, normally appearing to be so unsophisticated in that regard, could have such wisdom when it came to romantic relationships. Liao Yifang really had a knack for acting as a relationship expert. If he was assigned to the Civil Affairs Bureau, the divorce rate might drop a lot.

It was a pity that Zhou Feng didn't cherish him. Ye Qin intended to persuade Zhou Feng some other time. He applied what Liao Yifang said to his relationship with Cheng Feichi, and decided that since the past can no longer be changed, he would treat Cheng Feichi better in the future. He should drop the habit of always getting mad at him for no reason.

But after waiting for Cheng Feichi alone in the apartment at the Jiayuan Compound until nearly ten in the evening, Ye Qin forgot all about how he wanted to be kind to Cheng Feichi. When Cheng Feichi opened the door quietly, he saw a black shadow flying towards his face. He raised his hand and caught a pillow.

Ye Qin stood at the door, hands resting on his waist, shouting angrily, "Why don't you come back tomorrow? Just miss my birthday all together, wouldn't that be better?"

Cheng Feichi put down the box in his hand, opened it, and revealed a beautiful cake. Seeing that, Ye Chin wasn't as angry anymore. He slowly got up from the sofa and moved forward to the table, feigned an inadvertent glance at the cake and said with pretended disgust, "Too small. It's not even enough for a bite."

Though his birthday was not today at all, Ye Qin still stayed up with Cheng Feichi until midnight. Then he put on the candles, made a wish, and did whatever a birthday boy should do. Finally, he held his chin up and stretched out his hand.

"Where's my gift?"

"Close your eyes," Cheng Feichi said.

Ye Qin hadn't seen him for half a month. Now he couldn't see enough of him and was unwilling to close his eyes. But he was also curious about what gift Cheng Feichi had prepared for him, so he closed his eyes, having decided not to play honestly. He silently opened his eyes a tiny little bit to take a peek.

Through the crevices of his eyelashes, he could vaguely see Cheng Feichi taking out something from his pocket. While Ye Qin was trying to figure out what it was, Cheng Feichi held up Ye Qin's left hand and turned it into a palm-down position.

Then, a metal ring, warmed by his body temperature, touched the pad of his ring finger and was pushed smoothly to the base.

Before Cheng Feichi bade Ye Qin to open his eyes, Ye Qin opened them himself, staring at the radiant ring for a long time, overwhelmed.

"Your fingers are thin, and the clerk said that a narrow ring would look better." Cheng Feichi was still holding his hand, rubbing the base of his fingers with his warm hands and turning the ring around. The diamond on the ring was shining brightly. "I only have enough money to buy one with one diamond. If you don't like it, I'll buy a new one for you in the future, with as many diamonds as you want."

The last sentence brought Ye Qin back to reality from romantic sentiments. Ye Qin didn't know where to start, so he responded with a depressed expression. "Can you stop ruining the atmosphere like this...?"

Cheng Feichi smiled and said, "But one diamond is good

enough. I have one heart, which is reserved for you, and only you."

While taking a bath, Ye Qin realized in hindsight that Cheng Feichi had been busy these days. Could it be that he was saving the money made from working part-time in order to buy this ring? Wrapped in a bath towel, he hurried to ask. Cheng Feichi refused to admit it, only saying that he was busy taking care of his mother.

Then Ye Qin discovered that an injury on the palm of his right hand which had not healed completely, and was more than an inch long.

"I accidentally grazed it while riding," Cheng Feichi said lightly.

Ye Qin, whose IQ was insulted, was dizzy with anger. "Are you riding with your hand on the ground?"

In the past, Cheng Feichi used to take care of him, but this time their roles were reversed. Having dipped a cotton swab in alcohol, Ye Qin carefully wiped Cheng Feichi's wound, asking him if it hurt. After disinfection, he held Cheng Feichi's hand to his mouth and blew a small breath.

Seeing Cheng Feichi's confused face, Ye Qin took the initiative to further the cause of science. "Don't you know? If you give a wound a couple puffs, then it won't hurt that much. Isn't it winter? The wind is so cold, and breath is hot, so now it won't be cold anymore."

He blew a few more breaths.

He looked up and found that Cheng Feichi's expression was even more weird now. He even hid his face from Ye Qin, as if trying to avoid something.

In any case, they had been in a romantic relationship for so long. Even though opportunities for physical contact were few, Ye Qin gradually realized that now the time was just right.

It was exactly what he wanted: the right time, the right place, and the right person.

Therefore, when he stood up, he jumped up, spread his legs, and sat on Cheng Feichi's lap.

Thanks to his quick reflexes, Cheng Feichi was able to support Ye Qin's butt with his own hands. Feeling the softness under his palms, his breathing became heavy in an instant. Immediately he looked away, moving his hands up while trying to push Ye Qin away.

"Get off. Put on your clothes."

Ye Qin wasn't wearing anything. The bath towel that had been wrapped around his body had also been flung away, revealing a white and tender chest. His skin was still hot from the bath. Knowing that he had come this far, he pushed Cheng Feichi towards the direction of the bed, his arms circling him. Not letting him move, he boldly leaned over to ask for a kiss.

The little guy kissed without rules. One second his lips fell on Cheng Feichi's cheeks, the other at the roots of his ears, yet he was never able to align their lips. Cheng Feichi pushed him again, touched his bare waist, held it to prevent him from twisting, and shouted as if trying to stop him.

"Ye Qin."

Ye Qin was not used to being called by his name. He raised his head and looked down at him, panting quickly because of the violent movement just now. He licked away a half drop of saliva from the corner of his mouth and announced, "I'm an adult now."

Cheng Feichi seemed infected by his sudden solemnness. He stared at him for a while, but still decided to remove his hand. Ye Qin grabbed it and pressed it against his pliable waist.

"Don't move," Ye Qin ordered.

He was a little bit disappointed with Cheng Feichi's "resistance," but he was not going to give up just like that. When it was confirmed that Cheng Feichi had been bluffed into captivity and could not escape from him for the time being, Ye Qin put his left hand in front of Cheng Feichi's face and showed him the ring that he had just put on.

"Do you know what this ring means? You must, since you dared to put it on me."

Cheng Feichi glanced at the ring. The faint rose gold color matched Ye Qin's slender white fingers. When he turned his eyes back to Ye Qin's face, his gaze got darker and darker. His Adam's apple rolled up and down, as if he was trying to say something, but Ye Qin took the lead.

"You put this on me, so now you have to take responsibility for me." Ye Qin was afraid of being led away if he let Cheng Feichi talk, so he didn't give him a chance and played his trump card. Again, he gave Cheng Feichi a taste of his own medicine. "Even students know they need to take responsibility for what they did."

As soon as the words fell, a sudden dizziness came with it, as if the sky and the earth were spinning round. Ye Qin's body was flipped over and he was pressed to the mattress below.

Cheng Feichi put one arm around his waist, another supporting his face. His gaze pointed straight down, surrounding him.

It was not until then that Ye Qin realized his face was hot, and his body began to burn as well. He rolled his eyes to avoid Cheng Feichi's overly focused gaze and bluffed, "Why are you looking at me?"

"Pretty," Cheng Feichi answered without hesitation.

A low, raspy voice hit his ears at close range, causing his eardrum to tremble. Ye Qin wanted to raise his hand and touch his over-heated earlobe, but Cheng Feichi was holding him too tight and his waist was completely pressed down. It wasn't possible to move even an inch away.

Ye Qin's bent leg brushed Cheng Feichi's tented crotch. Ye

Qin was so ashamed that he was about to explode, and he hid his face while trying to adjust his expression with difficulty.

"You first..."

As soon as he uttered those two words, the black shadow shrouding him from above suddenly enlarged, and Cheng Feichi leaned over and kissed his bright red lips.

They had kissed many times before. Some were light and short, some were affectionate and lingering, but never had they ever had such passion. Every inch of skin that touched seemed to spark; all their senses were infinitely extended. Ye Qin could almost hear the sticky sound made by their rubbing lips and teeth.

As soon as the clench of Ye Qin's teeth loosened, Cheng Feichi's tongue took the opportunity to stick inside, and he swept every inch of his mouth slowly yet aggressively. It should've looked silly, yet he did it with extreme seriousness, as if he was religiously engraving his mark.

Hot breath ghosted their cheeks, so close to each other now, accompanied by the wet sounds of mixing saliva. Ye Qin gave a tiny snort, and his bare arms spontaneously looped around Cheng Feichi's neck to bring him down to himself.

He didn't know that his unconscious behavior had prolonged the kiss. Indeed, the overwhelming lust wouldn't allow him to think about it.

When Cheng Feichi finally retreated, he stared down with misty eyes from above. Ye Qin panted with his mouth half-open, and his own blurry gaze fell on Cheng Feichi's face. Releasing one hand, he tried unbuttoning Cheng Feichi's shirt. It was a little tight. It took Ye Qin a long time to undo only two buttonholes, and he bit his lower lip angrily.

"What kind of lame clothing is this?"

Cheng Feichi curled his lips, propped himself up, and raised his hands to unbutton himself.

His hands were very beautiful, and very different from Ye Qin's slender and delicate ones. His palms were wide and long, and the knuckles were distinct; beautiful, but full of power. His revealed chest was also not as thin as Ye Qin's, and the smooth but distinct muscle lines could be seen even when lit from behind.

As Ye Qin watched, he swallowed unconsciously. He twisted his waist and moved towards the edge of the bed.

Cheng Feichi held his shoulders. "Where are you going?"

Ye Qin took a plastic bag from under the pillow and closed his eyes with embarrassment. "I was getting the tools, tools!"

Their first time was a little bit more tortuous than Ye Qin had imagined.

Even while still in the process of stretching, Ye Qin shuddered and screamed from the pain. Yet he refused to let Cheng Feichi stop and, hooking Cheng Feichi's neck, he insisted that he continue.

"Slowly, slowly... Go ahead, hurry up... How many fingers are there now? ...Don't move, don't move... Hey, why are you not moving anymore?"

Perhaps because of nervousness, Ye Qin talked a lot, but he had lost his usual aura. The sounds he made were like a mosquito's humming, making Cheng Feichi's heart itch with desire.

He squeezed the flesh on Ye Qin's inner thigh. Ye Qin let out an "Ah," and his eyes immediately became wet. "What are you doing?"

"Distracting you," Cheng Feichi said, rubbing his big hands on the tender flesh a few more times, leaving red marks in different shades wherever he went.

Ye Qin felt comfortable with the squeezing and kneading, though he still held onto his habitual airs. He said, pursing his lips, "Thank you."

Even if it did hurt a bit, he didn't plan to back down. It wasn't easy to have gone this far, and today he was determined to renounce his virginity.

The fingers inside him were still moving slowly. Ye Qin pushed Cheng Feichi's arm and said anxiously, "Why don't you take off your pants?"

Cheng Feichi smiled, removed his fingers, and began to untie his belt.

Now he's obedient, Ye Qin thought angrily. Not knowing where to look, he gazed around and glanced over Cheng Feichi's lower body, and was startled by the bulge that was half-hidden in shadow.

Unconsciously swallowing his saliva, Ye Qin curled up his legs, clamped onto Cheng Feichi's waist, and asked nonchalantly, "Hey, have you done it with anyone else...?"

Cheng Feichi was stunned, and then smiled again. He leaned forward and brought Ye Qin into his arms. The two of them were naked, lying skin to skin, and they could easily sense the other's heartbeat.

Inadvertently, the words "disoriented and delirious" slid through his mind. Cheng Feichi, who had known its taste for the first time, felt a plectrum in his heart being strummed. He looked at the corners of Ye Qin's wet, red eyes.

"Guess."

Ye Qin was not only dissatisfied with the answer, but even a little bit ashamed into anger. He twisted his buttocks to get out of Cheng Feichi's arms, only to be grabbed by a forceful hand at his bare, slender waist. Dragging him back down, the hand pressed his open legs upwards.

"Hey, don't..."

He stopped abruptly. Ye Qin's face flushed in an instant. He felt a cylindrical object against his hip. It was thick, hard, and hot.

Cheng Feichi kissed his burning face, leaned against his ear, and said in a low voice, "There's no one else, only you."

It wasn't until that thing entered his body that Ye Qin was agitated by the pain, as if he was about to be split in half. But in the same moment, his mind also became clear, and he slowly realized how stupid his question had been.

The answer was obvious. This guy was normally so busy. Wasn't it already enough, dealing with only Ye Qin? How could he find any time to sleep with other people?

He was ashamed of getting upset for no apparent reason, and then he was made powerless by the sudden swelling pain. Only his five senses were under control, and his tears flowed like a spring that had just been opened.

Hurriedly, Cheng Feichi moved to pull out, when Ye Qin yelled and wept at once, "It doesn't matter that you're taller than me, but why did that thing have to get so big too... Hey, don't move yet!"

Seeing that he still had the strength for scolding, Cheng Feichi felt relieved. He freed one hand to touch his face, and received a handful of tears. He found the scene funny, but also felt sorry.

"Forget it today, next time..."

Ye Qin hurriedly hooked his neck. He sobbed a few breaths, gritted his teeth, and said, "Stop talking about next time! I want it *now*! Just come inside!"

So, Cheng Feichi pinched his waist, and that enormous and hard thing directly broke through and pushed inside.

Ye Qin wailed and indiscriminately kicked his legs, which had been pushed towards each side of his waist. Tears flowed more fiercely. "No, I didn't tell you to go so fast..."

In short, no matter what Cheng Feichi did, Ye Qin was dis-

satisfied and had something to complain about. Now that he'd understood this, and had been assured that he hadn't hurt Ye Qin, Cheng Feichi moved slowly and following his instinct.

At first, Ye Qin continued to cry a bit from discomfort. Later, when the pleasure began to grow, he started mewling like a kitten. "Move a little...faster... Ah...don't go too fast. Hmm..."

Ye Qin's voice was already soft, and now every word seemed almost coquettish; with a long, drawn-out tail that whirled into Cheng Feichi's ears, scratching his eardrum like a tiny hook. Cheng Feichi was so aroused that he abandoned his usual calmness. With self-taught precision, he grabbed Ye Qin's legs and moved his hips at a fierce, fast pace; as if he wanted to use all the strength that'd never found a target on the person beneath his body.

The resulting scream was impatient. Ye Qin was stupefied by the pleasure precisely hitting his sensitive spots with every thrust, and his whole body was numb with electricity. Even under such circumstances, he was still able to find fault with others. Pushing at Cheng Feichi's shoulders, he complained, "Don't, don't make that sound."

He was talking about the slapping sounds of skin and flesh clashing, as well as the squishing sounds made by the lubricant. Whispering and whistling, they made Ye Qin blush, and his heart beat faster.

Cheng Feichi's movements stopped. With one hand he held Ye Qin's cock, which had already been hard for a long time and was now resting stiffly against his lower abdomen. He squeezed it in a light, distracted manner, yet the squeezes still elicited repeated hums. He slammed his hips down, and his own cock, which had been half out, was now wholly inside Ye Qin again.

Ye Qin arched his neck and screamed, and a thrilling, over-whelming pleasure almost dispelled all his remaining rationality.

As he continued squeezing with his hands, Cheng Feichi

leaned down to touch the tip of Ye Qin's nose with his lips. He asked him, "Who was making that sound?"

From Ye Qin's angle, only the vague outline of the person pressing him down could be seen, as if he was shrouded in a layer of delicate light.

The fingers resting on Cheng Feichi's shoulder moved, and then lifted. They slid through the air and slowly traced his profile. The distance between the two of them was infinitesimal, and the hot breath that sprayed on the palm of Ye Qin's hand seemed to have turned into an entity in itself. It struck his heart with a deafening noise.

Ye Qin felt as if he had been trapped in an illusion; awake, but still asleep. All senses lost, his heart was swelling full of eagerness and sincerity.

He wanted to reach upwards, wondering if the person in front of him felt the same. Yet as he was about to touch Cheng Feichi, he became inexplicably flustered and timid. He curled his fingers and retracted his hand. Hugging his legs instead, he spread his lower body even more, nearly folding himself in half.

"I was making that sound," he confessed frankly. Licking his lips, he curled up the corners of his mouth. "Do you want to hear more? Then...hurry up."

After their lovemaking, Cheng Feichi's back was scratched to bits, and he had to help the offending sharp-toothed cat to take a bath. The kitten had been begging for pleasure beforehand, but had now lost the ability to move. He couldn't even apply shower gel to his own skin, asking his "gege" for help.

Right now, he seemed quite well-behaved. Feichi-gege's heart melted like a humid fountain in spring. How could he refuse the request? Having played the role of a dutiful bathing attendant, Cheng Feichi wiped his body dry with a towel.

Putting on his clothes, Ye Qin hung on Cheng Feichi's shoulder as if boneless, licking and biting, and occasionally breathing out a long hot breath.

They were both healthy young men. With their blood already boiling, it was impossible for them not to let things get out of hand. Ye Qin had hardly put on a sleeve of his pajama shirt before they were embracing again, and they kissed while staggering back into the shower compartment. There was still white steam in the narrow place, and with his dim vision, Cheng Feichi grabbed Ye Qin's waist from behind, and slowly pressed his stiff thing inside.

Ye Qin, who had just had a taste of lovemaking, reacted fairly straightforwardly. He was uncomfortable being pressed against the wall, so he lifted his ass and used it to push the person behind him. "Too deep, not comfortable...I want to face you."

Cheng Feichi took the opportunity to guide his speech without a hassle. "Me?"

When Ye Qin called out "gege" in a sultry voice, Cheng Feichi released him and helped him turn around.

Although Ye Qin was willing to be the bottom, he still had a grudge about the fact that he couldn't take control. With one leg slung over a strong arm, Ye Qin lay on Cheng Feichi's shoulders, opened his mouth, and took a bite of the tight muscles. The flesh did not feel delicate, and he muttered disdainfully, "I know you're proud of these muscles. They look nice, but what are they even useful for?"

He regretted it as soon as he said it. Ye Qin heard Cheng Feichi chuckle, and then his leg standing on the ground was also vigorously lifted. His whole body was now completely suspended. Except for his back against the slippery wall, only his legs hanging on Cheng Feichi's arms could find some support.

"You...What are you doing?" Ye Qin widened his eyes,

suddenly realized something, and changed his wording. "Gege, put me down, I'm scared..."

They were both in a state of undress. Cheng Feichi gazed at Ye Qin from head to toe, his desire undisguised. There was a little smile hiding at the corner of his mouth. "Yes, they're not as useful as what you've got."

Realizing what he was talking about, Ye Qin was both bashful and angry, struggling to get off him. But unfortunately, he was not strong enough, and he couldn't push Cheng Feichi away at all even if he used every limb.

That hard thing was like a soldering iron pushing against the hole that had not yet closed. Ye Qin's mouth flattened, and he was ready to start crying.

"You, you... You bully!"

Cheng Feichi's big hands supported Ye Qin's squishy buttocks, slightly relaxing his arms so that his cock, half of which had been resting inside, slid right to the hilt when Ye Qin's body fell.

Ye Qin opened his mouth wide. His breathing was stagnant for a few seconds; he couldn't say a word, and his eyes could not focus.

Cheng Feichi neither admitted nor denied the accusation. He leaned close to the corner of Ye Qin's lips, gave that corner a peck, and called out, "Ye Xiaoruan."

At the sound of that bewitching voice, Ye Qin quickly threw his last bit of resistance behind him. He was willing to be a fish on the chopping board at the mercy of the knife, and his boneless arms wrapped around Cheng Feichi's neck. He let Cheng Feichi take him, and floated up and down in the sea of desire.

The real end came at half past two in the morning. Ye Qin was about to fall asleep the second he hit the mattress, but he

was pulled up by Cheng Feichi so that his hair could be dried. With the hot air blowing, Ye Qin lost his bones again. Holding Cheng Feichi's waist, he nested in his arms and pulled his arm around his own waist. This gesture meant "my back hurts, so give me a rub."

Lying back on the bed and enjoying Cheng Feichi's service, Ye Qin yawned and played with Cheng Feichi's other hand. He touched the knuckles one by one and found something missing. Immediately, he found energy again.

"Where's your ring?"

Cheng Feichi said, "I only bought one."

Ye Qin could guess the reason, of course: he did not have enough money.

Excitement lost, he lay back and suddenly felt less happy about receiving the ring. The series was named "Love." What was the point of having only one from a pair?

"You liar," Ye Qin mumbled.

Cheng Feichi raised his eyebrows. "Huh?"

"Not showing up for so long, just because of this damn ring. You lied to me that something happened at home."

"There really was something at home. Otherwise I wouldn't be in such a hurry," Cheng Feichi finished explaining, and changed the direction of the conversation without warning. "You haven't ever lied to me?"

Ye Qin's heart started to beat fast again. Though he knew that Cheng Feichi didn't know anything, he was so nervous that his throat hurt. He stammered, "I, I...I didn't. When did I lie... lie, lie to you?"

Cheng Feichi pretended to be serious. "You said the word 'lie' three times. You did lie to me, three times."

"How could it have been three times?!" Ye Qin jumped up.

"Then there were at least some?"

Not only were there some, but it was far more than three times. Ye Qin didn't dare tell the truth. Seeing that Cheng Feichi was attentively waiting for his confession, he racked his brains to pick a less serious one.

"That...that girl isn't my sister."

Cheng Feichi gave no reaction for a while. "Sister?"

"The little girl I took to your house. Your mother was tutoring her," Ye Qin said, pulling the bed sheet. "She's Zhou Feng's sister, not mine."

Cheng Feichi froze for a moment, then suddenly smiled. "I know."

The little girl had introduced herself as Zhou Jiang when she first came. How could she have a brother whose surname was Ye?

Ye Qin's eyes went round. "Then why didn't you expose me? You even pretended that you'd been tricked!"

"Why should I have?" After rubbing his waist and tucking him under the quilt, Cheng Feichi squeezed his face. "It's interesting to watch you bounce around making trouble."

Ye Qin was pursing him at the time, carelessly and slovenly. There were no rules, only recklessness from beginning to end. But he hadn't hated it at all, and even secretly looked forward to it; guessing every day before going to bed, wondering what new trick Ye Qin would come up with tomorrow.

Even long before today, this eye-catching little sun was probably already shining in his heart.

Ye Qin also recalled how stupid he was back then, coming up with all sorts of strange tricks. He felt so abashed, yet there was nowhere to hide. He pushed away Cheng Feichi's hand and raised the quilt to cover his head.

When the day was about to dawn, the radiator suddenly failed to produce heat, and the central heater was too inefficient; it buzzed for a long time, but the room still couldn't warm up.

Ye Qin shrank his head and drilled into Cheng Feichi's arms, putting his feet between Cheng Feichi's legs for warmth.

"The climate of the capital isn't good at all. It's deadly hot in summer and deadly cold in winter." Nestling in Cheng Feichi's embrace, Ye Qin complained, "I'll settle on a tropical island in the future and never come back."

Cheng Feichi responded, "Okay. Wait until the college entrance examination is over."

Ye Qin touched his chest with his forehead. "The college entrance examination can go to hell. Can you think of anything other than study, study, and study?"

Cheng Feichi laughed. *Didn't I do all those things in order to go to the same university as you?*

"Wait until the college entrance examination is over," he repeated what he just said. "I shall take you to a tropical island."

Ye Qin didn't care about the cold now. He raised his head hurriedly. "Really?"

"When have I ever lied to you?"

Ye Qin felt his conscience stabbed again. He buried his head back into Cheng Feichi's chest. After a while, he poked out quietly, then touched Cheng Feichi's injured hand and held it tightly as he muttered, "Don't buy things for me in the future... The time you spent making money could've been spent with me instead."

Maybe because they were head over heels in love, or because they had done the most intimate thing in the world, but Ye Qin was itching to stay with Cheng Feichi 24 hours a day.

However, in reality, there were still many "trivial" matters waiting for them to deal with, such as Cheng Feichi's mother's illness, or Ye Qin's half-dead academic performance.

In the last monthly exam this year, Ye Qin stayed in his

previous rank, stuck as the 28th in class. Cheng Feichi asked him to send over pictures of the wrong answers he had written and gave him a loving education remotely.

"I asked you to write the formula for circular motion from memory last time, but this time you made mistakes again. Copied that twenty times... Last week I also explained verb-object construction. You should copy the sentence pattern thirty times... 'Liquid hydrogen chloride cannot conduct electricity, but hydrogen chloride is an electrolyte.' Copy that sentence fifty times.'"

Ye Qin wanted to cry. "How come there are more and more?!"

Cheng Feichi had his reasons. "The ones I ask you to copy more are also the ones you've encountered more often, and I explained them to you more recently. You shouldn't make mistakes again so quickly."

Well, well, you are the Straight-A student. Of course you're right.

Ye Qin copied furiously, and fell asleep in the process. When he opened his eyes, the new year had already come.

Following New Year's Day came the annual Winter Games of High School No. 6. This time Cheng Feichi was busy taking care of his mother, so he did not participate. Ye Qin wasn't busy at all. Therefore, empowered by the fine spirit to win glory for the class that he'd inherited from the class monitor, he signed up for the long jump contest.

In the middle of the games, the student who seemed most likely to win first place accidentally sprained his ankle and quit. Thus, Ye Qin inexplicably took first. Liao Yifang pinned a big red flower onto his chest, pushing him onto the podium and taking numerous pictures from various angles.

Ye Qin chose the one which he considered the most handsome and sent it to Cheng Feichi. Cheng Feichi replied with two words, "Getting married?"

As Ye Qin looked at those two words, his heart beat violently and shouted, *I do, I do!* Yet he refused to admit his enthusiasm and said proudly, "I took first place. Can't you see?"

Cheng Feichi could not reply in time.

Today, Cheng Xin was transferred to another ward. Having run upstairs and downstairs a few times, Cheng Feichi finally tidied the place up. When he went out to fetch water with a thermos bottle, he ran into the old woman who used to occupy the bed next to Cheng Xin's.

Having heard that she and Cheng Xin had become neighbors again, the old woman beamed with joy. "I was dying for someone to chat with, and now you and your mother arrived."

When Cheng Feichi returned to the ward, Mrs. Feng had already left after helping out, and Cheng Xin and the old woman were chatting happily.

Cheng Xin could have been discharged from the hospital last month, since the doctor said she could go home for recuperation. Cheng Xin, on the other hand, said nothing about leaving the hospital; probably because she didn't want to encounter *that* woman any more. Instead, she stayed there longer for recuperation.

Seeing the long-lost smile on Cheng Xin's face, Cheng Feichi felt that the hospitalization this time was worthwhile.

He peeled two apples and gave them to his elders. Not wishing to interrupt their conversation, Cheng Feichi planned to find a corner and stay there. Picking up her cellphone, Cheng Xin glanced at him and said, "I lost one of the chopsticks, but I need it for dinner. Buy a new pair; there is a small shop near the door."

Unsuspectingly, Cheng Feichi stood up and walked in that direction.

Out of the inpatient ward, he was on an unavoidable path

that led towards the hospital's main entrance when he met someone head-on.

Cheng Feichi had not seen him for a whole year, yet the man looked the same as he had this time last year. He was still in a suit and leather shoes, and wearing a crisp overcoat. He was just standing there, exuding the aura of the elite.

Unaffected, Cheng Feichi kept his eyes ahead and kept moving forward, away from him. But he had not gotten far when the man called out from behind, "Xiao-Chi, Dad wants to talk to you."

CHAPTER 14

THERE were many fast-food restaurants near Hospital No. 3, but there was only one coffee shop suitable for conversation.

The wind was strong outside. When he entered the shop, the man straightened his clothing, and noticed that Cheng Fe-ichi was wearing an old white-washed cotton jacket. He said, "Why don't you wear the clothes I bought you last year? Dad will buy you new ones when they're worn out."

Cheng Feichi didn't answer, but found a seat to sit down. "If you have anything to say, say it now. I should return soon."

Even when greeted by his unceremonious attitude, the man seemed unembarrassed. He signaled the waiter to take their orders, and said slowly in a negotiating tone, "Your mother says that you don't like sweets? I don't like them either. Then there's no need for desserts."

Ever since their first meeting, everything the man said had been too intimate, but his attitude was so natural that it was hard to find fault with. Cheng Feichi could only respond with silence.

The topics ranged from life to study, and the man did all the talking. Cheng Feichi's eyes went through the window and fell on the street trees; it was hard to tell whether he was listening.

When talking about the double first prizes won in last year's competition, the man smiled.

"When I told that to my friends at the dinner table, they didn't believe that my son was so capable; they thought I was bragging."

Cheng Feichi couldn't stand it anymore. He looked the man directly in the face and said, "I am not your son."

The man was stunned for a moment. He probably hadn't expected him to be so direct. After taking a sip from the coffee cup, his complexion returned to normal, and an undying smile returned to the corners of his mouth. "Your mother said that you act on impulse. Sure enough."

At this point, Cheng Feichi was certain that this "chance encounter" with this man had been arranged by Cheng Xin. They probably kept in frequent contact with each other in private. Cheng Feichi frowned almost imperceptibly and said, "Not as impulsive as your lady wife, I'm afraid."

He wasn't good at sarcasm, but in a situation like this, he had to say it. He didn't want the man to keep speaking to him as if everything was in his control.

Cheng Feichi thought this remark was bitter enough. No one with any self-respect could stand it. Unexpectedly, the man let out a small laugh.

"You really resemble your mother."

Cheng Feichi had not agreed to come here in order to give this man a chance to study who he resembled. The man noticed his impatience and finally cut to the point before Cheng Feichi got up and left.

I heard that you don't want to go abroad. What are your concerns? Tell me."

Cheng Feichi was eager to make his attitude clear, so that they could give up on their plans. Therefore, he told the truth.

"My mother is in poor health and cannot leave home."

The man nodded. "That's filial piety, good boy. What else?"

"Also, I don't want to spend your money."

After saying this, Cheng Feichi thought that he would encounter a series of persuasion attempts to the theme of "This is for your own good." Yet the man showed no intention to try and convince him, and he softly knocked the table twice with one finger, as if he was thinking.

"Anything else?"

"Nothing."

"Really?"

Cheng Feichi's expression was as calm as ever. "What else could there be?"

The man leaned back on the chair, his confidence in controlling everything never disappearing. He replied slowly for Cheng Feichi's benefit.

"There's also the Ye boy."

On his way back to the hospital, Cheng Feichi called Mrs. Feng.

When the call connected, he opened his mouth and took in a cold breath, which sent shivering down his throat that reached his heart. He heard his voice tremble. "Auntie, what happened back then? Can you tell me now?"

Hearing that the man had come for him directly, she sighed after her feelings of surprise passed. She repeated again and again, "I didn't know that she was still holding on to this after all these years."

Cheng Xin and Mrs. Feng met twenty years ago. At the time, Cheng Xin was already pregnant. She had moved to the Yulin Compound by herself. Mrs. Feng had just returned from a grocery shopping trip and passed by the door. Seeing a pregnant woman moving house all alone, she took pity on Cheng Xin and went over to lend a hand. Later, she discovered that Cheng Xin lived alone and often came to visit her. The two were of the same age, with a lot of shared interests to talk about. Over the course of several encounters, they became close acquaintances.

"What happened back then? I asked her that in passing, but she refused to answer, so I didn't ask again. But I remember a time when she had been pregnant with you for more than five months; it was very cold and there was heavy snow. She bought a ticket for herself, saying that she was going to S-City. I asked her if she was going to find the father of the child. She didn't give me a clear answer, only asking me to look after her house; saying that if she didn't come back, she would call me and I could do whatever I wanted with the apartment.

"Actually, I hoped that your mother wouldn't come back. Not because I wanted the apartment; it wasn't easy for her living alone. It would've made things easier if she had a man with her. I also suspected that your mother was probably trying to give birth to you in secret; seeing that she had finally changed her mind, I was happy for her. I didn't expect that she'd come back less than two days after she left. She'd taken the green train back, and stood on that thing for over ten hours. She was skinny, and the pregnancy didn't show when she was in a cotton jacket. No one gave their seat to her the whole way; it's really a crime."

Taking pity on the difficulties Cheng Xin had been through over the years, Mrs. Fang often said to Cheng Feichi that he should "be a good son for your mother; it really isn't easy for her." Even if Cheng Feichi couldn't experience them in person, he still felt uncomfortable when he heard these old tales—as if Cheng Xin had suffered purely because of him.

"Then, did my mother say what she was going to do in S-City?"

"She has such pride. How could she have ever told me?" Mrs. Feng said. "What happened there was probably not pleasant.

After coming back, she couldn't eat or sleep for a long while, as if she had lost her soul. Her health also collapsed; otherwise, it should have been much easier to give birth to you. It hurt all night, and she almost lost half of her life."

Before she hung up the phone, there came the usual persuasions. "You should listen to your mom and accept him as your father. Don't make her angry anymore. Her body can't afford it." She concluded the conversation like every woman who was willing to sacrifice herself for her family. "Oh, so many years have passed. Fortunately, that man still has a conscience. You and your mother could finally say goodbye to past suffering and lead a good life."

Before returning to the ward, Cheng Feichi stopped at the flower bed near the department, immersing himself in the cold wind for a long while.

Who did Cheng Xin meet in S-City back then? Judging by her reaction when facing that woman after so many years, it must've been the first time Cheng Xin had ever let go of her pride and decided to compromise for the sake of everyone's interests. Putting this information together with the bit of the story that had been revealed by his grandparents, Cheng Feichi was almost amused by the old tale of a hoodwinking rich girl separating a pair of star-crossed lovers.

Had the story happened to someone else, forced by life, forced by the world's perspective, he probably wouldn't have even had the chance to be born. The funny thing was that the plot had developed completely in accordance with the script: just like it was on TV, in the end it was him, the superfluous one, that bore the condemnation of fate at the expense of freedom.

What was even more dramatic was that everyone still thought this was justified. Anyway, it was all for his future; anyway, that person was indeed his biological father.

He took the business card from his pocket. The name on it was both unfamiliar and familiar. It reminded him of the childhood days when he was ridiculed and bullied because he had no father. It reminded him of all the effort he had made as he gradually matured—everything he'd ever done was meant to shut the mouths of those who'd say that although he had a mother who had given him life, he had no father to give him an education.

Although in his mother's eyes, all his effort was still less important than that man's need to have his so-called "prodigal son" return.

No one knew that, as early as when he was just beginning to learn to read, he had secretly looked into his mother's photo album. There were three people in that photo. Only one man had his name written on the back. The elegant handwriting engraved the two words "Yi Zheng" deeply into his mind.

On TV, in the newspapers, from word of mouth, he couldn't ignore the name even if he wanted to. But he still couldn't associate the name with the title of "father."

Even if Yi Zheng had called himself "Dad" countless times in front of him today.

Cheng Feichi took a deep breath. Instead of thinning away, the heavy pressure turned into an entity that pressed on him like a mountain.

He glanced at the number on the card and picked up the phone.

In the evening, Ye Qin received a belated reply from Cheng Feichi.

He'd even been thinking about how he could lose his temper with him. There was nothing else he could do, but he could pull a small trick to be able to meet up with Cheng Feichi, right? Having to attend a patient at their sickbed didn't mean one

could never leave that sick person's side. At worst, he could go to the hospital gate and wait, then leave as soon as they met up. Not a big deal. He wouldn't cause Cheng Feichi any trouble.

Thinking about this, Ye Qin checked his phone while putting his jacket on. He clicked on WeChat and was stunned when he saw the line on the screen.

Cheng Feichi wrote, "Study hard, but we'd better not see each other for a while."

Ye Qin blinked. *What did I do? Why can't we see each other? Does studying hard conflict with meeting up?*

He gave Cheng Feichi a call, but Cheng Feichi rejected it without picking up. Ye Qin almost crushed the roots of his teeth when he heard the beeping busy tone.

Nor did he manage to call Cheng Feichi successfully over the next few days. Occasionally he received a text reply, yet they were all brief, such as like "nothing wrong," "do as I said," and "don't make trouble." Ye Qin didn't understand. He wanted to know why. How did he become the one that was "making trouble"?

Cheng Feichi didn't show up at the ceremony signifying the ending of the term before winter vacation came. A student from Class No. 1 knew they were on good terms and asked Ye Qin to bring the winter homework to Cheng Feichi. Ye Qin walked out of the school gate, raised his hand, and threw the books away.

After a while, he went back and looked through the trash can, picking up all of the books and scolding Cheng Feichi as a bastard while doing it.

Not that he didn't notice something had gone wrong. His wild imagination even led him toward the thought of abduction—on second thought, he was convinced that this couldn't be the case. Cheng Feichi was so poor that he could only afford one ring; who would kidnap him?

Could it be that the kidnapper knew that he was Ye Jinxiang's son? But Ye Jinxiang was so busy recently, thanks to the company's capital chain problem—what kidnapper couldn't even see that? *Besides, if you must kidnap someone, why don't you kidnap me first? Isn't a legitimate child more valuable than an illegitimate child?*

In the final analysis, one can only blame Ye Jinxiang. That unapologetic old scoundrel. It's not enough to cheat; is he also addicted to planting changelings?

Ye Qin couldn't stop himself once his imagination began to run wild, so he turned to Liao Yifang, an expert on relationships, for guidance.

"Could it be..." Liao Yifang closed his mouth as soon as he began the sentence. "No, no, Cheng-tongxue isn't that kind of person."

Ye Qin asked urgently, "What kind of person?"

Being Liao Yifang, he was able to get the words out. "Just, just like Chen Shimei in Chinese opera—who abandoned his first wife and married someone else?"

This analogy gave Ye Qin such a fright that his forehead became covered with sweat. When he was calm enough to think about it, he also found it absurd. How would it be possible for Cheng Feichi to do that? He wouldn't dare give up on him, even if his courage was multiplied a hundred times.

Ye Qin didn't know if he was too confident in himself, or too confident in Cheng Feichi.

In short, neither was a good.

After realizing this, Ye Qin did not take the initiative to contact Cheng Feichi for a whole week. The day before he was setting out abroad for the holiday, he couldn't hold back anymore. He took a picture of the crumpled transcript that had lain hidden for several days and sent it to Cheng Feichi. His class ranking had improved by three, which was worth showing off.

The other end replied with a word: "Good."

Because of that word, Ye Qin's mood brightened again.

At least he hadn't run away. He was no Cheng Shimei.

When helping him pack his things, Luo Qiuling said that she and Ye Jinxiang would not go with him this time. Ye Qin didn't pay this much mind. Instead, in high spirits, he asked her what cosmetics she wanted, and promised to buy them for her at the airport.

"My silly boy." Luo Qiuling laughed. As if moved by her son's thoughtfulness, she gave Ye Qin's face a soft squeeze, which was something she hadn't done for a long time. "Mom just hopes that every day in the future, you can be as happy as you are today."

Ye Qin quickly escaped. He was an adult now. How would it look if he still let other people squeeze his face?!

And *that* one also loved to pinch his face. It was really annoying.

Although he labeled it as "annoying," in fact he was still upset that Cheng Feichi hadn't pinched his face in several days.

When Ye Qin was about to board, Cheng Feichi still hadn't given him a reply, let alone come to see him off. In a rage, he threw down the schoolbag full of review materials, leaving it at the consignment area. Five minutes later, he turned back and looked everywhere for his bag. It contained all the quizzes and English essays Cheng Feichi had designed and prepared for him.

Zhou Feng, who was going with him, couldn't bear the sight of this new Ye Qin: he said one thing, but meant another; every minute he regretted something he had or hadn't done. "How can Straight-A Cheng stand you? If I were him, I would have already turned crazy."

Ye Qin regarded him with disdain. "How can the class monitor stand *you*? If I were him, you'd be already dead."

The plane took off on time.

At the same time, at People's Hospital No. 3, Cheng Feichi walked into the ward with a bag of breakfast. Cheng Xin was on the bed holding an A4 sized paper with both hands, carefully reading it through.

It was too late to stop her. With trembling hands, Cheng Xin held the paper high and asked, "What is this?"

It was the self-recruitment application for C University in the Capital; the one Cheng Feichi had put between two pages of his book. At the end of the document, the official seal was stamped, and names were signed. Everything was ready, short of his enrollment.

The old woman in the bed next door looked over, "Oh, why is it from C University? Isn't he a smart boy? Smart enough that he's even been recommended for top universities without taking their entrance exams?"

"No." Cheng Xin shook her head. "He will not enter a domestic university. He will go abroad."

Cheng Feichi exhaled and said helplessly, "Mom..."

Cheng Xin seemed to have guessed what he was going to say, and hurriedly interrupted. "You will go abroad, won't you?"

Facing his mother's urgent and pleading eyes, Cheng Feichi was not unmoved, but he still replied, "No, I will not go abroad."

Even among the domestic universities, the C University wasn't considered prestigious. Cheng Feichi had made the choice based on Ye Qin's final exam results, plus a conservative estimate of how much he could improve in the remaining four months. It was a choice made after he had taken multiple factors into consideration.

Had Cheng Xin and Yi Zheng not been pressing him so hard, he wouldn't have had to make decisions so quickly. Over these past several days, he had been communicating with both his head teacher and the admissions department at C University,

hoping to settle where he'd be headed before the coming of the new year. Despite his careful planning, the secret came out after all. Cheng Xin had discovered it.

Hearing him answer without hesitation, Cheng Xin's eyes suddenly went cold. She restrained her anger and said, "Why? Give me a reason."

Cheng Feichi's heart fell back into his stomach. It seemed that Yi Zheng didn't tell Cheng Xin about him and Ye Qin, so there was still room for reconciliation in that matter.

"I want to stay. To study in China," he said.

"For me? That's not necessary," Cheng Xin said. "I've told you since you were a child that feelings are completely useless, especially when facing major choices in life."

Cheng Feichi couldn't help but feel sad when he heard this. Despite what she said, wasn't Cheng Xin being ruled by exactly what she was condemning? Otherwise, Yi Zheng would not easily define her with a chuckle and the word "impulsive."

"Because it's a major decision," Cheng Feichi stressed every word, "one has to follow his heart, instead of making blind decisions based on what other people have said."

Cheng Xin frowned slightly, obviously disagreeing. "I am your mother. I am different from other people. Everything I do is for your own good."

Cheng Feichi couldn't help but pursed his lips, letting out a bitter smile. Again and again, this high-sounding preaching—delivered as if not listening to her would be treason.

If he were a child without a mature and independent mind, he might've been fooled by this; even felt ashamed of being so inconsiderate and unfeeling. However, he had long passed the stage when he was confused about right and wrong. He now clearly understood that what his mother wanted was never attentiveness, but unconditional obedience.

He swallowed a heavy sigh and said, "Is everything you do for *my* own good, or for your own unfulfilled wishes?"

Cheng Xin stared at him in disbelief. In her eyes, there was panic at having been seen through, but also a touch of indescribable resentment.

So many years had passed. It was not that she had never tried to persuade herself to let it go, but every time when she startled awake at midnight, chased by nightmares time and time again, those images dug deeper into her mind. She couldn't forget the humiliation she had suffered twenty years ago; the twisted, bloody past. Therefore, even if no one understood her, even if everyone in the world admonished her, she would take back what belonged to her.

"All of that *should* have been mine!" Cheng Xin's voice was sharp, and then she forced herself to relax, pleading eagerly. "And also yours. You're his first son, and all that should be yours."

Cheng Feichi shook his head. "All of it belongs to him. I couldn't care less. I can fight for myself."

"How? You're on your own. What can you win?"

Maybe it was because of her illness, but Cheng Xin had recently become a little volatile. Or it might be because, after that woman's visit, she had lost the calmness that she had used as a guise in front of her son. Now there was no need to conceal herself. She quickly tore the application form in her hand to pieces and threw the shreds into the air.

Looking through the flying paper shreds, Cheng Feichi saw his mother's savage face, as if she had lost all reason.

"You can go to C University when I'm dead!"

At midday, he met the old woman from the next bed in the hospital cafeteria, and she dragged Cheng Feichi to a secluded corner.

"What's the matter with your mother? Good boy, don't put your future at stake out of spite for your family."

Just when Cheng Feichi thought she was here to be a lobbyist for his mother, the old woman continued, "Your mother is a bit too hard on you. You are an adult. She shouldn't make decisions for you without consulting you. But if you have a disagreement, you should talk about it calmly. Don't make rash decisions about your future. I am an old woman now; although I haven't attended school for a long time, I know what sort of school C University is. I heard your mother say that you're very clever. Your grades would be more than enough for you to go to A University, right? If you apply to C University, you're more muddled than an old crone who has one foot already in the coffin."

Cheng Feichi was speechless. Even an outsider could find anomalies in the fact that he had applied to a university incompatible with his academic level. For so many years, he and his mother had depended upon each other for survival, yet she could only remember his so-called excellence when she wanted to use it to tip the scales in her favor, so that she could satisfy her own selfishness.

Times had changed, and their situations had changed. Maybe she herself also knew that Yi Zheng was no longer the Yi Zheng he used to be. What's more, the old him had been able to abandon his feelings for future prospects. Now, twenty years later, what could she use to regain his attention?

Taking stock of everything she had, only a son who excelled in the eyes of others.

Therefore, Cheng Feichi, whom she regarded as her only hope, had no way to escape. He had grown into what Cheng Xin wanted, yet Cheng Xin forgot that he was also an individual with independent thoughts and judgment.

Cheng Feichi leaned his back against the wall and pinched

his eyebrows wearily.

He refused to be objectified, thus conflicts arose and gradually developed to the point they became irreconcilable; just like what happened today. To reconcile, one of them had to compromise.

But if he compromised this time, he would be prey stepping into a trap. The further he walked, the narrower the space became, and the net tangled around him became tighter and tighter until there was no room for resistance.

And then he and Ye Qin would have no chance anymore.

Breathing heavy and hard, Cheng Feichi was still trying his best to find a square of land where he could grow freely in this foul air. He opened his eyes, got his spirits up, took out his cellphone, and dialed Yi Zheng's number again.

While Cheng Feichi was struggling to work out a plan for their future, Ye Qin, who was on vacation across the ocean, was not very happy either.

Having enjoyed themselves on the island for a few days, he and Zhou Feng relocated to New York. Being loyal to their brotherhood, Liu Yangfan and Zhao Yue, who were studying on that continent, both skipped class to accommodate them. For two successive nights, they squandered their time in nightclubs.

By nature, Ye Qin wasn't one for pleasure-seeking. Tonight, he was again drenched in the disgusting smell of tobacco and alcohol. He frowned and was about to leave when Liu Yangfan stretched out his arm to stop him from leaving, while asking Zhou Feng, "When A-Yue and I aren't around, where do you take A-Qin to hang out? How come he looks as if he's becoming a Buddhist, and all earthly pleasures are beneath him?"

Zhou Feng threw the beer onto the table. "It's not that I don't take him out to play. He's busy all the time. Apart from studying, he's been staying with that straight-A student; thick as thieves. After class, you can't even see the back of him. Even though he's on vacation right now, he brought his homework! You remember last night how we got back really late? He found the time to complete two pages!"

Zhao Yue laughed out loud. "You're being so good for Straight-A Cheng! I bet our Qin-ge isn't faking it anymore—he is really in love!"

Ye Qin fell back to his seat and said stiffly, "Bullshit, I just think it's better than wasting time with you worthless losers."

Skeptical, Zhou Feng said while stroking his chin, "Why, I daresay that you're really under his thumb. Before we came here, he didn't even come to the airport to see you off, and you didn't even dare to fuss about it."

"Bullshit!!" Ye Qin said fiercely. "If I told him to come over no matter what, do you really think he'd dare not to come?"

Liu Yangfan flicked the ash from his cigarette, and said with a half-smile, "Then we'll have keep a look out when we return home next time."

The group of friends decided that they should all return home and hang out together for a couple of days. Feeling his dignity and his place in the gang greatly threatened, Ye Qin hurriedly sent a message before boarding the plane.

"I'm back! Come and pick me up at 8 o'clock Capital time, gege!"

When Cheng Feichi received the news late at night, he put down his phone and sat up on the folding chair in the ward. He added some hot water to Cheng Xin's teacup. When he laid back again, he began to think about the possibility of picking Ye Qin up at the airport.

He had not seen Ye Qin for more than a month. Even someone as cool as Cheng Feichi couldn't help but miss his beloved.

Especially while under this high-pressure surveillance that almost made him feel as if he'd been taken into custody.

While Yi Zheng seemed easier to talk to, after all these years in the business world, he had long developed a knack for speaking and acting in a way that appeared like he was open to negotiations but didn't actually give people any other options. These days, he and Cheng Feichi had been trying to outwit each other. Cheng Feichi demanded that Ye Qin not be harmed, and that Cheng Xin hear not a word about him. Yi Zheng had accepted these conditions easily, but he also asked Cheng Feichi to exchange terms with him.

His original words were, "When making a deal, each party should give something and receive something in return. If you do business at a loss, how can you avoid being laughed at by other people when they find out?"

Cheng Feichi thought what Yi Zheng was doing now was already absurd, yet he himself was without aid and resources. The only thing he could do was to stabilize the situation—to make Yi Zheng lose patience, or better, to make Yi Zheng abandon him. Only then would he be granted the opportunity to find his own way.

He had opted for this strategy because he had no alternative. Yi Zheng seemed omnipotent. He even knew the fact that he had contacted the head teacher, as well as how many times he had visited C University. A few days ago, in an attempt to shake his will, he even revealed that Ye Qin had employed a PI to investigate him.

Yi Zheng had been laughing on the phone. "The so-called private detectives he found were so clumsy, and they actually used their real names. That kid is like his father; full of trickery, thinking himself clever. He's not as simple as you believe him to be. And you're going to squander your good future for him—is he really worth it?"

It should have been a very powerful blow, but Cheng Feichi had long since guessed that Ye Qin had investigated him; otherwise, there would have been no tit-for-tat when they had first met.

Ye Qin couldn't hide anything. He wore all his emotions on his face. Despite the investigation, what kind of detrimental things could someone so simple and clear be capable of?

Thinking of this, Cheng Feichi again turned over and continued to ponder a legitimate reason for him to go out tomorrow.

The next day, he found the opportunity he wanted.

In the afternoon, his grandmother came to the hospital for a visit, bringing some side dishes that Cheng Xin loved. Cheng Feichi took the tableware to the sink outside, washing it while thinking about going out later in the name of escorting his grandma home. After that, he could catch one of the innumerable unregistered taxis at the entrance of the hospital and head to the airport. Even if a return journey took two hours, he could use a traffic jam as an excuse.

It would be good to stay there for only five minutes, he thought, seeking joy amidst the sorrow. If he continued to put off a meeting, it only became more and more likely that the little guy would make a scene.

Thinking thus, he couldn't help speeding up the washing. When he walked to the door of the ward with the dripping tableware, Cheng Xin's voice penetrated his ear even before he stepped into the room.

She was speaking extremely fast. "In what way am I inferior to her? She's just relying on her good family background. I also have a son. It cost half of my life to give birth to him, and I worked hard to raise him to be what he is today. Who dares to say he's not good? Who can say he's not excellent? Mom, do you think Xiao-Chi isn't good enough? That he doesn't deserve everything?"

Grandma's original plan was to stop Cheng Xin from being stubborn, but now she was overwhelmed by this irrefutable logic. Therefore she could only continue to persuade softly, "But that woman is innocent..."

Cheng Xin could no longer listen to anyone's advice. "She is innocent—then do I deserve it? I was with child first; she's the interloper. The only thing I wanted was to see Yi Zheng one more time, to hear him say in person that he did not want me anymore, and did not want the child. Then I could give up on him. But who gave that woman the right to treat me that way?"

Having said this, she laughed. "Sure enough, karma and retribution never miss. She deserves to have birthed an idiot for a son. In the end, who else can Yi Zheng turn to but me and Xiao-Chi? Heaven is never blind. Mom, aren't you happy for me? My son is so good. In the end, he's returning to where he should be."

In the room, Cheng Xin laughed like a madwoman. Outside the door, Cheng Feichi listened. Pressing upon the cold glazed tiles, his trembling fingertips turned blue and white, and his heart contracted cruelly.

He should have realized much sooner that in his mother's eyes, he was just a tool for revenge. To think that he had still clung to his delusions when comforting himself earlier; believing that at least part of the reason why his mother wanted to send him abroad was for his own good. Even her habit of praising him in front of everyone was not to show her pride in him, but to show off him as an object, for fear that others would not know.

The porcelain fell to the ground and shattered with an abrupt sound. The people in the room looked up toward the door. Grandma took a deep breath and called out in panic,

"Xiao-Chi..."

Cheng Feichi forced himself to ignore Cheng Xin's gaze. He turned around and walked out straight away. If he stayed here a minute longer, he was afraid that he would go as crazy as Cheng Xin.

"Where are you going?" There was chaotic movement from behind. Cheng Xin's sharp voice was still clearly audible. "Are you going to C University again? No, Mom forbids you to go!"

Cheng Feichi forced himself to stop, took a few deep breaths, and turned back slowly.

He saw Cheng Xin kneeling down by the door, holding a piece of broken porcelain in her hand. "If you dare to leave, then I'll kill myself here right now!"

All hell broke loose. Several passing nurses tried to grab the sharp shard in her hand, but were kept at bay by her ferocity and resolve.

Grandma was so frightened by the commotion that she burst into tears on the spot. "Xiao-Chi, come back quickly, come back and stop your mother; just listen to her and stop causing," she begged.

Right now, Cheng Feichi couldn't hear anything. Seeing the scene in front of him, his brain was empty, and his heart was numb. For a moment he even thought he was dreaming.

Even in his dreams, he had never seen such a ridiculous scene.

It was as if he, an ordinary person, was suddenly squeezed into a costume and pushed into the spotlight. The exit door was blocked, and the auditorium was full. Hundreds of eyes were staring at him, but he didn't even know what to say or what to do.

After finally regaining control of his limbs, his spine was still stiff. He walked back, step by step, and squatted in front of Cheng Xin. He raised his hand to grasp her hand with the broken porcelain.

Cheng Xin thought he had changed his mind. Her body relaxed. Even her facial expression became softer and more subdued. She was just about to say something when Cheng Feichi took the shard from her hand.

He spread open his right hand, palm up. Without any hesitation, he slashed the newly scarred wound there.

The young nurse standing next to him let out a scream. Blood gushed out, quickly dripping to the ground and gathering into a crimson puddle.

Cheng Xin was dumbfounded. Her mouth opened wide. There were intermittent breathy sounds in her throat, but she couldn't say a word.

Grandma hurriedly took the opportunity to help her up. She stood there, looking stricken. After a long time, she finally regained her senses and turned her gaze from the dripping hand back to Cheng Feichi's face.

"Mom." Cheng Feichi also stood up, controlling his trembling voice. "If you want my life, I'm paying it back to you now."

An hour later, Cheng Feichi was sitting in the car, looking at the rapidly receding landscape outside the window. Only then did he belatedly notice the pain.

Unlike the old, accidental one, the new wound he'd inflicted on himself was long and deep. The doctor had suggested stitches. Afraid of wasting time, he had refused, choosing instead to simply bandage it. Looking down, he saw the blood had already seeped through the gauze. He took out the spare gauze he'd been given by the doctor from his coat. On the narrow seat, he wound it with a few more layers using both hands and his mouth.

Last time, the little guy had been so distressed when he saw the wound on his palm. He couldn't let him see it this time.

When he got out of the car, it was already too late. The

main road leading to the airport was jammed during rush hour, and it was already twenty past eight by the time Cheng Feichi arrived at the airport. He looked around for a while at the pick-up point, then ran to the information desk to inquire. There he learned that the flight from New York had arrived on time at 8 o'clock, and all the passengers had already disembarked.

He called Ye Qin, but the line was busy. Maybe he had just gotten off the plane and hadn't had time to turn on his phone. When the call was able to get through, it was disconnected again and again. And then it could no longer get through at all. Likely Ye Qin had blocked his number.

Cheng Feichi knew Ye Qin must be angry. Not replying to his messages, not picking him up at the airport—anyone would get angry when faced with such behavior.

Standing in the waiting hall, he texted Ye Qin on WeChat but received no reply. Desperate, he looked into Ye Qin's Moments page. Surprisingly, there actually was a new post from Ye Qin: *Back already. Everyone come out and play!*

The accompanying picture showed two bottles of wine on a coffee table.

The pattern on the glass of the coffee table was unique, reflecting the circular lamp on the ceiling. Cheng Feichi only needed one glance to know where it was.

Before he had the time to think about it, he ran out to hail a taxi. He jumped into the car, and told the driver as he closed the door, "Zhongshan Road, Nanguo Mansion."

The airport was brightly lit. From time to time, planes with flashing signal lights rushed into the clouds, lighting up the night sky. When the car drove onto the elevated highway, a slight turn of the head would reveal a neon nighttime cityscape.

But Cheng Feichi didn't have the time to appreciate it. He was desperate to see Ye Qin. Not only was he desperate to offer an explanation, but he also wanted to soothe his own heart; his own heart that had been driven to the point of frenzy.

Apart from Ye Qin, there was no one else who could ease his heart that was on the verge of collapse.

Apart from Ye Qin, he wanted nothing.

In the private room of the club, Zhou Feng had finished howling the song "Friends" to welcome back the two friends who had just returned from overseas. He looked up, checking the time, and immediately put down the microphone. "I'm going to pick someone up."

"Did you call Yuanyuan over?" Zhao Yue asked

Zhou Feng slapped himself on the forehead. "Thanks for reminding me. I almost forgot about him." But then he waved his hand in dismissal and said, "Forget it. I'll call him next time. This time we're here to help our buddy Qin-ge with his game."

Ye Qin was still wondering who was coming when Zhou Feng pushed Sun Yiran through the door. Upon seeing Ye Qin, her face darkened and she turned to leave, but Zhao Yue and Liu Yangfan hustled her into the room from both sides.

"We rarely ever come back home now, Yiran-meimei. Give us some face."

With no choice but to stay, Sun Yiran chose the seat furthest away from Ye Qin to express how "unforgivable" she considered him.

Also upset, Ye Qin couldn't be bothered to pay her any attention. He took the wine Zhou Feng handed over with the intent for them to toast and reconcile, and instead, tilted his head and drink it all in one go. Afterwards, he slumped on the sofa and closed his eyes to rest.

A few people gathered around to play cards, but two of the five didn't participate, so the atmosphere never really livened up.

Zhou Feng lost three rounds in a row. Sorely disappointed, he looked over and urged Ye Qin to call Cheng Feichi there. "We're short of people right now and that nerd rocks at cards. Get him to carry me."

Ye Qin frowned. "Carry my ass. No."

The guy wouldn't even pick him up at the airport, let alone come for a card game.

"Don't jab at his sore spot," Zhao Yue told Zhou Feng. "A-Qin's obviously angry at him, and you're still bringing him up."

"So what?" Zhou Feng asked, puzzled. "Don't tell me he's scared of the nerd scolding him for not finishing his homework... Ha ha ha ha ha."

As he laughed, the others laughed along heartily, slapping their thighs. Hearing this, Ye Qin got angrier and kicked the coffee table. "Stop laughing!"

They were usually laid back with each other and could afford to joke around. Liu Yangfan keenly sensed that every time Ye Qin truly got angry, it was because of Cheng Feichi. He dangled a cigarette from his lips, lit it, and blew out smoke as he said, "By the way, A-Qin, when are you planning to dump him?"

At first, Sun Yiran was sitting a distance away and minding her own business. When she heard this, she suddenly whipped her head around.

Ye Qin also froze.

"He'll do it when it's time, okay?" Zhou Feng mediated, worried that the friends he'd spent a lot of effort getting together would start to quarrel. "Our buddy Qin-ge's not done playing yet. *He's* not even worried. Why do you care so much about his personal life?"

"Exactly," Zhao Yue chimed in. "A-Qin's already an adult... uh... on his ID, at least. He knows what he's doing. No need for us to worry 'bout it." He then tried to recount how many days Ye

Qin and Cheng Feichi had been together. "But I never expected our buddy Qin-ge to care about him for so long. It's been, like, what? A year now? And he's still not tired of this guy?"

Ye Qin hated it most when people took jabs at his young age, especially when Cheng Feichi was also involved. It made him look like the stupidest person in the world, who had tried to play someone only to get played in return. "I already got tired of him a long time ago," he retorted immediately. "I'm gonna dump him after New Year's."

"You're so kind-hearted, to let Cheng Feichi have a good New Year's Eve," Zhao Yue sighed.

"That's not true," Zhou Feng objected animatedly, reminded of something interesting. "I just remembered that the first gift he gave to Cheng Feichi had a secret hidden inside. If Cheng Feichi finds out, he'd die on the spot."

"Oh?" Liu Yangfan asked, curious. "What secret?"

Satisfied that Zhou Feng brought this up to boost his reputation, Ye Qin tilted his chin up and crowed, "He thinks I only put love notes in those stars. He thinks I'm really into him. Not only did he open them, he even showed me one and agreed to date me."

Zhou Feng gave everyone the lowdown of how the folded paper stars were mixed with a single one that had an insult, and Zhao Yue rocked back and forth with laughter. "You got some guts, bro. Weren't you scared that he'd just happen to unfold that particular one?"

"Why? I'm just playing with him. It's not like I was begging him to go out with me."

Ye Qin really did have these thoughts while folding the stars, so he didn't feel guilty at all by saying this.

But Liu Yangfan could sense that his words were different from his thoughts. "Why're you still wearing that ring, then?" he asked meaningfully.

He was referring to the Cartier ring that Cheng Feichi had given Ye Qin. Never able to keep things to himself, Ye Qin took a photo of the ring the very night he received it, which he posted as a WeChat Moment. A bunch of friends left likes and comments, and Zhou Feng even asked him if the straight-A student had proposed. Ye Qin wasn't brave enough to reply in the group chat, so he confessed in their private WeChat group that the straight-A student had spent several months' salary on the ring, so he couldn't not show it off.

His words had been saturated with a boasting tone. "Look how much he loves me! I've got him wrapped around my finger. Look how amazing I am!"

But now, he couldn't be that cocky. They hadn't seen each other for over a month, and Cheng Feichi didn't go to pick him up at the airport after Ye Qin had swallowed his pride and asked him to. Just looking at the ring made him upset. He took it off and tossed it on the table in anger. Metal hit glass with a sharp *clang*.

"Oh? You don't want it anymore? Don't be so quick to throw it away. It's worth at least ten thousand yuan. We could spend that on a bottle of wine here... Man, is this ring real or fake? What if it's a high-quality fake..."

Zhao Yue leaned over to pick up the ring and take a look at it, but Ye Qin snatched it first. Not wanting anyone else to touch the ring, he aimed it at the opening of the glass on the table and threw it in like a dart. Soda splashed out as the ring quickly sank into the murky liquid and vanished.

"Nice shot," Zhao Yue whistled as Liu Yangfan applauded.

For a while, Ye Qin stared at the glass filled with soda. Then, he snorted and looked away. "What a crappy ring!" he exclaimed, "There's only one diamond on it. Who'd want that shit?"

Right after he said this, Sun Yiran suddenly shot to her feet across from him. "How could you trample on his feelings like that? T-this is way too much!"

"He already gave it to Ye Qin, so it belongs to him. He can do whatever he wants with it," Zhou Feng said indifferently.

Sun Yiran was truly stunned. She gave Ye Qin a very severe look. When she saw him straightening his neck as if he didn't give a damn, she felt like he was a total stranger. Disappointed beyond measure, Sun Yiran picked up her jacket and purse from the sofa, about to leave.

Everyone other than Ye Qin tried to block her, but she was so determined that she stomped on them with her high heels and made them scream. No one was able to keep her there.

Sun Yiran slammed the door violently as she walked out in a rage, putting on her jacket on the way to the elevator.

She'd yet to get far before suddenly bumping into someone. When she looked up and saw who it was, her eyes went wide. She covered her mouth, and the purse she was carrying dropped to the ground.

Cheng Feichi was led upstairs by a waiter from the first floor of the club.

The staff here were well-trained and had very sharp eyes. Though he had only been here once, they all recognized him a friend of their boss's son. After all, he was going to the private room exclusively reserved for Liu Yangfan. Not many had been in there before.

After Cheng Feichi went upstairs, no one told Liu Yangfan and his friends of his arrival. The rules of the club were that waiters should never disturb guests unless a guest had a particular request. The waiter who led him up simply pointed him to the room and left.

The door of the private room had been left slightly ajar.

Cheng Feichi was about to knock when he heard the people inside talking loudly about him. His hand was only three centimeters from the door when he froze. Before he knew it, he had overheard the entire conversation.

He should have just left afterwards. If he hadn't spaced out for so long, he wouldn't have run into Sun Yiran as she came out of the room.

Sun Yiran was obviously panicked and kept her hand over her mouth for a long time. She looked at the tightly closed door of the private room and then back to Cheng Feichi. "D-did you hear everything?"

It was a simple question, but Cheng Feichi took ages to respond. Nodding, he hummed a confirmation.

Confusion and embarrassment rushed over Sun Yiran. She had never been in this kind of situation before, so she didn't know what to do. Turning again to look at the door, she debated whether she should knock and ask Ye Qin to explain, or do him a favor and take Cheng Feichi away.

Unaware of her inner struggles, Cheng Feichi headed straight for the elevator. After glancing at the display panel and seeing that it was headed for the lobby, he then turned towards the staircase.

Sun Yiran quickly chased after him. Luckily, Cheng Feichi wasn't walking at a crazy speed, so she could keep up and continue to talk. "I-I didn't mean to keep it from you."

Cheng Feichi stared at the floor expressionlessly. "Okay," he muttered.

"And I'm sure Ye Qin didn't really mean it," Sun Yiran continued, realizing that he would still listen to her. "I'll try talking to him. Don't...don't be upset."

With both feet on the last step of the marble staircase, Cheng Feichi suddenly came to a stop. Sun Yiran also stopped after him.

For a moment, she caught a trace of doubt in Cheng Feichi's eyes, but as soon as she blinked, those deep, amber eyes were left with nothing but a vast and distant emptiness.

Cheng Feichi shook his head very slowly, but he quickly sensed that this might lead to a misunderstanding. "No, you don't need to do that," he told her, and then fell silent for a few seconds.

"I'm fine," he added.

At 9:30 in the evening., the streets of Beijing were still bustling and heavy with traffic.

Every family was out shopping for the approaching Chinese New Year. As Cheng Feichi passed by the entrance of a supermarket, he saw a family of three leave with lots of shopping bags. He watched as they got into a cab, laughing. Then, he turned and stared at a display window adorned with big red Chinese knots for a while before continuing on.

For a long time, he had gotten accustomed to a fast-paced life. Normally, he didn't even waste time on the way to his part-time job, constantly planning trifles in his head, such as: *how much are living expenses for this month?* or *how can I earn more next month?* At this moment, he'd emptied his brain of everything, yet the sudden feeling of leisure made him even more confused. He didn't even know where he should go.

After waiting at the station for more than ten minutes, Cheng Feichi boarded an intercity bus. It was the last bus headed to the suburbs, so there weren't many passengers. He sat in the corner of the last row and tilted his head to look out the window. It seemed to divide the inside and outside of the bus into two completely different worlds. The outside was warm and lively, but inside, everything was cold and dispirited.

He was the only one trapped on this side.

Cheng Feichi called Yi Zheng on the bus. As soon as Yi Zheng heard him inquiring the specifics of what Ye Qin had investigated, he smiled knowingly. "Told you long ago that kid's not innocent. Do you believe it now?"

Cheng Feichi had learned from Yi Zheng that Ye Qin investigated him in September of the previous year, right after the start of his sophomore year of high school.

He didn't even know who Ye Qin was back then. For the first time, he hated himself for having such a good memory. He could still remember that Ye Qin had first gotten him breakfast on a Monday at the end of October, and that three incidents occurred in between: the convenience store framing, the tire piercing, and the gym class where Cheng Feichi caught Ye Qin as he was about to fall. During this period, there were no other interactions between them. Ye Qin began to pursue him for no reason.

Yi Zheng, being incredibly resourceful, even found out what Ye Qin had been investigating in detail. "In addition to investigating your family, he also investigated your mother, and even Ye Jinxiang's whereabouts during that period," he revealed without waiting for Cheng Feichi to ask. "As far as I know, Ye Jinxiang had a secret mistress. As for whether that kid investigated you in passing, or out of coincidence, or for some other reason, it's hard to say."

Cheng Feichi licked his dry lips and thanked him.

"You don't need to thank me for anything, you know? I'm your dad," Yi Zheng said pleasantly, able to put a worry to rest with minimal effort. Before hanging up, he recalled something else. "By the way, there's one more interesting tidbit. That kid's hiding his true age on his ID. He's not eighteen yet, but his birthday is real—November 29th."

The bus stopped at Jiayuan Compound.

When Cheng Feichi exited from the back of the bus, a cold wind blew in his face and stung him all over.

He thought it was because that his clothes were thin, but the whole time from when he got out the key in the elevator to when he went inside the apartment, his body continued to sting badly. It was like a steel needle piercing through his skin and desperately boring inward through his flesh and veins.

A few needles stabbed into his heart, and for a moment, he even thought that it had stopped beating. His fingers were so numb that they almost lost their sense of touch as he groped for the light switch and pressed it. The room suddenly lit up. Feeling icy air enter his lungs as he looked at the familiar yet unfamiliar decor in front of him, Cheng Feichi realized that he was neither dead nor dreaming.

Reality was a thousand—ten thousand times crueler.

The bedroom remained the same. He had folded the quilt and piled it at the head of the bed with the pillows. No one had been here since they parted on winter solstice.

Last year's winter solstice was on December 22nd, exactly twenty-three days away from Ye Qin's real birthday on November 29th. No wonder Ye Qin didn't need to go home and celebrate his birthday with his parents for two consecutive years.

Ye Qin was so attached to his family that he chose a nearby school to be closer to home. Every day, he went home to have lunch with his mother. Why would he spend such an important day with Cheng Feichi, who was neither a relative nor a friend?

Pampered since birth, Ye Qin must have seen hundreds upon thousands of luxurious gifts. Why would he even treasure the ring that Cheng Feichi had given him?

Looking around vacantly at the room that he and Ye Qin had decorated themselves, Cheng Feichi thought that he must have been insane to think this place felt like home.

His eyes fell sluggishly on the glass jar sitting near the bedside. He walked over and picked it up. The lights were off, so the stars in the jar glowed with subtle, fluorescent light. He opened the cap and poured them all out on the table. Under the tiny bit of light shining in from the living room, Cheng Feichi opened them up one by one.

Since his right hand was wrapped in heavy gauze, he couldn't curl his palm, so his movements were slow and difficult. Thus, Cheng Feichi simply removed the gauze and threw it on the floor, focusing entirely on taking apart the stars. The more stars he took apart, the stronger the inexpressible anticipation that rose in his heart; as if he could pretend he hadn't heard anything today if only he couldn't find that one star.

He just needed this one piece of proof to erase everything that had gone down today from his mind, and banish the piercing, heart-wrenching pain with it.

The glass jar was compact, and there weren't many paper stars inside. When only five remained, Cheng Feichi's eyes focused, and his fingers moved fast. His heart pounded heavily in his chest, yearning for this tiny sliver of hope.

Everything suddenly stopped when he took apart the third remaining star.

Cheng Feichi rolled the piece of paper open with his thumb and pieced together a string of words. For several minutes, he stared at it fixedly, breaking each word apart and putting them back together. He used all the strength he had to verify that this sentence meant what it did. Then, he refolded the stars and put them back in the glass jar.

When Cheng Feichi held the jar in his hand to examine it, he realized that it was now so smeared with sticky blood that he couldn't see inside. The smell of iron spread through his nose, and he wiped off the drying blood with the back of his still-clean hand. That star was still quietly sitting inside quietly.

As he breathed heavily, the cloth over his eyes blew away, and his vision suddenly became clear.

Now he understood. The reason Ye Qin had insulted and trampled on him in a million ways. How he constantly ran hot and cold, leaving Cheng Feichi at a loss for what to do. It wasn't because he was throwing a temper tantrum, but because he really hated Cheng Feichi—hated him so much that only by doing this could he vent his anger.

The entire time, Cheng Feichi was the only one who treasured this relationship. He was the only one who saw it as a little sun sent by the heavens to light up his dark and empty life.

In the end, this was just another castle built on lies. While he immersed himself in the light and warmth, a heavy hammer fell from the sky and smashed the faint, illusory structure to pieces.

In a mere moment, the blazing sunlight, the pulsing heart, the lively presence; it had all crumbled into dust and sand, carried away by the wind.

Ye Qin was right. What else was he, other than an utter fool?

Cheng Feichi thought he was laughing, but when he raised his head, a face devoid of all feeling was reflected in the window glass.

It turned out that even if a person hurt until they could hurt no more, it wouldn't necessarily show on their face.

CHAPTER 15

BACK at Nanguo Mansion, the four-people party went late into the night.

Ye Qin promised Luo Qiuling he'd go home that night. Right after midnight, Liu Yangfan asked if he should get him a cab.

"No, I still want to hang out for a bit longer," Ye Qin said, waving him off.

"Isn't our buddy A-Qin an obedient son?" Zhao Yue asked in surprise. "Why aren't you in a hurry to go home today?"

"I dare you to say another word," Ye Qin threatened, side-eying him.

"It's *so* annoying to speak and hear foreign languages every day," Liu Yangfan laughed. "We barely ever come back to China and you won't even let us speak Chinese?"

"Are you actually speaking in a human language right now? What have you said that's even remotely civilized? You even made me..."

—Spout a bunch of bullshit lies. The second half of the sentence reached the tip of Ye Qin's tongue before he swallowed it back down.

"Aren't we always like this?" Zhou Feng quipped. "We're

bros. What can't we say between us? It's just a few jokes for a laugh. Qin-ge, if you aren't happy about it, then come make fun of me. My arms are always open for you... Ow!"

Ye Qin had picked up the lighter on the table and whipped it directly at Zhou Feng's head. "Shut up, douchebag!"

"Hey, how 'bout we have a contest here to see who's the champion of douchebags?" Zhao Yue suggested to Liu Yangfan, shaking with laughter.

Two hours later, the jet-lagged boys lay crookedly on the sofa, dozing off.

Ye Qin was also so drowsy that he couldn't keep his eyes open, but he couldn't let himself fall asleep. As he lay on the sofa, he desperately pinched his thigh to stay awake, lest he slept all the way till dawn. If he moved now and the boys around him found out, how would he ever live it down?

Once the steady sound of snoring filled the air, Ye Qin sat up quietly, picked up the glass on the table, and tiptoed to the bathroom.

As he poured the drink into the sink, he carefully cupped the mouth of the glass with his hand, concerned that the ring would accidentally fall down the drain. When he finally got the ring, Ye Qin rinsed it thoroughly. Afraid that water wouldn't fully clean it, he applied some hand soap beside the sink. Then, he recalled somebody saying that the durability of metal products could be affected by chemical agents and quickly ran it under water again. Once the ring no longer smelled of wine, he wiped it dry with a paper towel before putting it under the dryer for quite some time.

Ye Qin closely examined the ring he'd put back on his ring finger in the back seat of the car on the way home. No matter which angle he looked at it, he kept feeling that something was off.

The color seemed darker. The diamond seemed less shiny than before. He knew the ring fit him perfectly, but why did it feel a bit too big right now?

Ye Qin examined it for some time, using his phone as a flashlight. The more he looked at it, the more he found faults, until he had an urge to call Liu Yangfan and ask if the drinks he served were corrosive and had ruined his ring.

Naturally, he was too embarrassed to make that call. Besides, *he* had been the one to toss the ring in. If it really did get ruined, there was no one else to blame. Wilted, Ye Qin decided to visit the brand counter tomorrow to see if the staff could get it looking good as new.

Speaking of the counter, Ye Qin remembered Zhao Yue's snide remark about the ring being a fake. He raised his hand again and looked it over, extremely unconvinced. This ring was so beautiful. How could it be fake?

Cheng Feichi had sent him a few messages on WeChat. Ye Qin read them one by one and tilted his chin up cockily. Cheng Feichi wouldn't dare buy him fake stuff.

Perhaps it was because the drinks had jumbled up his head, but Ye Qin had the same nightmare that night.

In his dream, Cheng Feichi was even farther away from him than before, so far away that his face was a blur. Ye Qin wanted to walk to the ginkgo tree, but the awfully strong wind kept him in place as if his feet were nailed to the ground. He wanted to call Cheng Feichi's name, but found that he couldn't make a sound. Ye Qin was about to go crazy, only able to look at Cheng Feichi from a distance, unable to reach him, to touch him.

He woke up gasping, drenched in cold sweat. Once his breathing returned to normal, Ye Qin turned to look out the window and saw that it was already light out.

The first thing he did when he got up was reach for his cellphone. The utterly blank screen with no notifications whatsoever stunned Ye Qin momentarily, and he tapped into "Contracts" to double-check. Cheng Feichi's number was already removed from the blacklist, so why hadn't he called?

Impatient, Ye Qin wanted to call Cheng Feichi but couldn't swallow his pride. Cheng Feichi was the one who hadn't messaged him back, who didn't pick up when he called. Ye Qin should be waiting for him to apologize first. What was he doing calling Cheng Feichi?

Ye Qin had only blacklisted him for a few hours and ignored some of his WeChat messages. So what? He never even got mad at Cheng Feichi for giving him the cold shoulder for so long.

When he thought about it this way, Ye Qin resisted the impulse. After double-checking that his phone had its ringtone set to maximum volume, he stuffed it in his pocket and went downstairs for breakfast.

Last night, Ye Qin hadn't had time to talk to Luo Qiuling, as he had passed out as soon as he'd gotten home. Now, he was too absent-minded. When Luo Qiuling asked about his trip, he couldn't be bothered to reply and used his spoon to stir the mushroom soup in his bowl instead. "Why are we having this again? Did we buy a whole cart of mushrooms?" he complained.

Luo Qiuling stopped talking. The silence lasted for the whole meal.

Ye Qin was about to go back to his room afterwards when she interjected, "Have a seat, Qin-Qin. I have something to say."

Ye Qin thought she was going to pass him another message from Ye Jinxiang, telling him to review his past term's successes and failures in preparation for the upcoming one or something along those lines. He was about to find a comfortable position to slump in while listening when he suddenly caught the words "studying abroad" leave her mouth. Ye Qin immediately perked

up, pointed at his own nose.

"Studying abroad? Me?"

"Well, your mom and dad were thinking, and we decided that it would be better to let you go abroad for university. Seeing as you often travel overseas, it'll take you no time to get used to..."

"I don't wanna study abroad," Ye Qin cut in before Luo Qiuling could finish. "I wanna stay in China."

"Foreign universities have a better environment than domestic ones, and you can make a lot of new friends. And it'll also be convenient if you want to take a vacation on a tropical island," Luo Qiuling advised tactfully, aware of Ye Qin's attachment to home.

"Was this Ye Jinxiang's idea?" Ye Qin asked bluntly.

When he last talked to Luo Qiuling about the national college entrance exams, she had told him to put down a local university so that he could come home more often. In less than three months, she had changed her mind. He could only conclude that Ye Jinxiang had been behind this.

For a moment, Luo Qiuling was stunned at hearing him call his father directly by name. Then, she quickly replied, "No, your dad and I came to the decision together after some discussion. You shouldn't be so angry with him, even if he's..." Here, she paused. Unable to find a suitable description, Luo Qiuling simply gave up. "When all's said and done, he's still your father. He really does love you. We wouldn't do anything to hurt you."

The moment as he heard words like these, Ye Qin felt annoyed. "So everything is set after you two discussed it?" he demanded, getting on his feet. "Did you ever ask for my opinion?"

Ye Qin had become used to doing whatever he wanted ever since he was young, so he hated being ordered around with a passion. He was convinced that this whole affair was trouble solely stirred up by Ye Jinxiang. That old man must have used some kind of sorcery to brainwash Luo Qiuling into agreeing to send him abroad.

Luo Qiuling chased after him, wanting to offer a few more words of persuasion, but Ye Qin pressed his mother back onto her chair. "Don't worry," he comforted her in turn. "In four months, I'll get into to a good domestic university and shut Ye Jinxiang up."

It wasn't that Ye Qin was overconfident, but that he believed in Cheng Feichi.

Cheng Feichi said that he would go to the same university as Ye Qin. Any university a straight-A student would go to couldn't be that bad, so Ye Qin just had to be good and listen to him.

Ye Qin found that ever since he started this relationship with Cheng Feichi, he became more and more used to leaving all the decisions to him. Before, Ye Qin had taken pride in being able to call all the shots, but he later cast this thought to the back of his mind subconsciously. He'd gradually come to experience the comfort of fully relying on Cheng Feichi and having to do nothing himself.

Everyone always said that you should leave the hard things to the talented folk. There was nothing that Cheng Feichi didn't know or couldn't do. Ye Qin would never rely on anyone else.

As he thought this, Ye Qin's anger towards Cheng Feichi dissipated and he waited for Cheng Feichi's call with the last bit of pride in him.

But the phone never rang. From dawn till dusk, he didn't receive a single phone call or WeChat message. Midway through, he even suspected his phone was broken and tried plugging in the charger a few times.

No call came the next day...or the day after...up until New Year's Eve.

Ye Qin thought Cheng Feichi was tied up with work again.

Plus, his mother was still in the hospital, so he might have been too busy to look at his cellphone. When New Year's Eve came around, he couldn't wait any longer. *If I call to wish him a Happy New Year, it won't be too embarrassing, right?* he thought. And just like that, he convinced himself, cleared his throat, and made the call.

Voicemail. It didn't go through.

Ye Qin tried again, but the call still didn't go through.

He loaded 200 RMB onto his cellphone and called again half an hour later. Still voicemail.

Cheng Feichi, how dare you block my number? he thought, jumping to his feet.

Ye Qin called using his landline, but still couldn't reach him. The rapid beeping sounds made his heart pound. Even though Cheng Feichi had been busy before and hadn't been able to find time to talk to him, Ye Qin would at least hear from him. What could keep him occupied for so long that he couldn't even find time to look at his cellphone?

Was his mother seriously ill?

No, no, no. How could he curse Cheng Feichi's mother like that? Ye Qin slapped his mouth. But then he remembered that Cheng Xin was Ye Jinxiang's mistress and immediately regretted it, feeling all jumbled up as he massaged his face.

Cheng Feichi hadn't blacklisted him. Ye Qin could still send messages. After sending Cheng Feichi a "Happy New Year," Ye Qin waited in bed holding onto his phone until he fell asleep. The next day, he woke up naturally to a bunch of good wishes. He scrolled through all of them, but didn't see the one he was waiting for.

Now, he could no longer sit still. On the afternoon of New Year's Day, Ye Qin went to look for Cheng Feichi at the hospital.

He didn't even know what Cheng Xin's condition was or

which department she had been admitted to. The nurses, being in charge of so many wards, couldn't offer him clear guidance either. He figured he might as well go search on his own; down the stairs floor by floor, down the hallways ward by ward.

After looping through the whole building in vain, Ye Qin heard that there were two more inpatient floors in the upstairs of the emergency department and hurried over. The nurse there flipped through the hospital records and said that the building had no patient named Ms. Cheng, but Ye Qin still insisted on taking a look at every ward. Once he went through all of them and double-checked that was no trace of Cheng Xin and Cheng Feichi, Ye Qin finally believed her.

"She might have transferred," one of the nurses said. "The transfer records aren't easy to check. You'll have better luck asking the patient's family."

It was only now that Ye Qin realized something was wrong and raced to the Yulin Compound in his car.

He knocked on Cheng Feichi's door for ages without anyone opening up to answer, which alarmed the downstairs neighbors. An old grandpa propped his cane on the staircase railing and craned his neck.

"No one's home. Stop knocking."

Ye Qin remembered Cheng Feichi saying that he once carried an elderly grandpa with weak legs up the stairs. This was probably him. "Where did they go?" he asked in a hurry.

The grandpa waved his hand dismissively. "I don't know. Maybe they went back to their hometown to celebrate the New Year."

Because he had previously investigated Cheng Xin and Cheng Feichi, Ye Qin knew that Cheng Xin's family came from around here in the capital; Cheng Feichi was even more of born and raised local. What "hometown" was there for them to return to?

He sat in the car and stared at the window of Cheng Fei-

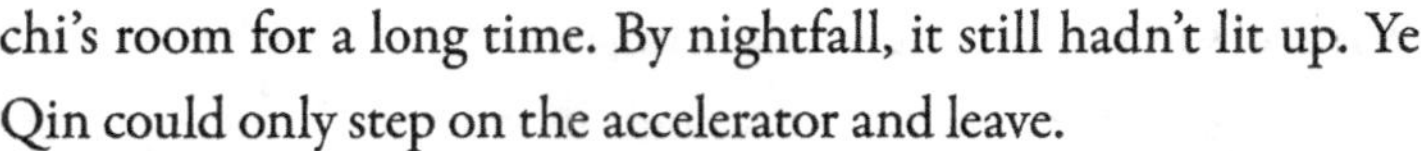

chi's room for a long time. By nightfall, it still hadn't lit up. Ye Qin could only step on the accelerator and leave.

As soon as Ye Qin got home, he asked around for news of Cheng Feichi. He checked with all the students he knew in the senior class, but they all told him something along the lines of, "How would I know? Aren't you closest with him?" Ye Qin asked Zhou Feng hopelessly. His sister had attended Cheng Xin's prep class, so maybe someone in his family knew something.

He also considered seeking Ye Jinxiang's help, but there were too many concerns, mainly that Luo Qiuling was current-ly unaware of the existence of Cheng Xin and her illegitimate child, Cheng Feichi. Telling her everything right now would inevitably lead to chaos. While others celebrated a happy, lively New Year's with their families, the Yes spent the holiday in a discombobulated mess. This was far too embarrassing.

Anyways, Ye Jinxiang hadn't returned after he'd left earlier in the morning. He was probably still busy with the company's affairs.

Let him be busy, then. Last night, he had been scowling at Ye Qin during their New Year's Eve family dinner and had scared everyone into silence, unable to eat with peace of mind. Ye Qin got angry at the memory and resolved not to turn to Ye Jinxiang for help.

Some time later, Zhou Feng got back to him. "My sister stopped attending her classes last term. Ms. Cheng said she couldn't teach anymore because of her poor health. My mom even tried to call her last night to send new year greetings, but her phone was turned off. She tried again today and it was the same."

Ye Qin instantly deflated. Then, nervousness and appre-hension engulfed him.

He kept flipping through his address book, not knowing who to call. Just then, Zhou Feng called back. "Guess what?!" he yelled as soon as it connected. "I'm at Nanguo right now and I just asked Yan Fan about the straight-A student. He showed up on the surveillance cameras. He was there that night we came back from New York!"

Finally, helpful news. All Ye Qin could think about was where Cheng Feichi could have gone. His head had no room for anything else. When he heard that Cheng Feichi had gone downstairs with Sun Yiran, Ye Qin immediately gave her a call.

"Did you run into Cheng Feichi that night?" he asked bluntly when the call connected, not even wishing her a happy new year. "Why didn't you bring him in? Why didn't you tell me? Are you my friend or not?"

For a while, Sun Yiran was stunned to silence by his string of questions. Once she got a hold of herself, she flew into a rage. "You jerk! You know full well what you said and did! Don't you?! *You* made Cheng Feichi angry enough to leave! And you have the nerve to blame me?"

Ye Qin was completely bewildered.

How could he have known that Cheng Feichi was listening outside the room at that time? He couldn't even remember what he'd said back then, just that it had been a bunch of nasty nonsense, not to mention he had thrown the ring into the glass in front of everyone.

Ye Qin opened up WeChat on autopilot and sent Cheng Feichi a message. "I'm sorry. I was wrong." Once he calmed down, he typed a sincere apology explaining how he had done stupid things that day because he'd been caught up in his friends' excitement and had also had a bit to drink. That was why he'd spewed a bunch of crap.

"I was just running my mouth, just joking around with them. It's all lies. Don't believe what I said that night."

After sending this message, Ye Qin added another line:

"Don't believe it, okay, gege~"

He added a heart at the end.

It wasn't like he'd never made Cheng Feichi angry before—they'd had gone through some pretty serious fights. But as long as Ye Qin called him gege, Cheng Feichi would instantly give in. Ye Qin thought it would be the same this time. After sending the message, he gave a huge sigh of relief and fell asleep holding his cellphone.

The next day, he still didn't get a reply from Cheng Feichi, and his phone calls still wouldn't go through.

Ye Qin had already graduated from initial panic to confusion. He had a vaguely bad feeling about this, but dismissed it with much effort to stop himself from delving deeper.

February 13th was Cheng Feichi's birthday, and he'd promised Ye Qin to keep that day free. Cheng Feichi said that he wouldn't lie to him.

Sure enough, Ye Qin got a message from him on the afternoon of February 12th: "Are you free?"

Lifeless only a moment ago, Ye Qin bounced on the bed the moment he heard back. But after tapping the answer button, he didn't want to seem too eager, so he forced his voice steady. "Guess."

Cheng Feichi didn't guess. "Where are you? I'm coming to you."

Ye Qin also didn't beat around the bush and told him straight out to meet up in the apartment in Jiayuan Compound in a little while. As soon as he put down the phone, he started to primp and get dressed. To make himself look even better, Ye Qin wore a pair of shoes that were nice-looking but had to be laced up.

Ye Qin still didn't know how to tie shoelaces. He re-tied

them once in the doorway of his house, once on the street as he was waiting for a green light, and once at the destination after getting out of the car. As he set one foot out of the elevator upstairs, the shoelace on his right foot loosened again. Desperate to meet up with Cheng Feichi, Ye Qin stopped caring.

Cheng Feichi would be there to help him in a moment anyway.

When he entered the apartment, Ye Qin first went into the kitchen to boil water. Before, he often stood in the kitchen door, watching as Cheng Feichi busied about. He hadn't been able to learn how to cook, but at least he had boiling water down.

After that, he washed both their cups. It was cold outside. Cheng Feichi, that broke guy, must have taken the bus again, and the bus was exposed to the blowing wind on all sides. When Cheng Feichi arrived in a bit, he'd be able to drink hot water immediately.

Once he was done with this stuff, Ye Qin washed a rag and used it to wipe down the dining table and chairs. *Cheng Feichi may just bring over groceries to cook,* he thought. *It all needs to be wiped down anyway.*

Young master Ye Qin, who had never done housework at home, got his first taste of the joy of labor. He toiled until he was sweating profusely and was about to go in the bedroom to wipe down the table and chairs in there when the doorbell rang.

Ye Qin threw aside the rag and scuttled over to get it. The floor had just been scrubbed and was quite slippery still, almost making him trip. Still panting, Ye Qin opened the door.

"Why even knock? Don't you have a key?" he grumbled mildly.

Cheng Feichi stood in the doorway wearing a black coat Ye Qin had never seen before. It made him look taller and straighter. When he held a key out in front of him, Ye Qin reached out and took it reflexively. Then, he pulled him into the room.

"Come in already, it's cold outside. I boiled some hot water."

Cheng Feichi didn't speak. Nor did he move. Ye Qin pulled until he couldn't pull him along, loosening his grip. Cheng Feichi had been waiting for that, and he freed his arm from Ye Qin's hand.

Ye Qin thought that Cheng Feichi was still upset over what he had heard at Nanguo Mansion. "I'm sorry, I'm sorry," he placated. "Didn't I already say sorry? Why are you so petty..."

"Let's break up."

Thinking that he was hearing things, Ye Qin blinked and looked up at Cheng Feichi's face. The corridors were dimly lit, so he couldn't fully make out Cheng Feichi's expression. He just got a vague feeling that something was different.

Perhaps it was his tone or the look in his eyes. He was just different from before.

Ye Qin's thoughts flew into a flurry and he pulled on the hand hanging at Cheng Feichi's side. "What's wrong? Why are you are still angry? I know I was wrong. I shouldn't have said those things. If you're still mad, then hit me..."

His voice went quieter and quieter because he realized that Cheng Feichi hadn't held his hand. None of the slender, powerful fingers had moved.

Whenever Cheng Feichi held his hand in the past, Ye Qin felt warm all over. Now, Cheng Feichi's hand was clearly still hot, but none of that heat transmitted to him. It was as if an invisible wall had gone up between them, harder and colder than a meter of ice.

Cheng Feichi slowly pulled back his hand, just like he had a moment ago. His breathing was shallow and even, with not a hair out of place. Once more, he parted his thin, pressed lips.

"Let's break up."

"Wh-what? Are you listening to me at all?"

Ye Qin tried pulling on his other hand and immediately shifted his attention when he noticed something strange. He leaned forward and grabbed it recklessly behind Cheng Feichi's back, but upon touching the thick gauze, quickly curbed his strength. "What happened to your hand? Hasn't that healed by now?"

Cheng Feichi pulled back his arm, slipping away nimbly.

Ye Qin was very dissatisfied with his continued indifference and resistance. He couldn't help feeling a little agitated. "What the hell's wrong with you? If you're upset, then hit me! Yell at me! Is there any reason not to let me touch you? And what's all that stuff about breaking up?"

To him, the words "break up" were equivalent to throwing a tantrum; on the same level as him blocking Cheng Feichi's number and ignoring his WeChat messages. It was a tactic he used to communicate his dissatisfaction, comparable to saying, "Don't be like this in the future."

But Cheng Feichi's "break up" obviously didn't have as many twists and turns. He merely went silent for a few seconds. "Just pretend you dumped me."

Ye Qin blanked out for a while. Then he remembered: that night at the club, he seemed to have said that he would dump Cheng Feichi right after Chinese New Year.

"That was just empty talk." Ye Qin became even more agitated, angry that Cheng Feichi had listened to what he shouldn't and even took it to heart. "Didn't I explain it to you on WeChat? Are you really gonna get hung up on it?"

He waited expectantly for Cheng Feichi to say no, to hear, "I'm not that narrow-minded." But he didn't hear either. Cheng Feichi offered him no response whatsoever, using silence as his answer.

Ye Qin was most afraid of his calm, silent persona that kept

other people a thousand miles away. Realizing that Cheng Fei-chi's condition was completely opposite to his, he suddenly lost his composure. He flew into a rage and shoved him.

"What the hell do you want?"

Cheng Feichi took two steps back before coming to a stand-still. He had no intention of moving forward, even if only by an inch. He repeated the same three words: "Let's break up."

Ye Qin realized that he was serious. He only agreed to meet because he wanted to make things clear in person. Everything had already been laid out when he handed over the key as soon as Ye Qin opened the door. Cheng Feichi had personally drawn a boundary between the two of them; one that he wouldn't cross, one that wouldn't allow Ye Qin to come close and touch him again.

What a responsible person! To take time away from his busy schedule and break up in person, when the issue could have been solved through a text message or a phone call. Was this what people called "seeing things through"?

Ye Qin clenched his back teeth inadvertently as his heart, once full of expectations, devolved entirely into anger. All he could think was that he'd been toyed with. His cheeks burned, and his head was jumbled up. What little patience and reason he had left also faded away, and he yanked the ring from his left ring finger.

"You wanna take this back then?!"

Cheng Feichi shifted his eyes to glance at the ring that Ye Qin was holding. "Since I already gave it to you, you can do whatever you want with it."

His calmness only served to make Ye Qin boil with rage. Without another word, Ye Qin whipped the ring at him. Cheng Feichi didn't catch it, letting it fall to the ground and bounce back up with a series of piercing sounds before finally rolling off somewhere.

"If you want to break up, then take it away." Ye Qin straightened his neck to look at Cheng Feichi, glaring so hard that his eyes were open wide. It was like he wanted compete with him: who could be crueler than whom? "I don't want your shitty stuff."

With that, he stepped back into the apartment and slammed the door.

Ye Qin sat on the sofa for a long time, so angry that he couldn't calm down.

The kettle in the kitchen turned off automatically with a *click*. The hot water was ready. Ye Qin looked at the apartment he had just tidied up and the teacups he had placed on the table side by side. It made him even more furious.

The anger eventually subsided into a feeling of injustice. So many things had happened between them before, and the two had only fallen out for a few days at most. Didn't he just crack a few jokes? Did Cheng Feichi really have to pull the breakup card to scare him?

Although Cheng Feichi's words and actions were always steady and reliable, Ye Qin still believed that he was only threatening a breakup to scare him into being more amenable and not losing his temper as often from now on.

Right? How could we really break up? Cheng Feichi treats me so well. He even said that he'd never lie to me, that he'll go to the same university as me.

He'd never lie to me.

Ye Qin injected himself with a dose of soothing thoughts. Then, he inevitably lost himself in the course of reflection, carefully going over to what he had done that could have made Cheng Feichi angry enough to mention the words "break up."

He had showed his condescending disdain for Cheng Feichi

in front of his friends. And he had thrown away the ring Cheng Feichi had given him. Even if he'd retrieved it later, Cheng Feichi must have felt awful when he'd heard and seen that from the door.

Ye Qin was accustomed to being alone, so he seldom showed compassion for others. He realized that if this had happened to him, he would probably be even more furious; so furious that he would blacklist Cheng Feichi's number for a week and make him apologize in person more than a hundred times. Then, for the sake of it, he would make Cheng Feichi kneel down on one knee and beg Ye Qin to put the ring back on.

Besides, that ring had been earned through Cheng Feichi's hard work, and the injury on his hand had yet to fully heal.

Starting to feel guilty, Ye Qin poured himself a glass of hot water. No one was there to remind him, so he burned his tongue on the first gulp and ran choking to the bedroom in search of the medicine box.

Before he found it, he first saw the glass jar on the table.

That was a birthday present he had given to Cheng Feichi. Although it did take some time to fold the stars, the thing wasn't worth much in his eyes. When he moved here temporarily, the jar took up a lot of space amongst what little luggage Cheng Feichi had. Ye Qin couldn't quite understand why he kept it with him.

During their first month of cohabitation, he slowly learned that Cheng Feichi truly treasured this gift. Every time Cheng Feichi cleaned the house, he would polish the glass jar until it sparkled and reflected the sun's splendid rays.

Once, Ye Qin lay on the bed watching him polish the jar. "That stupid thing is too ugly," he said with disdain. "Just as I thought, the convenience stand at the school gates has nothing good. I once saw a sapphire jar in one of the Times Square gift shops that came with its own stars inside. It was so pretty. I'll buy it and switch it for this one. It'll look super good in the apartment."

How did Cheng Feichi react at that time?

He shook his head and smiled. "I want this one."

Now, this crappy, worthless glass jar still shone as bright as a mirror, but only one star was left inside. The others had been taken apart and stacked neatly on the corner of the table.

Ye Qin stared blankly, hesitating for a second as he stretched his hand over. As he took the pile of paper strips, he discovered that the pile of stars which had once looked so big was really just this light and small.

He looked through them one by one. Each had the same sentence written on it: *Will you be my boyfriend?*

They had all been handwritten by him while he was either killing time in class or dozing off at home. There wasn't a single one that had been written with care. But afterwards, Cheng Feichi took one along while going out to find him, and put it in his hand like it was something precious. "Okay," he had replied.

Ye Qin knew what was written on the unopened star left in the jar.

His hands went clammy for no reason, unable to grip the jar steadily. As they shook, Ye Qin saw one of the star's corners was stained with a strange color. Switching the light on and pouring it out, he discovered that the spot was dark red and couldn't be scratched off. It was a bloodstain.

Ye Qin's pupils quickly shrank. It felt like someone was squeezing on his heart. He put down his things and ran back into the living room.

The sound-activated lights in the hallway of the building lit up in response to his flurry, but it was even quieter outside than inside. All he could see was the tightly closed, barred window and the elevator display screen indicating that it was stopped on the first floor.

Panicking, Ye Qin chased after him without even closing the apartment door.

A minute ago, he hadn't been worried at all. He had thought that Cheng Feichi would stand at the door and wait for him to calm down like always. He had thought that as soon as he opened the door, he could jump into that warm embrace and stay there for as long as he wanted.

As Ye Qin waited for the elevator to descend, he still held on to hope. Cheng Feichi must have not gone far, he thought. Cheng Feichi had waited for two hours in the rain before. He waited, even when Ye Qin had kicked him out, so it made no sense that he couldn't wait for more than ten minutes this time.

As soon as the elevator door opened, Ye Qin shot out like an arrow leaving the bowstring, running towards the compound gates along the road.

No one was taking a walk outside in the wintery night. The only things left on the road were a few lonely streetlamps that cast a still, gloomy light on the ground.

Even so, Ye Qin still thought that Cheng Feichi would be up ahead. He shouted Cheng Feichi's name hoarsely, feeling for the phone in his pocket as he ran, wanting to call Cheng Feichi to tell him not to leave. Tell him to wait up.

Ye Qin was so caught up in looking at his phone that he didn't pay attention to the path. He ran too fast. When his right foot stepped on the laces of his left shoe, his center of gravity shifted forward and he fell hard. His knees and palms collided heavily with the cement path with the same, heavy *thud* as the cellphone that had flown out of his hands.

The pain shot straight from his limbs to his head. As someone as scared of pain as he was, Ye Qin nearly burst into tears on the spot. Clenching his teeth and getting to his feet, he used the back of his hands to wipe away the wetness about to overflow from his eyes, afraid it would block his vision.

"Cheng Feichi, don't move!" he lifted his head and hollered out.

The only response was the whistling wind.

Ye Qin limped forward, dragging his tingling leg. The cold wind drained the color from his lips. Upon closer look, they even trembled as he huffed.

"Gege…" Ye Qin called out into the nothing. Afraid Cheng Feichi wouldn't hear him, he raised his voice and called out again, "Where are you, gege?! "

His voice seemed to contain grit—hoarse, broken, so choked he couldn't say anything else.

And the man who helped him tie his shoelaces, who smiled and told him, "I'm here," never turned back to look at him again.

Zhou Feng walked out of the elevator at a little past nine in the evening. When he looked up and saw the black shadow at the door, he almost threw away the stuff in his hands out of fright.

After walking closer, he discovered that it was Ye Qin squatting there and heaved a sigh of relief. "A-Qin, even if you have to spend the nerd's birthday with him, you don't have to be like this. This isn't a big surprise anymore, it's a big scare, okay?"

He passed his bags over to the other hand and tried to help Ye Qin up. "Hurry, hurry. Open the door. Let's go in and talk."

Ye Qin stayed in place for a long time. "I didn't bring the key," he said finally.

"…Shit." Speechless, Zhou Feng had no choice but to put down the stuff in his hands and crouch down beside him. "The nerd has the key, right? I'll be a good man through and through and carry you guys to the bridal chamber before I head out."

After waiting a while, he realized that Ye Qin wouldn't talk to him. Ye Qin didn't even look like he was grateful to Zhou

Feng for running his legs off at night to help him shop. Suddenly feeling bored, Zhou Feng pawed through the two paper bags on the floor. "This cake is freshly made. I saw the baker stuff it full of fruit and chocolate with my own eyes... The ring, I bought in the Dongcheng mall. It was out of stock in the Times Square boutique, can you believe it? Maybe cause it's Valentine's Day in two days. I was so worried that I also bought Yuanyuan... Hey, what are you doing?"

Suddenly reminded of something, Ye Qin shot up and turned on his phone flashlight. He bent over and searched the hallway up and down for something. Zhou Feng came over to help, asking what he was looking for, but Ye Qin didn't say anything, engrossed in his search.

Fortunately, the floor of the hallway was smooth. Ye Qin found the ring in a corner by the window. He placed it in his palms and blew on it, and then went to fetch the newly bought ring.

"Huh? Isn't this *that* ring? Didn't you already throw it away?"

Ignoring Zhou Feng's question, Ye Qin took a small box from the bag sitting on the ground and carefully opened it. Inside was the same ring in a bigger size, also adorned with a single diamond.

Ye Qin wanted to put his ring together with the new one, but the slit in the ring box was too small to put the two rings side by side. Regardless, he tried to shove it in several times to no avail.

Zhou Feng could no longer stand it. "Man, this is a box for one ring. If you want to put yours away, go find your box."

"I can't find it," Ye Qin said after a moment's thought.

He threw away his ring box the day after Cheng Feichi had given it to him. After putting on this ring, he never thought of taking it off again. He had even thought that, right after the clock struck midnight, once he revealed an identical ring, Cheng Feichi would put it on and never take it off again.

Just like how he thought Cheng Feichi would protect him

forever, and how, the moment Ye Qin turned around, he would be able to see him.

Ye Qin gave up in the end. He closed the ring box and put it back in the paper bag. His own ring, he clenched in his left fist together with that bloodstained star.

On the first day of school, the weather in the capital showed signs of warming up. The wind carried traces of warmth when it blew across the students standing in the schoolyard.

As soon as the opening ceremony ended, Ye Qin headed to office to find the senior class's homeroom teacher.

"Oh, Cheng Feichi? His school records have already been transferred. I don't know where he went, but in any case, it's not C University."

"C?" Ye Qin asked hesitantly.

"Yes," the teacher said, also looking puzzled. "He didn't want to accept A University's offer. He insisted on going to some second-rate C University and wouldn't listen to me no matter how I tried talking to him. He even filled out the application form. I still have a copy with me, which I need to find and shred as soon as I can."

On that note, he opened the drawer and bowed his head to search for it. "He has such good grades and a beautiful resume. Even the best major at C University is way below him. I don't know what he was thinking... Thank goodness he came to his senses. His family probably intervened."

As Ye Qin left the office with the nullified application form, his cellphone rang in his pocket. It was an unknown number, not saved in his contacts. He glanced at it hastily before picking up.

The person on the other side told him that Cheng Feichi had just gotten a passport and an American study visa. His flight was scheduled for today. Before Ye Qin even heard the exact

time, he broke into a run.

Since he didn't drive to school today, he got a taxi at the school gates. The whole way, Ye Qin repeatedly urged the driver to go faster, almost pissing off the ill-tempered middle-aged man.

After arriving at the airport, he realized that he didn't know the flight number and scampered to call the private investigator again. "His flight already left this morning," he was told. "We won't be able to keep track of his whereabouts once he leaves the country."

Ye Qin's bright eyes instantly went dull. For a while, he just stood in the crowded main terminal. It was only when he heard the person on the other end of the call bring up the matter of payment that he zoned back in gloomily and asked for the card number.

The online bank transfer went through quickly. The recipient, clearly happy, messaged that he would offer some information he had previously investigated part-way free of charge.

Ye Qin read the information three times, ultimately focusing on the line, "Cheng Feichi's biological father may be someone else." He burst out in sudden laughter.

Ye Qin unfolded the piece of paper clutched in his fist, and his eyes moved down in a straight line, falling on the applicant column. Cheng Feichi's signature, straight and bold, declared his resolution at the time of signing. Despite applying for a school far below his standards, despite all his effort going to waste, he didn't hesitate in the slightest.

Because he'd promised someone that they'd go to the same university.

Voices clamored in Ye Qin's ears. The entrance to the security checkpoint was less than twenty meters ahead.

Every second, someone left this country. Some said goodbye

for a short time; some left indefinitely. Some cried, reluctant to part; some smiled and offered their good wishes. In the constant stream of people coming and going, Ye Qin was the only one out of place, unable to even put on the mask of a normal expression and blend into the surroundings.

The black words on the white paper gradually blurred right before his eyes. A pea-sized teardrop fell on the paper, splotching the ink and smudging the three dots in "Chi" into a blurry patch.

And wasn't that it? Feichi was his name; he was never meant to be trapped here, by Ye Qin's side.

But the genius had just left, and Ye Qin already began to miss him.

"I'm sorry," he repeated over and over in his head. Ye Qin wished he could be as kind and generous, as calm and steady as Cheng Feichi. He wanted to be an adult, smiling as he wished Cheng Feichi a bright future. But the very thought ate away at his heart and bones, corroding the deepest part of his bone marrow. Just the words "Cheng Feichi" gently flickering through Ye Qin's mind caused him unbearable pain.

Everyone knew that young master Ye treasured his reputation above all else. No matter where or when, he refused to be beneath anyone. Afraid of being seen, he hid his face with the form and covered his eyes with his hands. But tears continued to overflow through the cracks of his fingers, trailing down the back of his hands into his shirt cuffs. Soon, they froze into ice. The ice wouldn't melt no matter how much warmth his new tears carried.

Spring that year came particularly early. It wasn't only new sprouts and life that accompanied the snowmelt, but also the Ye family's crisis spilling out from the duct tape patch-job.

When school started back up, Ye Qin seldom went out. He spent most of his time outside of school at home, and in doing so, got more opportunities to interact with family.

The first thing he discovered was that more and more guests came by his home every day. At the peak of this, he could hear door knocks five or six times daily.

One time, it got so noisy that he couldn't sleep. He ran downstairs to see men in black suits and ties standing in a row in the living room. Luo Qiuling was speaking to them with an anxious expression when she saw that he had come down. She hastily waved him off.

"Go back to bed, and lock the door."

Things started to go downhill at some point, until they were too scared to open the door when they heard knocking. Every day before school, Luo Qiuling had the family caretaker look around outside first. She also warned him not to come back home for lunch and dinner. A car would be there to pick him up from night class.

At the time, Ye Qin just assumed that Ye Jinxiang had gotten on someone's bad side. After all, the Ye company's predecessor was the Luo family, a family with stable roots that had been renowned for generations in Chinese herbal medicine. Even if its heirs had dwindled by this generation and its company's main line of business was behind the times, it was still superior to any ordinary family. It wouldn't deteriorate to the point of bankruptcy and fall from power. If worse came to worst, Ye Qin would just rein in his spending habits.

Besides, this was stuff that Ye Jinxiang should be concerned about. Ye Qin was better off putting more energy into studying. He wanted to get into C University so that when Cheng Feichi came back, he would at least have a legitimate conversation topic.

Even if he knew that Cheng Feichi probably never wanted-ed to see him again, and that the day Cheng Feichi mentioned breaking up was the last time he ever planned to see him.

"You're a little brat who deserves a beating. You should visit my place to get a loving lesson from my dad." When Sun Yiran got wind of Cheng Feichi leaving China, she thought Ye Qin had angered him into it. "You grew up without any problems. No one ever dared to say anything bad to your face. If you overheard Cheng Feichi saying those things, what would you think?"

Ye Qin had already thought about all of that. He even allowed himself to get lost in those thoughts. Gradually, he realized that even though his actions had been bad enough on their own, his intent had been even worse. With such tainted motives, everything he did become malicious. In the end, even the sweet, wonderful memories turned into knives piercing his heart.

To Cheng Feichi, his words were not frivolous as Ye Qin had thought. Rather, they were a fatal blow.

At the pitiful sight of Ye Qin—helpless, dejected, eyes unfocused—Sun Yiran lost the heart to continue scolding him. "Oh, don't be so disappointed. Back when I couldn't get him, I also thought the sky going to fall; that no one in the world was worse off than me. At least you were able to get him for a while. Hey, what's it like, having gotten to date the hottest guy in school?"

It was obvious that Sun Yiran was attempting to comfort him, but Ye Qin couldn't bring himself to laugh. He tugged up the corners of his mouth forcefully, looking uglier than if he had just cried.

Sun Yiran covered her eyes and hollered. "Whence cometh the evil?!

"I think you really care about him," she then sighed. "So why did you say those things? Now, wasn't that stupid? Okay, don't worry. When he comes back, apologize nicely. Even if you can't be his lover, you can still be his friend."

But Ye Qin only wanted to keep being his lover.

As this thought drifted through his mind, he laughed at

himself.

Cheng Feichi probably didn't even want to be his friend. The two of them weren't the same kind of people in the first place, and now, they weren't even connected by blood as Ye Qin had thought. They ought to be walking in two parallel lines, never crossing paths.

Ye Qin used to consider himself an optimist, but after Cheng Feichi left, he only sorrow remained.

Every day, he went to school, ate, and slept like nothing changed. Only those closest to him could sense the tiny differences.

When April came around, Zhou Feng invited him on a trip to Y Province in the glorified name of taking a break before the exam. Not wanting to go, Ye Qin claimed that he didn't like the cold climate, being high up on the plateau. Zhou Feng told him Liao Yifang was also going, but it'd be too boring with just the two of them. Ye Qin thought about it and agreed in the end, worried the class monitor would get bullied.

However, just before they left, there was an event that shocked the whole school.

Somehow the teachers found out about Zhou Feng and Liao Yifang's relationship, and the Dean's Office called both sets of parents to school that very day. The office door stayed closed for two full hours. When Ye Qin got the news and rushed over, everyone had already left, and both parties involved were un-reachable.

A few days later, Zhou Feng called Ye Qin on the down-low. "A-Qin, give me your PI's contact info," he whispered.

Ye Qin thought he was going to do something bad, so he asked why he wanted it. On the other end, Zhou Feng sounded awkward for quite a while. "To find Yuanyuan," he finally confessed.

Ye Qin learned from him that the class monitor hadn't gone

to school ever since that day; not because he'd been put under house arrest, unable to get out, but because he had transferred out of High School No. 6. He'd even moved, leaving without a single warning.

Ye Qin thought that it wasn't like Liao Yifang to wash his hands of this affair. "What happened that day?" he asked.

Zhou Feng took a few deep breaths on the other side of the call and finished preparing himself before he spoke. "He took full responsibility in front of everyone and said that he s-seduced me."

Ye Qin knew about Zhou Feng's family situation, so when he heard this, his heart did a complete somersault. "Did they believe it?"

"No," Zhou Feng said. "I kept saying that we were just good buddies; nothing like that 'improper relationship' they were talking about."

What he said sounded unfeeling, but it was indeed the best choice to make in those circumstances.

But the school had actually called their parents—even confronting a family with a background such as the Zhous, where anyone you picked came with an influential status. Evidently, they had come prepared with evidence, and it wasn't something that could easily be swept under the rug.

"My dad's probably behind this. All he thinks about is how to fix me and give me a taste of discipline." By now, Zhou Feng had shed his usual frivolousness, but there was no lack of cool deduction in his anger. "I just didn't think he would make Yuanyuan his first target. Yuanyuan must be so sad. I want to find him and tell him I'm sorry."

Zhou Feng's delayed regret made Ye Qin feel a little sympathetic, except this time he no longer did things one-sidedly in a fit of passion. Instead, he considered the feasibility of searching via his private investigator, and concluded that it was best not to

act rashly. Considering the Zhou patriarch's skills, he'd probably get wind of whatever the PI could find much quicker. If they went around looking for the class monitor, it might even set off alarms and do him more harm.

Zhou Feng thought for a moment and agreed with his opinion, deciding to give up on the idea temporarily. "We can't go to Province Y anymore. Let's meet up again when we have a chance," he said a little regretfully before hanging up.

For some reason, Ye Qin had a small hunch that this "again" would not come any time soon.

There was always a group of youngsters who thought they had to make the whole world revolve around them to show how brave and heroic they were. Only after running into a situation that didn't go their way did these people learn that life was not made of happiness and leisure, but instead helplessness.

Recently, the atmosphere was always tense at home. Luo Qiuling wore herself out running around outside to raise money, and it had been several days since she'd sat down for a good meal. Yesterday, she raised the topic of studying abroad again, but Ye Qin shut it down.

At the peak of his success, he hadn't wanted to leave home. Now, as his family was going through hardship, he had even more reason to stay.

Moreover, Ye Qin still had to wait for that person to come back.

In the evening, he made a trip to the Jiayuan Compound to pack everything there in bags. Luo Qiuling said the apartment would be sold soon. Just before leaving, he took one last look at the small apartment filled with traces of a couple living together. Holding onto that immaculately polished glass jar, he gently closed the door.

When he got home, he saw the gates of the estate were wide open. Workers in uniform carried things outside, including all those treasured antiques that Ye Jinxiang had carefully collected.

Luo Qiuling sat in the house, wiping away tears. From her mouth, Ye Qin finally learned that what happened to their company was far more complicated than a mere severing of the capital chain. Last year, Ye Jinxiang began playing the stock market; forward buying and investing with some woman. As if dosed up on ecstasy, he did every risky thing in the book and even went gambling in Macau. In his complete obliviousness, that woman swindled him out of all his family fortune.

The company had been reduced to an empty frame. The bank was already settling accounts with Ye Jinxiang's personal assets. Luo Qiuling just found out today that their house had been put up for collateral for quite some time now, and would soon be taken by the bank for auction.

After the house was nearly cleared of valuables, Ye Jinxiang came back with his tail between his legs. As soon as he walked through the door, he got tackled and violently beaten.

Ye Qin panted. His eyes bulged in anger, like he'd been waiting for this opportunity for a very long time. It was still beyond his capabilities to be an adult and keep a calm face despite his emotions. Apart from taking out anger on behalf of his mother, who had been mistreated for so many years, he was also seeking an outlet for his bottled-up pain.

He should have felt happy after he finished venting, but emptiness and a sense of loss leaked from his body, swallowing him up from the inside out.

What would beating Ye Jinxiang do? Could it stop his mother's tears? Buy back the house? Turn back time?

...Could it bring back Cheng Feichi?

Ye Jinxiang was wrong, but neither was Ye Qin above it all.

He was the one who refused a direct confrontation and instead sought revenge in the dark. He was the one who was so narrow-minded, who trampled on Cheng Feichi in a hundred different ways. He was the stupid, childish one unaware of his own feelings. He even haughtily treated this whole thing as an act, unaware that his heartfelt, joyous laughter and tears of heart-wrenching pain were because he had already become one with the act long ago.

And if he hadn't gotten lost in the act, Cheng Feichi also wouldn't have given him his heart. Neither would he have cut things off so resolutely when he left. A man that warm and kind wouldn't even give Ye Qin one last chance.

One day in May, Zhou Feng found time to meet up with Ye Qin at the diner by the school gates.

At first glance, Ye Qin almost didn't recognize him. His family had beaten him so severely that Zhou Feng's face was a motley of purples. Despite his skull swelling as big as a pig's head, he still had been given a crew cut that looked like it had been buzzed right against the scalp, leaving behind less than a centimeter's worth of blueish stubble.

"Grandpa buzzed it; he said the army's barbers weren't as good as him, that they'd shave off my skin and leave me permanently bald afterwards." Zhou Feng rubbed his head in embarrassment. "Actually, it doesn't look that bad. Yours truly is a handsome guy, after all. It's just that my head gets cold whenever there's a sudden gust."

It had already been a while since Ye Qin found out about his plan to join the army over the phone. Naturally, his first reaction was surprise. Just two months ago, this guy had still been hitting the books hard because he didn't want to be shipped off to the army.

Zhou Feng hadn't elaborated on their call. He only disclosed the truth now, in person. "I thought a lot about what you said before over the last few days. The more I thought, the more it made sense to me. At this critical moment, I have to listen to my dad, or else what'll happen to Yuanyuan? I can't let him be implicated anymore."

The door of the diner faced the sun, and its windows were wide open. In absence of the closed-off private club room's fragrant scent of luxury, they became more clear-headed and were able to face their deep, honest thoughts with candidness.

"You and the class monitor…"

Ye Qin had only begun when Zhou Feng made a T for "stop," as if he knew where he was going with this. "Please don't ask. For the past few days, my mom, my grandma, and my other grandma were all chasing me down to ask if we were a real thing. If I hear it any more, I'm going to throw up." After taking a sip of cold water, he continued, "I think…that we're still too young. We used to while away our days aimlessly. I don't even know if it was real or not. Right now, I just want him to be happy and no longer dragged down by me, or I'll really…"

Even if he didn't say the last bit, Ye Qin still knew what he meant.

For them, too many things in this world had unclear boundaries. If they never suffered a loss, if they never fell on their face, who knows what kind of irreparable consequences that would cause.

They ordered three stir-fried dishes and chatted as they ate.

Not even a full month had passed since they last saw each other, but the air was permeated with a subtle ambience of a reunion of old friends. There was even a rather conspicuous, solemn silence when it came time to part.

Zhou Feng poured Ye Qin a cup of tea. "Are you still looking for him?"

Ye Qin nodded, and then shook his head. "I can't find him, so I'm not looking for now."

Some time ago, he asked everyone he could, including students that Cheng Feichi had tutored. He even followed the line of contact down to Cheng Feichi's schoolmates in the university's affiliated middle school. Through them, he got in touch with that girl, Zhang Peiyao.

Zhang Peiyao was already in university when she got Ye Qin's call. When she heard him ask about Cheng Feichi, she was initially very guarded, telling him that she would not say anything no matter what, and he could dream on if he wanted to pry any words from her mouth.

The moment he heard her voice, Ye Qin knew she was the person he had been looking for. He explained his intentions, telling her that he just wanted to know where Cheng Feichi went and what exactly happened at the time. After hearing his honest approach, Zhang Peiyao slowly let down her defenses.

Regarding his questions, Zhang Peiyao said that although she sympathized, she was unable to help with where he'd gone, as she hadn't been in contact with Cheng Feichi for a very long time. For what had happened back then, she offered a vague description: in short, she was childish back then, and when she couldn't get him to go out with her, she allowed other peoples to instigate her into spreading rumors that he was gay. She never thought that it would force him to leave the university's affiliated high school.

Now that time had passed, even the most embarrassing things became easier to confess. "I've already explained everything. No matter who you are, don't harass him anymore," Zhang Peiyao even warned Ye Qin in the end. "He doesn't want to be disturbed."

Recalling up to this point, Ye Qin couldn't prevent a bitter laugh. Chase him down? He only wanted to make sure Cheng Feichi was doing well.

Unaware of Ye Qin's thoughts, Zhou Feng cocked his head and pondered for a moment. "Don't look for him for now then," he echoed. "Wait for me to climb the ranks in the army, and I'll get pops to help you search."

Ye Qin grunted and took a sip of water. Suddenly, he tossed out an unrelated question. "When did you realize that you'd fallen for him?"

Zhou Feng froze, somewhat at a loss. "F-fallen? For who?"

"Anyone."

Zhou Feng put down his chopsticks and thought back solemnly. "It's...almost like a chemical reaction. When I see him, when I see that he cares about me, my heart bubbles up. Steam rises from my stomach to my throat. It gathers in my head. It's as if every nerve is enveloped in it. It's almost coming out of me."

Ye Qin chalked this utterly unappealing explanation up to a joke to ease the tension before they parted. In no time, he forgot about it.

That night, when Ye Qin couldn't sleep, he took out his mobile phone and went on the campus forum. He scrolled to the post that he had browsed many times before, once again looking through the photos of Cheng Feichi that had been secretly taken by someone else.

He didn't save the photos on his phone, because this wasn't the Cheng Feichi that he knew. But he couldn't use one-dimensional words to describe what Cheng Feichi was like in his eyes.

It drizzled the next day, and the small van couldn't carry much stuff. The driver impatiently told them to hurry up and

that he had to move stuff for another client later.

Various boxes of household waste were tossed into a garbage pile. Ye Qin's last remaining bit of luggage was mostly packed with books and clothes. The glass bottle was wrapped in clothes, and a tiny, still-intact piece of Lego Technic was piled on top of the books.

When the van started, Ye Qin suddenly remembered something and jumped out recklessly. He ran to the garbage pile, squatted, and rummaged through it, shutting out his mother's calls behind him.

Finally, he found the cellphone that he had thrown out last year in the pile of miscellaneous junk. When he pressed down the power button, Ye Qin was so nervous that his heart almost jumped out of his chest. It wasn't until he saw the screen light up that he finally let go of a long breath that he had been holding in his throat.

After turning on the phone, Ye Qin quickly navigated to a picture through memory alone.

The desk. The window. The winter sunlight. The teen photographed in secret.

Ye Qin stared at the photo almost greedily. He hadn't wanted to cry at all—he'd cried enough lately; it was so embarrassing. But the chemical reaction Zhou Feng had spoken of, the steam and bubbles and whatnot, clogged his nose and made it burn; it made his eyes swell, too.

Also, there was this annoying spring rain, pitter-pattering without end.

Despite this, Ye Qin forced out a tearful smile and moved his lips, giving the blessings he never got a chance to tell the man before his eyes: "You have to study hard, eat well, sleep properly, and be happy every day. D-don't ever..."

Don't ever get mixed up with bad guys again. Ye Qin tried

to say these words aloud several times, but couldn't, because he was one of those bad guys. He was selfish, stupid, arrogant, and conceited. Not only did he have the additional crime of weaponizing love, but he still vainly hoped to go back to how things were before.

Ye Qin wiped the tiny raindrops off the screen and stared at the man in the photo for a very long time. He wanted to transcend space and time to come face to face with him.

The young man's brows were gently furrowed, and his mouth was half open. The slightly stupid expression he made in response to the sudden incident couldn't hide his handsome, gentle eyes.

In that moment, they only had eyes for each other, and everything was still perfect and new.

CHAPTER 16

SUMMER, five years later.

The alarm rang five times, only to be snoozed again and again by the man lying on the narrow bottom bunk.

Once 8 o'clock had passed, his cellphone automatically came out of "do not disturb" mode and immediately rang again. The man in bed was sleepy. Still thinking it was the alarm, he felt for the lower screen and pressed down, which allowed the incoming call through.

"You're still in bed?" the woman on the other side probed. When five seconds passed without response, she immediately howled like a devil urging for his death. "Ye Qin, get over here! If I don't see you awake and neatly dressed when I arrive at 8:20, I'll throw you off the twenty-third floor!

Five minutes later, Ye Qin stood in front of the bathroom counter with a head of short, unkempt hair, brushing his teeth while he squinted and fiddled with the strands. "Good morning," he slurred to the half-asleep man in the mirror.

This was a habit he'd maintained over these few years. As ever-changing and colorful as his dreams were, after waking up, he still had to deal with the same reality as yesterday. Saying this was to wake himself up, to forcefully remove himself from the imaginary world and go to work with a good attitude, in a good state.

Even if he didn't like his job at all.

Fifteen minutes later, the dormitory door got a punctual knock. Zheng Yueyue *clip-clopped* in on high heels and saw that Ye Qin, who was frying an egg in the kitchen, had just barely managed to get his clothes on neatly. Only then did she rein in the menacing air. She quickly checked the time and said, "Hurry, let's go. Leave the egg. I'll buy you a scallion pancake with a sausage, tenderloin slices, and two eggs added on."

Ye Qin accepted this offer, but still finished frying the egg. He banged open the bedroom door, put the dish on the table next to it, and said to the man still sleeping in the neighboring bed, "I'm bestowing you with an egg. When I come back, I'm going to ask how cooked the yolk is. Don't secretly throw it out."

Curling into a ball inside his blanket on the bed, the man stuck out a hand and gave an OK sign. In a muffled voice, he said, "Okay, Qin-ge."

On the way to work, Ye Qin wolfed down the richly packed pancake. Zheng Yueyue prattled on for nth time.

"Even though I bought you breakfast this time, you have to remember to avoid these greasy foods. You're twenty-three. Don't think that you can still compare physiques with those young men like Song Xu. Did you forget that time when your face broke out and you lost an endorsement? Also, get up earlier for work in the future. Don't always push it to the last minute and wait for me to call. Are you fused to the bed or what..."

Ye Qin, who had been staying as quiet as a mouse, protested at this point. "Yesterday, we wrapped at 2 a.m. I already told you that I won't be able to get up when I don't get enough sleep. That's why I asked you to buy a box of chocolates to put next to my pillow... Never mind." Halfway through, he changed the topic. "Besides, last time, what kind of 'endorsement' was that? Acne cream? Everlasting acne-free skin after applying the cream to your face for seven days? You can tell from a glance that false advertising. Wouldn't we clearly be deceiving fans?"

"Are you fully aware of how few fans you have? If not for your good prices and easy negotiations, how many companies would choose you?" Tired and angry about Ye Qin's high-minded moral consciousness, Zheng Yueyue said, "So what if it's fake? Doesn't stop you from making money. Do you still want to repay your debts? Do you still want to go back to school?"

These words were too on-point, and Ye Qin froze for a second, unable to enjoy his pancake anymore. After some time, he looked down and replied, "I do need to earn money, but at least...I can't betray my conscience..."

Today's job was a photoshoot and interview for the inner pages of some magazine.

Upon arrival, Zheng Yueyue personally applied Ye Qin's makeup. Seeing the dark circles that couldn't be concealed by several layers of makeup and his vaguely sunken cheeks, she felt a little sorry. While circling behind him to help fix his hair, she said, "Just now, I was a bit harsh. Don't take it to heart. When you leave work today, go back and get a good night's sleep. Treat yourself to whatever you want to eat. You're different from them—no matter how much you eat, you don't put on weight."

Ye Qin, resting with his eyes closed, snapped them open upon hearing this and stretched his lips into the first smile of the day. "Okay, Yueyue-jie!"

The shoot was scheduled for 10 a.m., but the interview with the previous guest took longer than originally planned. It was already noon when they officially began.

It was right at lunchtime, and the staff on-site were completely disengaged. Naturally, they were in a bit of a bad mood. Originally, Ye Qin had three outfits planned, but in the end he was shot in only one to quickly make do.

Nowadays, with the rapid development of internet publicity, print media was facing a predicament. The few remaining entertainment news magazines had to depend on fans' purchasing power for survival. Those that featured interviews and reviews dwindled; using celebrity pictures to get attention and make sales became the new way forward. With Ye Qin's current level of fame, the number of sales his fans could contribute to the magazine could be counted on one hand. Without the commercial numbers to back him up, he couldn't get any respect; just like how one had to already be famous to get cast in dramas.

Even so, Zheng Yueyue was utterly displeased and said that she was going to have a discussion with the editor-in-chief. Ye Qin didn't care whatsoever. No one could stand wearing formal clothes and shooting pictures on the grass under the blazing sun. After hearing that the currently trending star who was interviewed before him had seven or eight outfits, he optimistically thought that being a nobody was not bad. Money came in slowly, yes, but at least he didn't have to suffer through something like that.

When the time for interviewing came, the reporter had an even lazier attitude. Halfway through the script, he realized that he hadn't even started recording. Eager to have lunch, he roughly picked out a few random questions from the top of the list to fulfil his obligations and even yawned continuously in between, making Ye Qin tired as well. The official answers which he had recited until daybreak were jumbled up into paste in his head. Ye Qin had to use a lot of effort to anchor himself and not let his mouth run.

"There's a rumor online saying that you were born with a silver spoon in your mouth. What made you choose this career path?"

"It's been almost five years. Do those rumors still exist?" Ye Qin spread his hands and said, "If I were a trust fund baby, why am I not at home drinking, gambling, and talking big? Why would I come here to sit under the sun and eat boxed lunches?"

The reporter, put to laughter by his answer, continued, "I heard that you have a very good relationship with He Hansong on your team, yet he didn't bring anyone with him when shooting 'First Challenge of Love.' Any thoughts on this?"

This question wasn't on the script he had received last night. Sitting in on the interview, Zheng Yueyue shot to her feet. Ye Qin indicated for her not to act rashly by raising his eyebrows, as if saying: *I can handle this.*

After all, he had been finding his way around in showbiz for four years. Of course, Ye Qin could see that there were a few landmines lurking in this question. Magazines had to have selling points, and those were equivalent to commercial value. If a tiny celebrity like him didn't offer some gimmick, why would the publisher invite him? For afternoon tea?

Actually, Ye Qin had already been through a familiar sequence of events four years ago when he had just debuted in the entertainment circle.

At the time, he had not yet turned eighteen, and the training and heavy pressure he carried day after day made him unbearably depressed. During some press conference celebrating the team going public, he was already sleepy from the warm air filling up the room when a reporter raised a microphone and asked him, "Someone said that He Hansong didn't show up for today's team trip because he went to film a variety show at the Beijing television station. Do any of you other team members here have anything to say to him?"

Back then, even though Ye Qin had wanted to lay low, the reporter still latched on to him. On top of that, he didn't have a favorable impression of He Hansong, and so he snapped back in a very bad mood. "There's nothing to say. Where he goes isn't my business."

As soon as he got off the stage, he was pulled into the backstage lounge by Zheng Yueyue for a scolding.

"If you don't have connections or supporters in this circle, you have to establish them on your own. He Hansong already has a devoted fan-base, and you all rely on his resources. Rein in your spoiled temper and don't lose sight of the situation again."

Fortunately, the company had packaged Ye Qin's character as frank and honest, so what he said could somewhat be put down to his personality. However, He Hansong had already garnered a lot of popularity from two commercials he had shot before teaming up with them. During that period of time, Ye Qin was cursed out by He Hansong's fans for being jealous of his popularity, so much so that it hit the trending topics. For a while, Ye Qin was too afraid to even go outside.

It was approximately from that point on that Ye Qin became silent and withdrawn, ignoring anything outside of work; as if he had completely sealed himself away. He stayed in this state until two years ago, when the members of the group began to take off on solo careers and group activities diminished. Only then did he break free and reopen his heart to the public.

Zheng Yueyue had only become his manager again in the past year, too. The company big-shots believed he still had potential, and thought that they could give him another chance to explore it. As a matter of fact, everyone clearly understood that if it wasn't for his good looks—which had not deteriorated over the years, but had rather grown prettier—as well as the lack of

scandals attached to him, Ye Qin would have been kicked off the team long before He Hansong's fans smeared him.

In the public eye, Ye Qin had curbed the foolishness and arrogance that he used to don when he first joined the circle; he had become polite and thoughtful. His movements, however, retained his youthfulness. One could find easiness and confidence that very uniquely belonged to him in his every gesture and expression.

Now he picked up the beverage on the table and took a slip. Blinking at the reporter, he said, "How could Song-ge forget us? He promised to bring back local specialties for us. We're still counting on him for tonight's dinner."

When he left, he ran into a few waiting fans who didn't get a chance to see their own idols and greeted him instead as he got off work. Ye Qin received a bar of chocolate. Once he was in the car, he peeled off the wrapper and was about to stuff it in his mouth when Zheng Yueyue blocked it with her deft hand. She held it up to the window and carefully checked it against the natural light for quite some time. Only when she was sure there was no problem did she let him continue eating.

Seeing his mouth become smeared with chocolate as he ate, Zheng Yueyue sighed. "Such a little kid. Smart and perceptive one moment, and thoughtlessly stupid the next. How are you going to muddle your way through your future?"

But Ye Qin's mood was much improved by the bar of chocolate. He licked his lips and smiled until his eyes were like two crescent moons. "You just said this afternoon that I'm not young anymore. Now I'm a kid?"

Zheng Yueyue, who was managing several artists at the same time, dropped him at the first floor of the building and was about to go to another artist's shooting location to take a look. Before leaving, she warned Ye Qin, "He Hansong might come back to the dormitory today. Whatever he says, pretend you don't hear it. Don't pick a fight with him."

Ye Qin answered with a mouthful of yesses. While waiting for the elevator, he lifted his gaze to the ceiling and recalled in stifling boredom that if He Hansong hadn't provoked him with curses involving his mother, who'd care to waste their breath on him?

Ye Qin could take anything if those curses were only targeted at him.

When he entered the room, Song Xu, who had stayed inside for the whole day, came over to greet him. As he handed over indoor slippers to Ye Qin, he leaned over and whispered in his ear, "Song-ge came back. I couldn't keep him out, so he... Qin-ge, don't get mad yet. You can still save that thing."

Ye Qin quickly entered the room and scrambled to the upper bunk without even taking off his shoes. Another member of the group used to sleep on the upper bunk. After that person moved out, it became Ye Qin's storage rack.

It was only upon seeing that the Lego Technic under a glass cover just had a broken middle beam that Ye Qin put his heart back into his chest. He kneeled on the upper bunk and patiently put it back together piece by piece.

The dorm was small. After everyone in the group debuted solo, the only members who still stayed there regularly were Ye Qin, Song Xu, and He Hansong, who came back when he was having fights with his "patron." It seemed that every time He Hansong came back, it was purely to give Ye Qin a hard time. As expected, very soon, the cellphone in Ye Qin's pocket rang.

"Qin-Qin, have you finished work?"

Ye Qin only felt repulsed when faced with such an excessively intimate nickname. "I told you not to call me again. If you have so much free time, look after that loverboy of yours. Don't let him cause trouble in front of me again, okay?"

Not only did the man on the other side of the call not feel ashamed, but he even laughed. "And you still say that you don't care? Still say you're not jealous?"

Ye Qin almost rolled his eyes, but since the guy had a lot of influence and couldn't be offended so casually, he didn't curse him out. But the words he spoke were not polite, either. "Before, I thought He Hansong watched too many idol dramas. Now I know you're the one who believes in those. If I accidentally spared you a glance, would you start imagining that I was in love with you?"

The man burst into laughter and switched to negotiation mode. "Are idol dramas so bad? If you say 'yes' to me, I can give you anything you want. You can get good scripts and become popular. I can even promise that He Hansong will never bother you again. How about it?"

Ye Qin sneered. He was about to refuse when he heard that man continue, "If you really wanted to turn me down, why did you pick up my call? Why not change numbers?"

Hanging up, Ye Qin sat on the top bunk for a while, looking fixedly at the Lego Technic he'd rebuilt into its original form. After a while, he placed the glass lid back carefully.

He received a call from Zheng Yueyue that night, telling him she had arranged a guest appearance on a reality show for them. To be frank, it was more piggybacking on He Hansong's limelight. If it were up to him, Ye Qin would refuse to go on a show with him, but what right did a no-name pawn like him have to say "no" to the company's plans?

Before going into the bathroom for a shower, Ye Qin heard He Hansong smashing things to the ground in the next room. Following the principle that it was better to avoid trouble whenever possible, he pretended not to hear. Yet, without warning, when he finished showering and returned to the room, he heard Song Yu say, "Song-ge just came by our room again. He took a spare phone and left."

Ye Qin went back to the room and scoured the drawer. His heart immediately shot into his throat. He threw down the towel and went to the next room, kicking in the door without another word.

The door banged open. Sitting inside, He Hansong jolted. His hands shook momentarily, dropping the cellphone on the ground.

Ye Qin took two steps forward and picked it up, threatening nastily, "If you ever touch my stuff again..." Then he abruptly whipped his head around and left, turning a deaf ear to He Hansong's curses behind him.

It was a good while after returning to his room that Ye Qin slowly move past his lingering fears.

He Hansong had entered the circle earlier and he had a better way with words. Many renowned heads in the entertainment circle liked him a lot and loved to invite him to conferences and whatnot. Even if He Hansong's patron had started liking him for some absurd reason, he couldn't act rashly in front of He Hansong.

Moreover, that man received ridicule from Ye Qin every time he called. By the time he finally truly lost patience, Ye Qin's demise would be pretty much imminent.

Ye Qin inwardly sighed. After mixing in the circle for over four years, he'd still failed to learn how to control his temper. In Yueyue-jie's words, he would "suffer a big loss sooner or later".

Song Xu watched him charge an old cellphone model that had been out of the market for many years and asked curiously, "Qin-ge, why do you keep that crappy phone? It's too old to serve as a backup, even."

Ye Qin ignored him. When he turned on the phone, he first looked at the photo album. Seeing those photos were still there, he let loose a held breath.

"Old pictures? Don't keep them on that phone. It might no longer turn on someday," suggested Song Xu. "Back them up to a computer or USB. It's safer."

Ye Qin was submerged in one particular photo. "I already have a backup."

"Oh, that's good then." Song Xu moved closer to take a look and asked, "Who's this?"

Afraid that if he stared for too long, the cellphone really wouldn't turn on next time, Ye Qin pressed the power button.

When Song Xu turned around to do something else, he answered in a voice which only himself could hear, "My gege."

Perhaps because those two words had come to his lips again today, Ye Qin had that dream again.

The wind that picked up from nothing, the youth under the ginkgo tree, and himself, desperately wishing to catch him even though his legs wouldn't obey.

Ye Qin woke up drenched in sweat. He looked down at his palms, curling and uncurling his fingers. He repeated this motion several times before slowly gaining control over the shaking and suppressing the fear that had recklessly spread through his mind.

He finally appeared once again in his dreams, but last time Ye Qin had dreamt of him, he had left not long after showing up. Thinking of this, Ye Qin was torn between happiness and dismay: he did not know whether he should keep his hope, or just continue to lose himself in inescapable memories.

It was already very bright outside. Ye Qin got out of the bed and poured out a cup of water for himself. Hands still somewhat weak, he accidentally let the cup lid fall. Despite the ruckus,

Song Xu remained in deep slumber on the neighbor bunk, not even stirring.

Ye Qin laughed in spite of himself. *This kid wouldn't probably wouldn't even wake up if you threw him off the twenty-third floor,* he thought.

In their so-called group, He Hansong was the oldest, turning twenty-four this year, and Song Xu was the youngest. When he made his debut, he was only a fifteen-year-old kid; so anxious before getting on stage that he would cry. Thus, Ye Qin normally looked after him pretty closely. Having lost his parents when he was young, Song Xu knew to be thankful for receiving his kindness. After many interactions, the two became friends.

Today, there was an audition for a TV series that Song Xu had passed to Ye Qin. At first, Ye Qin still had misgivings, but Song Xu said, "I've got enough on my own agenda and no family to feed. I'm in a good situation right now: I've got work to do, and time to sleep. Ge, you should have a go at it. If you get picked, I'll get a reputation for having a keen eye."

Indeed short of money, Ye Qin thought for a moment and accepted his offer.

The audition took place in S-City, so Ye Qin notified Zheng Yueyue and went by himself to buy a high-speed train ticket. Having put on his backpack and face mask, Ye Qin hesitated when his hand was already on the doorknob. He turned back and took the cellphone in the drawer with him.

It took six hours by high-speed rail. He used to take a plane ride of similar length to go on vacation abroad. On the train, Ye Qin thought of a method that Song Xu had taught him. He set up a hotspot with the phone he was using nowadays and the old cellphone unexpectedly received the signal, connecting to the web.

He had no hopes of logging into WeChat, thinking that his account would have long been locked. But much to his surprise,

he logged in smoothly: the app even loaded a long string of unread messages.

Holding his breath, Ye Qin scrolled down slowly and stopped at the first conversation which had no replies. Then he slowly let the heavy breath out of his lungs.

Still, he moved his fingers and subconsciously opened his Moments page. As before, the last post was the picture of four lollipops from six years ago. Back then, WeChat didn't have options for choosing who could see what, or have a time limit for what was displayed in Moments. He hadn't been blocked, either. It was obvious that no one had logged onto that account in the past few years.

Ye Qin couldn't help laughing at himself. *What are you thinking? He knows the full truth. He could only hate you. How could he reach out to you again?*

He left neatly and completely, cutting off all avenues of communication. It was already nice enough of him to leave behind a place that held memories, that proved the short period of time once existed.

In just a few short minutes, he seemed to have spent all the energy in his body. Exhausted, Ye Qin put down the cellphone and took a rest against the back of the seat.

At this exact moment, the old cellphone suddenly vibrated in his palm. Before he opened his eyes, Ye Qin's heart already began to pound wildly in response. Without clearly seeing the name on the display screen, he pressed the receive button on instinct.

"Shit, you're fast!" On the other side of the call, Zhou Feng, evidently unprepared, pointed the camera at his face and fixed the hat on his head. He laughed. "Celebrities behave differently, after all; up and at it so early in the morning. Your xiao-di just made a dangerous escape from heavily guarded troops. Does the big celebrity have free time to see me?"

The audition went pretty smoothly.

It was for a role that could barely be considered the "second most important supporting actor": the inconspicuous brother of the female lead who had no romance subplot. Hence, not very many people fought for the role.

As soon as Ye Qin went in, the director sitting amongst a whole line of people immediately smiled. Rumor had it that this director, when casting actors, weighted looks most heavily. Ye Qin had only recited two lines when the director said "good" three times and bade him go back to wait for news, without any other comment.

In these four years or so, Ye Qin also shot some TV shows. He knew that, in this circle, you couldn't put too much faith in a casual remark. Before a contract was signed, it was best to have no expectations at all, because anything could happen.

After auditioning, he rode a car back to the high-speed rail. He hadn't even had time to have either breakfast or lunch, so his stomach suddenly began to hurt on the way. Thus he bought a sandwich at the rail station and ate as he walked, messaging Zhou Feng at the same time.

The two of them agreed to meet up at a coffee shop in the northern part of the city. In the afternoon of the following day, Zhou Feng arrived first. When he saw Ye Qin walk in with a mask on, he waved his hands at him. "Here, A-Qin."

Ye Qin walked over and took a seat, taking off his mask.

Zhou Feng stopped him fussily. "Hey, don't take it off yet. Aren't you afraid that people will recognize you?"

"Have you been living in the deep mountains for the past five years?" Ye Qin laughed. "I'm really not some big celebrity. I'm the kind that, even if I stood on the streets and yelled 'I'm Ye Qin,' no one would recognize me."

Even after not seeing each other for years, the two only had

to make a bit of small talk to recover the familiarity and tacit understanding they had when they were younger.

Zhou Feng still had that cheeky grin, only now there was less unreliable frivolousness and more steady enthusiasm. His tanned skin and strongly built body made him look steadfast and robust, and extremely manly.

When asked why he didn't reach out even once in the past five years, he hit the table and said bitterly, "My dad was dead set on throwing me somewhere that doesn't even have signal towers. It's truly a desolate place, where you can only yell into the void. I tried to run away three times, only to get caught and brought back. I couldn't use my cellphone, and could only write you guys letters. I wrote for several nights under an oil lamp and walked twenty miles of mountainous trail before I found a mailbox to send them out. Who knew that none of you would write me a reply!"

Ye Qin smiled at this. "I'd already moved by then. Who knows where your letter was sent."

"Both Liu Yangfan and Zhao Yue were abroad, so it's not strange they didn't get my letters, but you didn't even goddamn tell me that you m..." Halfway through, Zhou Feng realized something was wrong. "Wait, you moved? Where did you move to?"

Ye Qin said, "An apartment in the suburbs, but now that's been sold too."

It wasn't hard for Zhou Feng to guess from the word "too" that the cottage their family had been living in had been the first to be sold. Looking at Ye Qin's attire now and his constantly hustling state, he'd really be an idiot not to realize that something had happened to Ye Qin's family.

The atmosphere suddenly quieted. Zhou Feng took a sip of coffee that was so bitter it made him frown. As he tossed sugar cubes into the mug, he asked Ye Qin in a feigned casual tone, "What, you moved into a bigger house?"

Ye Qin didn't take his lead and bluff his way through. Instead, he truthfully recounted how his family went bankrupt, including how Ye Jinxiang had been publicly persecuted for illegal earnings and remained in jail to this day. He also told Zhou Feng that because he had no money to go to school, even after receiving his acceptance letter, he didn't register at C University. He chose to become an artist because he could make money fast this way.

Even though he could have avoided the burden of the family debt by giving up his inheritance rights, he hadn't. He had promised his father's victims to repay them on Ye Jinxiang's behalf, so for a time he had been deep in debt. It'd been slowly paid back over the past few years, and only then did the situation improve somewhat.

Zhou Feng received waves of shock as he listened. Seeing Ye Qin play down the situation in words that held no trace of resentment whatsoever, he also kept the shock from showing on his face. Coughing lightly, he asked, "Then, where are you living now?"

"A dorm arranged for me by the company," Ye Qin said.

"What about auntie?"

He was asking about Luo Qiuling. Ye Qin looked down at the table for a few seconds, and then lifted his head again. "She passed away."

In summer five years ago, Ye Jinxiang was put behind bars. To settle the family debt, Luo Qiuling had run around trying to raising money. Ye Qin, however, had kept his face buried in books, his head only filled with the goal of getting into C University. He hated Ye Jinxiang, and he knew very well that the current situation was also related to Luo Qiuling's weakness in their marriage.

On the last day of the national college examinations, it rained heavily. Ye Qin had just come out of the exam venue when a hospital called and asked him to identify a body. When he saw his mom's face, mangled beyond recognition after she had been hit by a car, his heart was slowly torn apart with a searing pain, much like a thousand needles sticking into his flesh.

From that day on, he no longer had anyone dear by his side. From that day forth, he could only face the world on his own.

The atmosphere became even more quiet. Zhou Feng was too shocked and could only feel sorry for Ye Qin. Ever since the minute they met today, he had realized that Ye Qin was very different from before. The old Ye Qin would think that keeping up appearances was the most important thing: that Ye Qin would talk tough all the way through, rather than show anyone his weakness and helplessness. He had to have gone through a lot in these past five years to become like this—at peace with life, while still resilient to life's obstacles, no matter how miserable and beaten down he was.

"Let's stop talking about this." In the end, it was Ye Qin who changed the subject, breaking through the heavy atmosphere. "Why did you come back this time? Is there anything I can help with?"

Zhou Feng, who also happened to be at a loss for how to proceed, seized this exit ramp and replied, "No particular reason. Just to see you guys, and..." He produced a postcard from his pocket. "...to find someone."

Three days later, Ye Qin and the two other members of the group left together again for S-City to shoot the reality show that they had been inserted into.

Zheng Yueyue put a lot of weight on this shoot and bought business class tickets for all of them, saying that it would help keep up appearances especially if they happened to run into fans. For the 4 p.m. flight, the group of people got dragged to the airport at

2 p.m. He Hansong was having tea in the VIP lounge, while Song Xu was snoring on the chair. Ye Qin found a corner to sit in to ask his private detective how the investigation was going.

The only clue they had this time was a thin postcard, with the postmark indicating that it had been sent from H Province; a province adjacent to the capital. However, the sender didn't leave a name or a date. It was already hard enough to trace it back to that post office, let alone a specific address. The PI said that if he wanted to try doing that, he'd need some more time.

Ye Qin relayed all the information to Zhou Feng. Zhou Feng asked him how much, and then transferred an amount far above that number. Ye Qin knew Zhou Feng wanted to help him, but he still only took funds for the investigation and returned the rest.

Zhou Feng messaged over WeChat, "This is what I earned as a soldier. We're friends. Take it. Don't struggle on your own."

How could he not? Five years ago, when all other roads were blocked, Ye Qin once turned to Liu Yangfan and Zhao Yue for help. Because they'd been friends for many years, they lent him money from their families. Even though he had repaid them very quickly, there was a rift in their friendship from that point on. Over the past few years, he hadn't once contacted those two.

Social circles were divided by class. Ye Qin's life had been completely overturned. Without his outstanding family background, he was nothing.

Ye Qin sent Zhou Feng a reaction of a fist against a hand. "Mighty Boss Zhou," he typed.

Then, he calmly guided the topic to the search, asking Zhou Feng why he didn't look for the man himself. Wasn't it foolish to eschew the Zhou family's powerful sphere of influence and probe around blindly on his own?

Zhou Feng sent a sighing emoji, either as a helpless response

to Ye Qin's stubbornness or trying to show his disappointment towards the unsuccessful search. Perhaps it was both. "Dad still wants to send me back to the army for the full eight years. I just got home and haven't gotten re-accustomed to things, so I can only act like a good boy for the time being."

Ye Qin scrolled back through the photo album to the picture of the postcard. The handwriting on it was light. The words "Happy New Year" were vaguely distinguishable in the photo, yet he could still tell that the handwriting was elegant.

He switched back to WeChat and asked, "Did our class monitor write the postcard?"

This old title seemed to evoke Zhou Feng's memories and he only replied with certainty after a long pause, "It's him. I'd never forget his handwriting."

The plane was much faster than the high-speed rail. When they reached S-City, it was still light out. As Ye Qin didn't bring a suitcase, he waited for the others to get their luggage at the baggage claim.

They were going to stay here for three days, including two nights, and they carried many changes of clothes and toiletries in their bags. The company was a bit short-handed at the moment, so they had no assistants. Zheng Yueyue had stuffed Ye Qin's backpack with two additional outfits to be used on the program, as well as a makeup bag.

Many flights were arriving, and passengers crowded around the baggage claim area. Ye Qin waited for ages without seeing anyone come out. He put the heavy backpack on the ground temporarily, kneaded his shoulders, and looked all around. *Who said there would be fans?* he thought. *Yueyue-jie clearly overthought things.*

As his eyes flicked past the exit, he caught sight of a straight, tall figure.

Ye Qin's eyes suddenly widened, and he subconsciously took a few steps in that direction. The backpack at his feet lost its support and thudded onto the floor. Only then did he come to his senses and put the backpack back on his shoulders.

When he lifted his head to look again, the figure was already gone.

On the ride to the hotel, Ye Qin pressed his head against the window and looked out at S-City's bustling streets, thinking that perhaps he hadn't been getting enough sleep recently. He was so tired that he was starting to see illusions.

That one had left for America five years ago and might not ever come back. The great wide world was filled with people. Ye Qin had already lost a person as good as him; why would he find him again so easily in the crowd?

Serves you right, Ye Qin mocked. At the same time, he urged himself to be at ease. In any case, he no longer had the right to self-confidence and certainty that Zhou Feng did.

In recent years, apart from having learned how to live independently, Ye Qin had also acquired the useful skill of comforting himself. However, this brief episode was like a sudden gust of cold air during summer. It still somewhat affected him at the shooting the day after.

It just had to be an outdoor sports segment, too. There was no way to hide in a corner as a wallflower. Toughing it out, Ye Qin entered the venue on ice skates, falling on his butt several times on the way. On top of that, he had to consider the filming cameras, trying his hardest not to make ugly, grimacing expressions.

Fortunately, the hostess was kind and took good care of him, as he was a newbie who was on the show for the first time. She even circled the topic back to him repeatedly, telling him,

"Handsome people look good even when they fall."

Unexpectedly, this made He Hansong unhappy. Several times he passed by and took advantage of the camera being aimed elsewhere to purposely give Ye Qin a hard time. Now and then, he gave him a push or clipped him on the shoulder. Finally, he managed to make Ye Qin fall, the latter's tailbone hitting the ice hard. Ye Qin sprawled out on the ice in so much pain that his face drained of color.

When a camcorder came over for a closeup, He Hansong squeezed closer to steal the shot. "Qin-Qin, what happened? Didn't you say that you learned how to skate in a club at university... Oh, sorry, I forgot that wasn't you. You didn't even go to university."

Ye Qin had nothing to say to such a farce. He lay there resting for a moment before being helped up by a staff member. The hostess, who had witnessed the entire incident from beginning to end, told him in private that this part would be cut later. She also persuaded Ye Qin to not take it too personally and added that education wasn't the only criterion to measure a person's quality.

Nowadays, the masses put more value on an artist's internal and external qualities. Ever since debuting, Ye Qin had been denounced for his low level of education. Within their team, He Hansong was currently enrolled in the capital's Theatre Academy, dropping by from time to time for a meal or a selfie. Song Xu had a widespread reputation as an honor student: having exceeded the highest cut-off in national college examinations by thirty points, he was already the industry paragon for excelling in work and study. He had even been invited on "The Brain: China." The other two members were music majors. After leaving the group, they returned to campus to resume their studies. In the whole group, Ye Qin was left to be the ignorant clown.

And so, Ye Qin could not find a good retort. He forced out

a smile as he kneaded his backside. "I really didn't go to university, and didn't participate in any sort of society. Promise that you won't make fun of me for not being able to skate, won't you?"

After the chaotic day, Ye Qin thought he could finally rest. Once he was back in the car, he took things out and began to remove his makeup.

"Stop, stop," Zheng Yueyue ordered them as she got in the car. "We still have to go somewhere else. Don't be in a hurry to change and take off your makeup yet."

Ye Qin had a hunch that this wasn't anything good, yet he didn't protest too violently. Contrarily, He Hansong wasn't as cordial and he scoffed, "Half an hour. Not one second more."

"President Tang is there as well," Zheng Yueyue stated.

On hearing this, He Hansong sat up straight and took out powder foundation from his bag, fixing his face while checking the mirror.

Song Xu was the last to realize what was happening. He leaned into Ye Qin and asked, "Do we have to d...do *that*?"

Ye Qin turned aside and whispered back, "Lil' fella, don't jump to any ridiculous conclusions. Just take it as an invitation to dinner and bring your empty stomach."

Naturally, it wasn't Ye Qin's first time in this situation: they were being trotted out before the bigshots. To be brutally honest, he wasn't so big of a celebrity that he was "trotted out" often. He mostly tailed behind He Hansong, taking advantage of the latter's popularity.

On previous locations, they had all been wallflowers whenever He Hansong was present. After all, as a male artist, Ye Qin wasn't worried about certain difficult predicaments that could happen. Most situations only required them to nod, bow, and greet, "President Zhang, President Wang, President Li" in suc-

cession, and at most to drink a few glasses to show their respect. So Ye Qin wasn't nervous at all.

As he walked into the hotel, Ye Qin stretched his long neck to look around, one moment thinking of getting a salonpas for his tailbone, the next moment marveling at how the hotel looked after its renovation. Both the floor and the ceiling flashed with shining gold, as tacky as ever.

Ye Qin hid his mockery in his head. Naturally, he wouldn't say it out loud. Unless they knew that he had once stayed here seven or eight years ago as a guest in the top floor penthouse, anyone hearing his comments would think that he was being envious.

When he entered a wide, luxurious private room, Ye Qin merely stayed behind He Hansong, looking down as if he was determined to carve the carpet pattern into his memory and then go home to find a similar one on Taobao. Zheng Yueyue tapped him from behind for several times, hinting at him to raise his head and give a smile. Thus he quickly finished making greetings along with He Hansong and then continued to study the carpet.

The director of the show, the upper management at the TV station, and several sponsors sat at the table. The sponsors were led by He Hansong's most major financial backer, Tang Chong. Everyone at the table knew about their relationship, and they pressed He Hansong to sit beside President Tang and have a few drinks with him.

Unexpectedly, Tang Chong didn't agree immediately today. Rather, he said with a smile that there were too many people present and he didn't want to make a fool of himself. "Why not let them put on a performance to liven things up?"

Ye Qin's eyelid twitched. When he felt Tang Song's gaze lingering on him, his blood went cold.

Zheng Yueyue, who was used to this kind of scene, pushed the three of them forward. "Sing something happy. That single from last summer will do. Perk up. Don't kill the bosses' mood."

As the main attraction, He Hansong was the first to sneer. Song Xu was also shocked by this humiliating request.

But be that as it may, singing and dancing was their job. Even if they were somewhere else, their social status wouldn't change. In front of this group of bigshots who couldn't be offended, they had to put on pretend smiles and fawn no matter how unwilling they were.

It was just a song. It wouldn't hurt. If they didn't do it, their wages might get deducted.

Ye Qin bit the bullet and took the microphones. He handed one over to Song Xu and whispered in his ear, "It'll only be three minutes. Just bear with it."

One of the bigshots even found a background track to play on his cellphone. After the lead-in, the three of them were about to start singing when Tang Chong suddenly stood up and interrupted. "A very important guest is yet to arrive." He looked at his watch and continued, "He's almost here. Let me go pick him up."

Ye Qin, who had almost choked at the sudden interruption, patted his chest. When he heard people at the table discussing some gossip about "the eldest son of the esteemed Yi family," "...just came back from overseas," he was too occupied to think deeply about it.

When the door opened again, everyone in the room stood up in welcome and respect. A few people called out, "President Cheng," with faces full of smiles. Ye Qin made no note of it. There were as many bigshots in the country with the last name Chen as there were hairs on an ox. If he yelled "President Chen" on the streets, there'd be seven or eight people turning to look. This President "Chen"—or did they say President "Cheng"?—

likely had a good father, just as Tang Chong had, but so what? As soon as he entered this vanity fair, he would blend in with the rest of them and become exactly the same as everyone else there.

But as soon as the arriving guest spoke, Ye Qin was hit by a giant hammer. He was left trembling from head to foot, outside and in.

"Sorry for being late. I ran into a traffic jam on the way."

The male voice was deep and layered, hitting against Ye Qin's eardrum in a familiar beat. That simple courtesy made his head shake, as if he had instantaneously tumbled into a foggy dream.

Then, a gust of wind blew past. Ye Qin straightened his rigid neck. Under his gaze, the man entered and sat down on the empty seat specifically reserved for him. In a calm, composed, and polite manner, he looked at every person in the room.

Even though he had no hope, every time when Ye Qin couldn't sleep—when he felt broken-hearted, when he felt like he couldn't hold on—he secretly fantasized about their reunion.

Over one thousand seven hundred endless nights, he'd imagined more than a hundred preset scenes: normal ones, wondrous ones, and even awkward ones. He'd thought of every single one.

But reality always surpassed imagination. At least, in all of his presets, there was no scenario as embarrassing and humiliating as the present one.

"President Cheng, you came at a great time. This idol group was about to sing for everyone," said the director of the show. "Since you've just gotten back from overseas, you probably wouldn't know them. Come, come, young Mr. He, bring your brothers over and introduce yourselves to President Cheng."

He Hansong announced his name first and Song Xu followed closely. When it was Ye Qin's turn, he didn't know how he managed to open his mouth. He couldn't even hear his own voice clearly. All five senses rapidly broke down, with only his vision still holding on by a thin rope.

It was this dwindling sense that enabled him to detect Cheng Feichi gazing at him.

That completely tranquil gaze stopped on him for less than a second before moving away, as if he was looking at a stranger whom he had met for the first time.

Ye Qin never thought a song could last this long.

Thankfully, after performing it countless times, the lyrics, tune, and rhythm had become muscle memory and were carved deeply in his mind. Even with his mind floating in outer space, he could still sing a rehearsed routine.

When they finished the performance, Tang Chong led the applause and then invited the three of them to sit down and have some drinks. He Hansong plopped down beside Tang Chong, while Song Xu was pulled aside by a female producer whom he was acquainted with. Initially, Ye Qin wanted to flee amidst the chaos, but as soon as he turned around, he ran into the waiter on his way carrying additional chairs. Zheng Yueyue pushed him from behind and he dropped onto a chair clumsily.

There was a lot of space at the big, round table, enough for the three of them. As the waiter brought out the dishes, Ye Qin peeked to his right. Cheng Feichi sat less than two meters away from him. They were only separated by a person sitting in between.

Before arriving, Ye Qin had been the one to say "bring an empty stomach"; looking at the magnificent feast both for the eyes and for the stomach, he lost all his appetite. Twice he toasted for the health of the bosses, along with the other two members of the group at the table. Then, Ye Qin remained quietly at his seat, praying for this dinner to quickly come to an end.

But the heavens just wouldn't answer his wishes. Less than half an hour later, the guest sitting on his right departed early, saying that he had another dinner party to join. The waiters immediately brought out more dishes, cleared his dining set, and took away his seat. Now the two of them had nothing separating them but air. Wherever they looked, they could catch the other at the corner of their eyes.

Ye Qin sat on pins and needles, dying to become invisible. He suddenly remembered that he had makeup on. When he introduced himself a while ago, he'd also lowered his voice. Maybe Cheng Feichi didn't recognize him at all.

This thought made him instantly more relaxed. He relaxed his frozen joints and straightened his back, which had been arched from the moment he sat down.

Once he broke free from the initial awkwardness and embarrassment, the overdue happiness spread through his heart. Cheng Feichi came back. Just the thought of this made him so excited that he couldn't sit still.

And he seemed to be doing well. Ye Qin lifted a glass of water from the table. As he tilted his head back and drank, he peeked at Cheng Feichi. His face was as defined and handsome as before. The white shirt he had on had the top two buttons undone, showing his Adam's apple, yet his cuffs were tightly done up in a way that led others to admire his slender, beautiful hands.

As everyone else drank and chatted merrily, their attention elsewhere, Ye Qin examined Cheng Feichi's hands with his eyes, looking at the distinct knuckles and veins that moved up and down as Cheng Feichi lifted a wine glass. The warm memory of being led by that hand reemerged.

In the dark theatre, down the autumn boulevard, on the schoolyard basking in the sun... That hand had once pulled him along as if it was holding the most precious treasure in the world.

Ye Qin had to clench his teeth until his cheeks were rigid. Only then was he able to keep back the wetness in his eyes, not letting himself lose control in front of such a big crowd.

He really was back.

Nothing special happened in the latter half of the dinner party. It was the habit of the Chinese to talk business while drinking, so the topics were inevitably dry and dull. Ye Qin only pricked up his ears when he heard them fawningly ask for Cheng Feichi's opinion.

Cheng Feichi came to this occasion via invite, without any business duties, so he spoke very little. However, practically everyone at the table knew the Yi family's status and influence in S-City. Even if he didn't take the initiative to speak, there was no lack of people to strike up conversations, trying to butter him up.

"President Cheng, are you left-handed? I heard that left-handed people are all very smart."

Everyone knew that this was boot-licking under the guise of curiosity, but they all carried on with the flattering comments. They blurted out things like "The president of such and such country is left-handed," or "this and that celebrity is left-handed," or "left-handed people think more actively," and so on.

With flattery coming from all directions, there was no joy on Cheng Feichi's face. He put down the glass in his hand and said calmly, "No, I injured my right hand in the past. It's inconvenient to use it."

After the party disbanded, Ye Qin was still trying to recall what had happened to Cheng Feichi's hand. At the time, their separation had been hasty. He reached conclusions for half his unanswered questions after slowly pondering them throughout the years. The other half flew into the clouds, along with the airplane which he ultimately hadn't caught sight of; the plane which had disappeared without a trace.

The five-year gap pulled a long, thick curtain between them, completely blocking the countless threads of connection that had once linked them, before severing them entirely.

How could a short reunion overcome the long separation? Absent-mindedly, Ye Qin deluded himself into thinking that time had started over after he'd forgotten everything—even if he had been even more torn down and embarrassed, even if this had been their first meeting.

Ye Qin washed his face in the bathroom and deliberately stayed behind. Still, he ran into Tang Chong, who was lying in wait at the turn of the corridor.

Ye Qin instinctively lifted his head and looked for surveillance cameras. Tang Chong smiled and said, "Qin-Qin, baby, don't panic. I just want to have a chat with you."

Frowning, Ye Qin asked, "Where's He Hansong?"

Tang Chong said smugly, "So you *are* jealous. I told you before, as long as you come with me, everything that's his will be yours instead. Why are you still hesitating? A little birdie told me that...he gave you a hard time again today?"

He then approached and reached a hand behind Ye Qin to grope his butt. His hand had just touched the fabric of his pants when Ye Qin slapped it away.

Seeing Ye Qin glare menacingly at him with his dark eyes only made Tang Chong more excited. He grabbed Ye Qin's waist and pushed him into the corner. "I love to see you playing coy, like a wild kitten."

It wasn't like Ye Qin had never been harassed by Tang Chong before. This guy took advantage of what little power his father had to do whatever he wanted. Normally, he just bullied the weak and feared the strong, but today, he'd had a few more drinks and became more daring. As he pushed Ye Qin, he even puckered his lips to kiss him. The smell of alcohol was so strong that Ye Qin almost wanted to throw up. He raised his hand and slapped Tang Chong across the face.

Ye Qin wasn't controlling his strength; Tang Chong's head sprung sideways. Tang Chong took several steps back in succession and covered his face in shock for a good moment. Expression changing from disbelief to indignant anger, he surged forward and grabbed the collar of Ye Qin's shirt, pinning him to the wall.

"Fuck. I give you face and you don't want it. Do you think you're still the young master of the Ye family?!"

Ye Qin's eyes sightly widened. Without waiting for his response, Tang Chong forced his head up by the chin.

"There are countless people who want to get into my bed. Don't think too highly of yourself!" he mocked. "If it weren't for that face of yours, which does get better by the year, to be fair... Ow!"

There was a dull thud. The first thing that Ye Qin did when he broke free of the restraint was to put all of his strength into a headbutt, making Tang Chong let go of him. Then he seized this chance to push him away and flee.

In the staircase, Ye Qin ran while pondering what he should do next.

Should he tell Zheng Yueyue and ask for her help? No, she worked for the company and put profit above all else. If she knew he'd pissed off Tang Chong, she might not only refuse to help, but even urge him to submit to Tang Chong.

Should he find an opportunity to apologize, then? He was afraid that he himself was incapable of tossing away his pride and pretending to be sorry. That guy had a mouth full of shit and liked to jab at his weak spots. What if he apologized and they just wound up fighting again?

After being worn down for five years, Ye Qin had long since

changed from the insolent young master of the Ye family. Even if he still lost control of his temper from time to time, he could prepare an escape route for himself very quickly.

After all, the people who would always accommodate his needs unconditionally were no more.

With his thoughts in disarray, Ye Qin made a turn on the staircase while looking down and carelessly ran into the chest of a man in a suit.

Cheng Feichi had just finished a phone call and was about to go back to the private room to get his things. As the elevator was at full capacity, he chose to take the stairs. He hadn't expected that he would run into Ye Qin.

Ye Qin was obviously taller than before. When he stood up straight, he reached Cheng Feichi's ears perfectly. He also looked different from before. The baby fat had gone away and the lines of his features became more solid and well-defined. On the whole, he still appeared pretty and refined; completely different from his character.

His first reaction after running into someone was panic. When he saw that it was Cheng Feichi, he scrambled back a few steps to a distance that just happened to allow Cheng Feichi to see his red forehead and messy collar.

He'd gotten into a fight with someone, thought Cheng Feichi.

The *clip-clop* of high heels sounded behind him as a woman approached. "Why does it take you so long to come out? We've been waiting for ages... What happened to your head? Did you fight with He Hansong again?"

Ye Qin turned away as if he didn't want anyone to see his head. Cheng Feichi heard him mutter, "No."

Realizing there was someone else present, Zheng Yueyue told Cheng Feichi politely, "It's just stuff between kids. Sorry if this startled you." Then she gave Ye Qin a push. "Hurry up and apologize to President Cheng."

Ye Qin raised his head and glanced at him before quickly looking away. He stammered for a while, unable to say a single word.

Cheng Feichi was about to tell them there was no need, when the elevator on the other side stopped on the ground floor and Tang Chong stormed out in a rage. He rolled up his sleeves and made a beeline for Ye Qin, yelling, "You fucking little shit, you have the guts to hit me?!"

Ye Qin turned and ducked, while Zheng Yueyue also opened her arms and stepped in Tang Chong's way. Before asking what happened, she first mediated, "President Tang, please calm down. Let's talk this out. There are so many people watching here..."

Though people came and went in the hotel lobby, no one took note of what was taking place in the corner.

With Zheng Yueyue covering for him, Ye Qin was about to slip away along the wall. It had not occurred to him that Tang Chong suddenly got smart this time. Rather than fight the person in front of him, he pushed Zheng Yueyue aside and took huge steps towards Ye Qin, using his right hand to grab Ye Qin's wrist and pin it behind his back. Tang Chong lifted his left fist high and was about to smash it into his face.

He was stopped by the man standing at the side, who had been silent this whole time.

Cheng Feichi stopped the fist that was just about to land on Ye Qin's face. He said expressionlessly, "President Tang, this is a public setting."

Actually, Tang Chong was a bit afraid of this young master from the Yi family, whom he had only met twice.

His appearance in this circle had been abrupt. At first, all the other bigshots laughed behind his back for having Cheng as a surname instead of Yi. Afterwards, they heard that he had been given an important position right after coming back from

overseas: now it was he who ran all of the Yi family's hotel and restaurant businesses in the Yangtze River Delta. Everyone knew that the Yi family had made their fortune on hotel chains. Whoever took over this crucial part of the business was equal to the heir declarant.

Only after this did all the families attach importance to their dealings with Cheng Feichi. However, this young master of the Yi family, Mr. Cheng, never joined the other local young masters in living the fast life. Normally he only appeared at business gatherings, and wherever he went, he put on a cold face and acted in a businesslike manner. The circle of hedonic young masters, with Tang Chong as their head, had to make nice with him on the threats of their fathers and had to genuflect to him for fear of offending the Yi family. They were truly miserable beyond words.

Now, Cheng Feichi was sticking his nose in other people's business. Tang Chong burned with anger, yet he had to compromise and let go of Ye Qin. At the same time, for the sake of keeping his own face, he said, "That little star is a little punk. He stole my stuff and injured me." He pointed at his own forehead and said, "Look, he did this."

"Bullshit!" Unable to hold back any longer, Ye Qin finally seethed. "You know full well who the punk really is."

Cheng Feichi finally understood how the two identical bumps on their foreheads came to be. He glanced at Ye Qin and asked Tang Chong, "He stole your stuff?"

Tang Chong's eyes darted back and forth between the two of them. If good at nothing else, he was an expert in reading body language. At once, he deduced, "You two...know each other?"

"No."

"Yes."

Completely opposing answers came out of their mouths at the same time. Having blurted out "no" without thinking, Ye Qin was taken aback. He turned and looked at the person with whom he hadn't dared exchange a glance with for this whole evening.

He finally realized that his judgement had been clouded by the joy of reunion—to actually think that Cheng Feichi couldn't recognize him!

How could he not? Ye Qin had hurt him so much. It was just like the injury on his palm. Even after it healed, scabbed, and grew new flesh, each hand flex and finger curl served as an everlasting reminder of the pain and hatred from those days.

The greatest revenge was recognizing him at first glance, but wearing an expression of complete calm, not letting his eyes linger even for a moment.

Tang Chong was also taken aback, but quickly smiled and said, "Pardon my bad memory. I didn't see you interacting earlier, though we were at the dinner party for such a long time."

Zheng Yueyue was completely dumbfounded. She looked at one and then the other, asking Ye Qin, "Are you friends with President Cheng?"

"No," Ye Qin objected again.

Tang Chong's smile grew even more profound. "Oh? I don't understand, then. Are you long-lost brothers instead?"

It was a light joke, but that word seemed to morph into a sharp steel needle, stabbing Ye Qin's heart quickly and precisely.

Before Cheng Feichi could speak, Ye Qin cut in first. "Old classmates."

Despite knowing how miserable he looked, Ye Qin still took a deep breath, straightened his back, and added, "High school classmates."

He didn't dare listen to Cheng Feichi's response.

He wanted to keep the last bit of dignity he had.

CHAPTER 17

IN the car, Zheng Yueyue was asking, "Are you really President Cheng's high school classmate?"

Ye Qin grunted.

"Isn't he from S-City?"

"He used to live in the capital."

"You two went to the same high school?" Zheng Yueyue still wasn't fully convinced. "I heard that President Cheng graduated from a famous university in America. I thought he grew up overseas."

Ye Qin thought for a bit and said, "He was already outstanding when he went to school here. I would not be surprised to see him get into any good university."

Curious, Song Xu also leaned in to gossip. Ye Qin told them everything that he could, including how Cheng Feichi got awards for many competitions in high school and was a worthy honor student.

Having heard this, Zheng Yueyue said suspiciously, "Seeing that you know him so well, I doubt you two were normal classmates. He even stepped forward to save you a moment ago." Then, she persuaded, "If you have such a powerful friend, hurry up and get into regular contact with him. Don't stupidly pretend not to know him. Cheng Feichi already has no shortage of former classmates currying favor with him and leveraging connections."

Ye Qin shook his head wordlessly.

The bright lights of S-City flickered in the night, making the downtown as bright as daytime. But the light that reflected in his eyes was cold.

He knew that if it had been a total stranger back in the hotel lobby, Cheng Feichi would still have lent a helping hand. That action didn't serve as his protection; it was just a normal reaction he made following his conscience.

That's why Ye Qin's heart churned when he heard Cheng Feichi's frank admission that the two knew each other.

He suddenly recalled how, when he first debuted, the company had taken advantage of his family's hype to paint him as "a golden boy stuck in a bind." He had laughed on the spot, thinking that he could at most be called "a fallen young master who had lost his halo."

The real golden boy was Cheng Feichi. He was upright, big-hearted, kind, and gentle. He would never bully the weak, and it was further beneath him to use the dirty, despicable methods Ye Qin had once used for revenge.

Cheng Feichi was so different from him that neither monstrous waves nor endless swamps could keep him down.

The shoot in S-City lasted three days this time.

On the afternoon of the second day, Ye Qin's injured tailbone hurt more than the day before and was still bad after he put on a salonpas. After leaving it on for several hours, he could finally sit down and rest. Less than five minutes later, he stood back up, and the explosive pain in his joints shot straight up to his brain.

Ye Qin's vision suddenly blanked out and he almost fainted. Afraid that something would happen if he stubbornly persisted, Zheng Yueyue quickly cleared his schedule and dropped him into a taxi headed for the hospital. She also instructed him to buy a bottle of Thousand Flowers Healing Oil to rub on his forehead.

On the way there, Ye Qin was still pondering if his earnings would get deducted for shooting two fewer photos. When he reached the Patient Registration and Payment desk, he couldn't even bear to get a specialist number that cost more than ten yuan and got a five-yuan normal patient number instead.

S-City's hospitals were overcrowded, just like the capital's. Ye Qin waited half an hour outside the consultation room before he was called up. When the doctor heard that he'd injured his tailbone, he wrote him a slip for an X-ray without taking a single look.

Ye Qin adjusted his face mask at the nose, thinking that it was fortunate he didn't need to get examined. Taking his pants off on the spot was too embarrassing.

He joined another long queue. The doctor in the imaging department told him to retrieve the photos from the machine himself in an hour. Ye Qin had nothing to do, yet sitting down was also uncomfortable. Finally, he decided to go back to the consulting room and look for the doctor.

The elderly doctor didn't find him pesky, and chatted with him in between examinations. He said that more and more young people were getting spinal problems, especially fashionistas like him who didn't even notice when their bones got damaged from low temperatures. They were really going to feel it once they got old.

Ye Qin looked down at the costume underneath his vest, which almost fully opened up from his abs to his sides, even exposing his bellybutton. He raised his head and chuckled. "I have to wear this for my job, can't help it. Gotta eat somehow."

Beside him, the auntie waiting to see the doctor looked over in surprise.

When it was almost time, Ye Qin pulled the front flaps of his vest closed and rode the elevator to the first floor to fetch those pictures.

While waiting in line, an ambulance stopped outside the front doors. Doctors, nurses, and a few family members of the patient gathered around the wheelchair, forming a path. The surrounding people also stepped aside on their own.

Ye Qin didn't know that his shoelaces had come undone. When he stepped back, he tripped. Thankfully, someone held him up from behind so that he didn't fall.

He turned back to say thanks, but as the word left his mouth, he froze in shock.

The person holding him up was Cheng Feichi.

There was a time when the proud and arrogant Ye Qin believed that, if it weren't for him stooping down to Cheng Feichi's level, their worlds would never intersect. One was the world of the elite who went in and out of first-class restaurants and private clinics; the other belonged to the commoners who went in and out of crowded street stalls and public hospitals. They were separated in different hierarchies from birth.

Now that situation had switched, he finally knew how ridiculous and childish he was in the past, using money to hold up his status.

"Thanks," he ended up saying the word which was the most suitable for warding off embarrassment at present. Then, he wrapped the flaps of his vest tighter, hiding the exposed belly-button, and said in an attempt to make conversation, "What a coincidence. Are you here to see the doctor?"

Today, Cheng Feichi wore a simple T-shirt and long pants, yet he felt as distant as yesterday when he wore a suit and leather shoes. He hummed and glanced at the medical record that Ye Qin was holding. "Are you sick?" he asked.

"Huh? Oh...a minor problem. I fell while skating and accidentally hurt my tailbone. I just came to get some salonpas but the doctor made me get an X-ray."

Ye Qin didn't know why he explained in such detail. Clearly Cheng Feichi was just casually asking. As soon as he finished, he regretted it, feeling like a base person who kept going back on his own word. Yesterday he had just put up a front, saying that they didn't know each other, and now he was in such a rush to get close with him.

Cheng Feichi hummed again and fell silent.

Ye Qin hung his head, not daring to look at him and fixing his stare at the medical record. His thoughts suddenly floated to the summer vacation of six years past.

At that time, they were deeply in love and stuck to each other even as they slept at night. He remembered one time when he got sunburnt from walking under the blazing sun for too long. Cheng Feichi had stayed by his side throughout the night, wiping him down with a wet towel to help him alleviate the sting of sunburn, taking him in his arms and gently patting his back, whispering comforting words in his ear, "Pain, pain, go away."

Actually, it hadn't hurt that much, but because he wanted to be coaxed by Cheng Feichi, he acted as if it hurt a lot and tried every way to crawl into Cheng Feichi's embrace.

Afterwards, Cheng Feichi heard somewhere that the scientific way to treat sunburnt skin was to keep it cool, exposed, and kept away from sources of heat as much as possible. Thus, whenever Ye Qin crawled over, he pushed him away. Every time Ye Qin came, Cheng Feichi pushed him. He was completely cold and unfeeling and almost made Ye Qin angry to the point of tears. After getting pushed away for the last time, Ye Qin kicked Cheng Feichi, telling him to go sleep outside and stop being annoying in front of him.

Cheng Feichi really left. Not even ten minutes later, Ye Qin regretted it. He tiptoed to the door on bare feet. He put his hand on the handle and his ear on the door, listening for movement outside. Not hearing a single noise, he hurriedly opened the door from fright. As soon as he lifted his head, he saw Cheng Feichi standing outside, arms wide open. He said, "Now you can hug me."

Within those ten short minutes, he had gone to the bathroom and taken a cold shower. Even though he knew that he might catch a cold. Even though he knew that his temperature would slowly rise again and they'd only have five minutes to hug at most.

To date, Ye Qin remembered what he felt when he threw himself in Cheng Feichi's embrace. The word "sweet" didn't portray even one ten-thousandth of that abundant bliss.

But now, the two of them stood in a line, maintaining a meter of personal space in between. Cheng Feichi neither evaded him, nor showed him excessive care. It was as if he had returned to his original guarded state.

No, it was a type of intangible separation more severe than police tape. It was like Ye Qin's existence no longer had any connection to him, and he no longer wanted to know him either.

The many "thank you"s and "sorry"s Ye Qin still owed, words that he had never swallowed his pride to say at the time, were never to be said. He no longer had the right.

When it was time to get the X-ray photos, Ye Qin said goodbye to Cheng Feichi. Not caring that his tailbone still hurt, Ye Qin turned and ran.

He relied on his lack of popularity to push and shove through such a huge public hospital. When Zhou Feng called, he immediately pulled off his mask so that he could speak freely.

"I've found him! I've found him! I've found him!"

The moment he connected, Zhou Feng yelled madly, sounding like the rush of a flood. Ye Qin thought he had accidentally pressed the repeat button and held his cellphone away. Covering his ears, he said, "If I didn't know better, I'd think you were about to become a dad."

"I already found him. Is becoming a dad that far off? Never mind, I'll keep being a brother." Zhou Feng was immersed in happiness and unable to break free. "We both got it wrong before, thinking he had to be in H Province because that's where the postcard was sent from. He's actually in the capital!"

When Ye Qin heard from him that Liao Yifang was teaching history at a middle school in the capital, he couldn't help but be surprised. "Our class monitor's grades were so high, and he planned to go abroad. Isn't it too much of a waste of his talent to be a teacher?"

Hearing this, Zhou Feng fell silent for a while, and then said, "It's all my fault. It must be because he transferred right before the college entrance exam. It affected his prospects." A moment later, he regained confidence. "No problem. I'll give him a good life in the future. When I get his forgiveness, I'll bring him to the registry. You can be our witness when we get married."

The country had just legalized same-sex marriage not long ago. Zhou Feng vowed to be part of the first group trying it out. Ye Qin reminded him to figure out his family issues first and Zhou Feng said dismissively, "Me and him love each other. Our relationship is within the bounds of law and reason. I already listened to them and joined the army. What more could they ask for?"

Still feeling something wasn't quite right, Ye Qin asked,

"This time you're for real?"

"Shit," Zhou Feng swore. "You don't think I went through so much trouble just for fun?"

"Then what about Sun Yiran?"

Zhou Feng couldn't help but feel guilty towards these past affairs. "Yiran has a boyfriend she intends to marry. She's doing quite well. A few days ago we talked over the phone and she said to let bygones be bygones. She even wants us to hang out together when we're free... I was thinking, when I see Yuanyuan, I have to be one hundred twenty percent sincere; more sincere than when I took my army oath. Nothing's impossible if you're sincere. Surely he'll forgive me?"

Ye Qin had a thought that made his eyes go distant for a moment. He said, "That's not a sure thing."

Short of an affirmation, Zhou Feng complained, annoyed, "I haven't seen you for years. A-Qin, how did you get like this? Can't you give me some encouragement?"

Ye Qin laughed bitterly. He couldn't even handle his own affairs; how could he give encouragement to someone else?

Zhou Feng suddenly sighed and then switched to a grave tone. "Every day for the past several years, I faced a never-ending wilderness, a land of dust as far as the eye can see. He's what I think about the most. Before sleeping, I think about whether he's sleeping. Before eating, I think about whether he's eaten. When the commander gets up to make a speech, I can imagine him speaking under the national flag. Maybe the contrast it what does it. The corps is filled with rough fellas; which one of them has a smile as sweet as his? Which one of them treats me so wholeheartedly well?"

He talked himself into a smile, gently massaged his throat, and continued, "Then, why don't you pass me some of your advice, A-Qin? I'm scared that when I see him, my legs will shake and I won't be able to say anything. Then I'll become a joke to that class of his."

Ye Qin, who just met the person he'd been thinking of for five years, now had the authority to speak.

He lifted his head to the white hospital ceiling and mulled over this for a long time. Afraid Zhou Feng wouldn't understand, he put as much as he could in simple language. "Don't speak without thinking. Hold in every word until you've thought it through. Also...don't be embarrassed about what's been in your heart for the last few years. Say every sentence in earnest for him to hear."

Say it now, while you still have the chance.

The day he returned to Beijing, Ye Qin happened to receive the contract sent by the production team that held the last audition.

Zheng Yueyue couldn't contain her joy. She made Ye Qin sign the contract and send it back early in the morning, and then started coming up with a plan to find him an assistant. Despite it being just an idol drama and not any big production, and despite only filming in S-City for less than a month, at least he had the reputation of a third male lead. Having an actor carrying bags and checking in by himself would be embarrassing.

After spending a lot of effort reaching out and finally settling on an assistant, Zheng Yueyue pulled Ye Qin along to the supermarket for a shopping spree.

Ye Qin had been shooting that outdoor activity program for three whole days and didn't even get to sleep after coming back to the dorm. He yawned while following Zheng Yueyue around, watching her toss kitchen utensils and household products into the shopping cart unstoppably.

"It's not even my first time shooting a drama. There's no

need to prepare this much."

When all was said, Ye Qin had been on the scene for almost five years now. He'd never shot a proper drama series, but he shot bucketloads of low-budget web dramas, amateur films, and whatnot. He thought that Zheng Yueyue was being too nervous and making a big fuss over things.

"How is there no need?" Zheng Yueyue grabbed a few bottles of mosquito-repelling aromatic water, reading the labels. "You're shooting in the mountains in the suburbs of S-City, where it's inconvenient to shower and stuff. And don't you know how bad mosquitoes are on the mountain? They can bite your soft skin and fine flesh into a sieve, so that when you drink water it'll sprinkle out like a showerhead."

Ye Qin was so scared by her descriptions that he paid for all those bottles of aromatic water eagerly. The next day, when he climbed the mountain, one of them was in his pocket.

It was close to the anniversary of his mother Luo Qiuling's death. Afraid that he would have to go to the set early when shooting the drama later and not have time to return to the capital, Ye Qin went to see her first thing.

Luo Qiuling had been buried in the Luo family grave, at the heart of the mountain, just like his grandfather.

Previously, a car had always given him a ride to the Luo family villa on the mountaintop; the next day, he could get there after walking a few steps. Now, there was no car and no villa. Ye Qin walked up the mountain, booking a single bedroom in a guesthouse at the top.

At his walking speed, night would fall by the time he reached the mountaintop. Therefore, he had to stay there overnight. Tomorrow morning, he would get up and make offerings to the grave.

The air quality today was bad. The mountain was permeat-

ed with fog. After climbing halfway up, Ye Qin lifted his head and gazed afar. He couldn't even see the winding road going up the mountain in front of him.

It was already sunset. Hikers who passed by once in a while were all heading down. It was then that he thought of turning around and coming back another day. He took out his cellphone and was about to cancel the room when he found that the refund would not process. After going back, he discovered that "special discount, no refunds" was written on the webpage.

Ye Qin couldn't spare the money. After deliberating for a moment, he clenched his teeth and continued climbing.

The free-floating clouds gradually turned into dark fog coiling around the mountains, while the jade range turned into a gloomy darkness as the last of the sun's rays disappeared.

Amidst the nightfall, surrounded only by the sound of rustling leaves and light wind, Ye Qin found himself lost.

He didn't remember when he had left the flagstone trail, only this wasn't his first time seeing this particular clutch of trees. Last time he passed by, there was still sunlight pouring out between the perfectly straight trunks. Now all that was left were dark, broken shadows.

After going in a few more circles, Ye Qin became scared.

Before he started hyperventilating, he took out his cellphone and made calls. He couldn't get a hold of Zhou Feng or Song Xu. Zheng Yueyue was working, and told him to call the police for help immediately.

He input the three numbers "110," which stayed on his screen for a long time. Insects gradually began chirping, and the night chill pierced into his heart. Still, he didn't push the call button.

Tang Chong did call midway though. Maybe he had heard something. That mouth of his probably wouldn't say any kind words anyway, so Ye Qin rejected the call.

Another gust of wind blew past. Licking his dry lips, he slowly deleted the numbers off the screen and entered a sequence of digits he knew by heart.

For a while after Cheng Feichi had just left, Ye Qin couldn't sleep for nights on end, sheltering himself in the apartment in Jiayuan Compound. As soon as he heard the slightest stir, he thought it was Cheng Feichi coming back. He moved the pillow and covers to the door and listened to the outside movements at all times—from the elevator, from the staircase, even sounds of the wind moving the window and cars starting at the foot of the building. He didn't miss a single one.

Later, he realized his mental state wasn't normal and used all sorts of methods to calm himself down, telling himself over and over: *Cheng Feichi went to America. When he wants to come back, he will. He loves it the most when I behave. I just have to wait for him.*

And then?

And then, his mom passed away. He got into C University, but couldn't continue his studies. He muddled his way into the entertainment circle, lived the kind of life that he never would have thought of before, experienced all kinds of ugly things in the human world. Reality wore away at him, making him stronger every day, as if he had put on a mask and then covered the mask with a thick layer of oil paint.

But what use was that? Didn't it break into jagged pieces at the first glimpse of him?

His so-called "strength" was built on nothing. It was hollow on the inside and its foundation was unstable. All the hero-ism and fearlessness came from a soft center that could shatter in one strike.

He never ventured outside that barrier. He'd been stuck inside all along, burying his head in the sand and living out an empty life.

Five years. He put his all into making himself grow up, and yet still ended up in this wretched state.

Actually, he hadn't grown up at all. He still remained as he was: cowardly, selfish, hypocritical, and greedy. Now, he even vainly tried to rely on Cheng Feichi's return to find a reason to bounce back.

Ye Qin slowly crouched down in the darkness, burying his face in his hands.

The surroundings were completely deserted. At this moment, he no longer wanted to use smiles to pretend like he didn't care. He no longer wanted to use optimism to pretend that all was well and peaceful. He let out the fear and panic that he'd bottled up from the first time Cheng Feichi reappeared to today.

Everything in the world was a source of fear.

He was afraid of the dark, afraid of being alone, afraid of being manipulated, afraid of Cheng Feichi leaving, even more afraid that Cheng Feichi would never look him in the eyes again after coming back.

Icy, shaky hands dialed that number. Before hearing the urgent, piercing busy signal, as a teardrop slid along the corner of his lips into his mouth, Ye Qin choked, "I... I miss you so much... Gege."

An hour later, Ye Qin stumbled along the muddy mountain path, looking at the back of the person walking in front of him. It still felt surreal, as if he were in a dream.

Hearing the footsteps gradually slow down behind him, Cheng Feichi turned around and asked, "Too tired?"

The sudden eye contact gave Ye Qin a jolt, and he quickly

shook his head. "I can keep going."

When he sensed that Cheng Feichi had slowed his pace significantly after turning back, Ye Qin's heart overflowed with a burst of warmth. Without knowing whether it was clean, he wiped his face, not wanting to leave any trace of tears.

Just thinking back to a moment ago made Ye Qin beside himself with embarrassment. He had been counting on the fact that no one was around to abandon all reservations and cry. Loudly and recklessly. With tears streaked all over his face.

He wasn't sure if Cheng Feichi had heard him.

Ye Qin carefully went over what had happened. It seemed that he hadn't heard the phone beep, and after he finished speaking, someone called his name from the other end.

"Ye Qin?"

At that moment, Ye Qin was scared to death. He covered his mouth in fear of making a sound. Suddenly, an unexpected hiccup came from his throat, followed by a series of coughs, and then, his tears flowed more furiously.

The person at the other end was not in a hurry. He waited patiently for Ye Qin to calm down before asking, "Where are you now?"

The moment he identified who it was, Ye Qin was no longer afraid.

Now that he had calmed down, Ye Qin took in the surrounding area. Although it appeared to be the middle of nowhere, there was constant chirping in the background, not to mention the whistling wind that lingered in the branches. It was no surprise that Cheng Feichi judged that he might be in danger just through a phone call.

It was just that Ye Qin thought this adventure would end in him calling the police. Who knew that Cheng Feichi was currently on the same mountain? After asking about Ye Qin's

surroundings and telling him to stay there with his flashlight on, Cheng Feichi found him in less than half an hour.

This particular mountain was neither very tall nor very big. Ye Qin momentarily teetered between feeling ashamed of his behavior and thanking his lucky stars for calling Cheng Feichi.

Even though he had absolutely no hope that it would go through.

When they reached a fork, Cheng Feichi glanced at the road signs, checked the time, and turned to Ye Qin. "I'm not familiar with the B&B you mentioned," he said. "It's really late right now, and we may not be able to find it. We're staying at a place just a bit ahead if you don't mind making do for a night."

Ye Qin naturally didn't mind. But he felt bad for seeming too straightforward, so he asked, "Are you spending your holiday here?"

"Yeah," Cheng Feichi said, "my mom wanted to come back to the capital and have a look around, but the air quality's poor in the city. It's bad for her health."

So it seems that they booked a B&B as well, Ye Qin thought. For him to encounter this kind of coincidence, it seemed that the heavens did not treat him too poorly after all.

A faint light at the end of the road ahead signaled they were approaching their destination. Ye Qin picked up his pace naturally until he walked side-by-side with Cheng Feichi. This rare opportunity, combined with his pounding heart, gave him an impulse to say something, yet he didn't know what he should say.

In the end, it was Cheng Feichi who opened his mouth first. "There aren't any wild animals here. Take your time, and mind your steps."

For a moment, Ye Qin was stupefied. He would never have thought that Cheng Feichi still remembered that he was afraid of the dark.

"Alright," he mumbled.

Again, misery and bitterness spread in his heart. Ye Qin didn't know if he was the only one who remembered the cramped back row of the classroom in a power outage, the chatter in the background, and a kiss that instantly calmed his panicked heart.

With his thoughts running wild, Ye Qin tripped. Cheng Feichi, whose sharp eyes caught the incident, gave his wrist a timely pull.

Ye Qin only wore a long-sleeved button-up. Cheng Feichi's warmth traveled through the thin fabric to his skin and seeped into his flesh until the blood flowing through his veins seemed to boil. The impulse that had been hovering in his chest transformed into courage. The words that had been buried in his heart for so long finally surged up into his throat.

He wanted to ask Cheng Feichi for a second chance. *You once changed yourself for me. Now, I can change myself for you. I'll become whatever you want me to be, okay?*

Ye Qin moved his fingers to grab the hand that Cheng Feichi was just about to remove. At the same time, he opened his mouth and was just about to speak when a blinding light flashed ahead.

"Ge, look here! I'm here!" a girl's bell-like voice immediately followed.

Mountain dwellings were always so filled with the fragrance of grass that you could even taste it in freshly boiled hot water. The persistent, familiar taste lingered on the tongue even after Ye Qin put down the cup.

When the Luo villa was still there, Ye Qin disliked the smell and would only drink drinks that he'd brought along. When he drank this water again just a few years later, all he could taste was nostalgia and melancholy.

"Finished? I'll get you another. Not a lot of people can

stand hot water in such heat."

The young lady named Yan Hong stood up cordially. She was about to refill his cup when Ye Qin quickly got to his feet as well. "I'll get it," he insisted.

"No need to be polite with me," Yan Hong said, snatching the cup from his hand. "Feichi-ge's friend is my friend. This is my role."

Her lady-of-the-house bearing put Ye Qin at somewhat of a loss. Eventually, he let her pour for him and squeaked "thank you" as he took the cup.

As Cheng Xin was resting in the bedroom, it was just the three of them in the living room.

When Cheng Feichi went to the kitchen to cut fruit, Ye Qin meant to help but ended up getting overtaken by Yan Hong. He was left to sit uncomfortably on the sofa like a guest and listen to quiet chatter and the girl's laughter coming from the kitchen.

"So you guys were high school schoolmates!" As the three of them sat around the table chatting, Yan Hong fetched a slice of watermelon for Ye Qin and an apple pealed by Cheng Feichi for herself. "High School No. 6, in the capital? I heard from Auntie that Feichi-ge got a scholarship every year."

Pinching the slice of watermelon, Ye Qin didn't know where to start. "Yep," he said. "His grades were very good."

Yan Hong playfully rolled her eyes. "Were there a lot of people trying to get with him?"

Ye Qin cast a glance at Cheng Feichi, sitting aside and scanning through some documents. "Yeah, a lot," he confirmed with a nod.

Yan Hong smiled with quite some pride and bit her apple. "So, was he just as unsmiling in school as he is now?" she continued asking. "I just told him a bunch of jokes, and his lips didn't even move."

It wasn't until now that Cheng Feichi finally showed some reaction. A tiny furrow appeared on his brow, and he raised his head a little.

Though Ye Qin rarely thought back on his own accord in the past five years, the Cheng Feichi in his memories was always gentle, never hesitating to give Ye Qin a smile.

He could be wrong, but he felt Cheng Feichi's eyes linger on him for a moment. Perhaps because he wished to keep those old smiles for himself, Ye Qin lied, "More or less. He never really used to smile either."

At dinnertime, Yan Hong helped Cheng Xin out of her room.

Cheng Xin was sickly and spiritless. Her face was sallow, and she looked even thinner than before. Cheng Feichi introduced Ye Qin as a schoolmate who had once visited their home, but she just gave Ye Qin a casual greeting without even recognizing him. After having some soup and a few noodles, she instructed Yan Hong to be a good hostess and retired back to her room.

Ye Qin felt uncomfortable from head to toe staying here, as if he were the only outsider in this house. The more cordial Yan Hong treated him, the more uncomfortable he became.

That night, despite going to bed very early, he couldn't fall asleep, tossing and turning. He turned on his phone and went on the High School No. 6 network for the first time in a long time.

Nowadays, people seldom used the school forum, and new threads appeared infrequently. Ye Qin found that the old thread asking where Cheng Feichi had gone several years ago had been bumped to the top of the page again.

The newest reply had been made three days ago by an anonymous user, saying that they had run into Cheng Feichi at a certain hotel in S-City. The attendants all called him "President Cheng" and even mentioned that there had been a pretty girl

beside him with round eyes, a slim nose, and a curly bob.

The simple, short description perfectly matched Yan Hong's features.

Ye Qin found it even harder to fall asleep. As soon as a faint light appeared in the sky, he got up to pour himself a glass of water.

This villa had three floors. Ye Qin's bedroom was located at the end of the second-floor hallway. After walking to the staircase, he craned his neck and looked up. The door to Cheng Feichi's bedroom was open. It seemed he was already awake.

Ye Qin couldn't help picking up the pace as he walked downstairs and into the living room, but there was only Yan Hong sitting alone, preoccupied, at the dining table.

She waved Ye Qin over. "Feichi-ge took Auntie out for a walk. We're gonna have breakfast first."

Ye Qin gave the excuse that he wasn't hungry and could wait for them to come back to eat, but Yan Hong pulled him into a seat regardless. "It's fine. Auntie's not here, so I call the shots."

Even if he could never get accustomed to it, Ye Qin had still somewhat learned to read faces over the past few years. For no reason, he felt that this girl put on a specific demeanor in front of him and spoke with hidden meaning.

Ye Qin hoped that this was just in his head. He took a slice of bread, bit it, and chewed in silence. *As soon as Cheng Feichi comes back, I'll say goodbye and leave,* he thought. If there were enough time, Ye Qin would like to have a word with him as well.

But Yan Hong didn't plan to let him have breakfast in peace. "You're probably the same age as me. Did you debut as soon as you graduated high school?"

As they were chatting yesterday, they had exchanged some details from their own lives. No matter how obscure Ye Qin was as a celebrity, his information could still be found on Baidu, so when he heard this, he nodded and hummed in affirmation.

"Were you very close with Feichi-ge in high school?"

Perhaps it was because he was a guest that Ye Qin felt like he got the short end of the stick in this exchange. "No. We were normal friends. That's all," he replied with his best attempt to stay calm.

"Oh, I see," Yan Hong said ambiguously as she stirred the milk in her cup with a teaspoon. Suddenly, she asked, "Yesterday, you said there were a lot of people trying to get with him. Were you one of them?"

Elsewhere at the same time, Cheng Feichi pushed Cheng Xin's wheelchair along a trail close to the villa.

Summer in the mountains was a lot cooler than the city, especially in the morning. Though Cheng Xin wore a jacket and covered herself with a thin blanket, she still coughed into her hand several times. "When we get back to S-City, it's high time to have your engagement party."

Cheng Feichi stopped in his steps. "I don't want to get married yet."

"You have to marry sooner or later." Cheng Xin tilted her head back and continued to persuade. "Yan Hong is from a good family, and she likes you. If you marry her, I'll have no..."

"You said the same thing then," Cheng Feichi interrupted. He paused for a second and then repeated, "You told me the same thing: if I go overseas, you'll have no reason to worry about me anymore."

Cheng Feichi's voice was quite cold and devoid of emotion. Cheng Xin used her arm to wheel around and face him, only to find his face as cold and hard as his voice.

This put Cheng Xin in a trance. She recalled that her son had been quite different as a teenager. He had called her "mom" back then, and would never use such estranged and distant language.

"Mom only ever wants the best for you." Cheng Xin

thought the five years he'd spent abroad had caused their relationship to become like this and was eager to rekindle the maternal bond. She leaned towards him, taking his hand. "Didn't you and Yan Hong already get to know each other abroad? You should know better than me what kind of girl she is. Your dad also thinks Yan Hong is a good choice..."

"You two thought going abroad was a good choice, so you forced me to go. Now, you two think that she's a good choice, so you're forcing me to marry her?"

"Mom's health is getting worse by the day," Cheng Xin said, immediately softening her tone. "My only wish before I die now is to see your place firmly established in the Yi family..."

Cheng Feichi couldn't help but inwardly sneer. Not even the word "die" could move him one bit. After beating around the bush for so long, wasn't this all just for the sake of her own selfish desires? Five years ago, he made the snap decision in depression and hopelessness, out of a pressing urge to escape. He had guessed even back then that this choice would lead to a chain of unending requests.

Yet five years had been enough for him to reach a clear resolution: his life should be in his own hands, and not for others to manipulate at will. He should neither concede nor compromise for anyone else's sake.

"Please don't impose any more of your expectations on me. I will do what I have specifically promised. I believe I have the right to make my own decisions regarding anything else."

Cheng Xin looked up after listening to Cheng Feichi deliver that statement as he would a report. His calm expression seemed to reflect the teen who had cut his own palm open in the hospital as a gesture of defiance against her. In a flicker of sunlight, the willfulness and rebelliousness fell away, leaving behind a man who had become steadier and more disciplined.

She almost felt like she didn't know him.

Cheng Xin suddenly realized that, rather than making Cheng Feichi grow up, forcing him to wander around overseas for five years had made him put up thicker walls around himself. The gates to his fortress were firmly shut. He was within reach, yet keenly guarded, allowing no intruders.

Indeed, Yan Hong had accompanied them to the capital because Cheng Xin had invited her in hopes that she and Cheng Feichi would grow closer. She thought that Cheng Feichi couldn't possibly ignore her wishes if she pressured him as his mother—just like how, five years ago, he had listened to her in the end.

But she forgot that she had been the first person to be walled out.

Cheng Xin rubbed her temple, feeling somewhat tired. Then, she slowly wheeled around. "Let's go back. Yan Hong's probably impatient by now."

When they got back to the villa, they found Yan Hong making tea in the courtyard. After leading Cheng Xin to the table for breakfast, Cheng Feichi glanced up at the second floor.

"He said something came up, so he'll be leaving early," Yan Hong said.

Cheng Feichi nodded, withdrawing his gaze.

It wasn't until after breakfast that he realized he forgot to ask Ye Qin yesterday why he had been on the mountain.

Cheng Feichi fished his cellphone from his pocket. After arriving in the capital yesterday afternoon, he fetched the items left behind from going abroad from his grandmother's place. His old phone was the first thing to catch his eye.

"I kept your old number for you, knowing you'll return someday and will want to catch up with your old friends," his grandmother told him.

Perhaps working around the clock ever since coming back

had made him unaccustomed to the sudden leisure he felt after arriving in the mountains that evening. For some reason, he pressed the power button.

Less than three minutes later, he got Ye Qin's call.

The old mobile phone couldn't stay on for too long. After just one night, it turned off on its own. Cheng Feichi plugged it in, turned it back on, and waited for a while. The screen stayed empty, with no missed calls or new messages.

Cheng Feichi left the cellphone to charge in his bedroom. As he went downstairs, he passed by the bedroom that Ye Qin had stayed in for one night. When Cheng Feichi went in to close the window, he found a bottle of aromatic water on the table.

There was a note under the bottle that read, *Thanks for your hospitality. I'm heading off.*

The writing was just as chicken scratch as before, but it ended in a period that was round and full.

The signature in the lower right corner said, "Ye Ruan," just like his nickname in the cellphone that Cheng Feichi hadn't touched in five years.

The supporting actor was set to start shooting on June 20th. Ye Qin joined the crew on the 15th.

"I'll cover the hotel costs for the first few days. I just want to ask you for an opportunity to observe my seniors acting," he said sincerely.

The director, deeply moved by his dedication, lamented that there weren't many new young actors with such professional awareness nowadays. And with a wave of his hand, Ye Qin was granted free meals and accommodation for this period.

True to his word, Ye Qin got up and reported early to the set every day. With the script in hand, he highlighted and took notes as he observed. When supplies came around, he even offered to move water and cargo, acting as a good student in every sense.

To tell the truth, what was there to observe while filming an idol drama shot for the sake of viewer traffic? He was only putting on a show to soothe his conscience for getting a few days of free meals and accommodation.

Ye Qin had only recently figured out the importance of maintaining good connections. If he made his presence known and behaved well in front of others, perhaps someone would think of him when the right opportunity came. Afterwards, he could return the favor. Once he established a network, his career would also go smoother.

This was what people called "humanity." Once, he'd disdained such pretenses, believing that he could accomplish anything with his own power. It was only after his family fell apart and no one was there to help him that Ye Qin realized he had never solely relied on his own power, but the "added values" attached to him—meaning, bluntly, money and social status.

Ye Qin had always been a man of action. After realizing this, he quickly convinced himself to accept it and then developed a method of combat suited for himself.

But against Cheng Feichi, whose return he hoped for day and night, Ye Qin was at a complete loss. He didn't know how to face him at all.

They were no longer lovers, and their social status went through drastic upheaval. He no longer had the right to pursue Cheng Feichi as freely as he had before. Neither did he know what Cheng Feichi thought of him, whether he still hated him or simply truly didn't care.

Either possibility made him tremble with fear. What little courage he managed to summon dissipated at the mere sign of things going awry, and it took leagues of effort for him to gather it again.

Just like how, when he heard the girl named Yan Hong proclaim, "I'm his fiancée," he didn't even have the guts to ask Cheng Feichi for confirmation. Who could he ask as? A friend? An old schoolmate? His ex-boyfriend?

Once, he treated Cheng Feichi as his boyfriend in every way and acted spoilt, unreasonable, everything under the sun with him. He should have known that there would be a day when Cheng Feichi's affection and patience ran out. When they faced each other again, Ye Qin didn't even dare speak loudly, afraid that Cheng Feichi would get annoyed and leave without ever turning back, leaving him there to wait to death by himself.

At least they had broken up properly then. If Cheng Feichi wanted to leave again, he wouldn't even need to say a word, as there was absolutely nothing between them anymore.

When the thought crossed his mind, Ye Qin opened the address book on his phone and gazed at the number saved as "Gege." He hesitated again and again but ultimately didn't dial.

Letting out a long sigh, he persuaded himself not to act on impulse. Cheng Feichi was in the country, in S-City now. It was only a matter of time before Ye Qin found an appropriate occasion to apologize and clear up past misunderstandings.

After that, he would leave the ball in Cheng Feichi's court. He would hand over to Cheng Feichi the respect and care that he had neglected to give him before most earnestly.

As long as he agrees and says he doesn't hate me, isn't tired of me, I can go back to being the old Ye Qin, who wasn't afraid of anything in the world.

At least in front of Cheng Feichi.

The idol drama adopted the popular theme of an inspirational comeback. The first shooting location was in the S-City suburbs, where the inexperienced first love between the village girl female lead and a male lead who had left the city to find himself was being filmed.

The place was quite inaccessible. There were no recreational facilities nearby, and restaurants were scarcer than hen's teeth. As a supporting actor, Ye Qin got very few scenes and barely any lines to remember. Every scene he did get consisted of him following behind the heroine, saying jiejie-this, jiejie-that, and acting cute. Even Zheng Yueyue thought that this was practically Ye Qin going on camera as himself, no need to adopt a specific mood or mental state.

Thus, Ye Qin remained quite idle. Other actors had to get in a car and ride off to a different set after shooting their part. What little free time they had, they used to carpool downtown and treat themselves to a good meal. Only Ye Qin abstained and remained cooped up in the hotel, sleeping, watching TV, and playing with Legos. Once in a while, he checked the news to get wind of the Yi family's advancements.

Whenever there were people interested in the stock market, there were people interested in the gossip mill of the powers running it. A family as influential as the Yis, who could make the S-City shake three times with a mere stomp, had as much gossip circulating through the grapevine as hairs on an ox. It was difficult to tell truth from lies.

Some said that the new heir had been born to Yi Zheng's ex-wife, and that Yi Zheng had discarded her to marry an heiress. Consequently, their child was born with a disability, making Yi Zheng recall his eldest son who was wandering about in the world. Others said this young Mr. Cheng had indeed been born and raised out of wedlock and was only able to obtain his public status as the Yi heir after receiving the family's recognition. But the fact that his surname remained unchanged indicated that the Yi family didn't fully accept him, and possibly hadn't even added his name to the family registry.

Discussion on this subject also circulated in the High School No. 6 forum. An anonymous user posted a new thread. "Anyone remember Cheng Feichi, who used to be the hottest guy in school? Did anyone know he's the Yi family young master?" The replies below ran rampant with wild speculations about Cheng Feichi's life story. Due to this thread, the number of visitors to the forum reached a two-year peak.

While many people envied him, there was naturally also no lack of those who responded with sarcasm. Under the cloak of anonymity, they posted replies everywhere.

"No wonder he could become president of a company at such a young age."

"I could do the same if I had a rich dad."

"Why bother discussing a bastard who doesn't even deserve to see the light of day?"

Ye Qin got angry looking at them. He went through hell and high water to recover his old account and password, and then dove right into the discussion with his personal account, slamming anyone who spoke ill of Cheng Feichi.

"If you can do it, go do it. If you can't, then shut up."

"Why don't you piss off and take a good, hard look in the mirror?"

"He can be company president because he has the skill."

Afraid he might only be bringing more trash talk down on Cheng Feichi, Ye Qin reined in half of his power and tried his best to reason with language that erred on the side of civilized and law-abiding.

But even when he kept such a low profile, he still got caught by an acquaintance.

One night, he got a phone call from Zhou Feng. "I knew Qin-ge was still my homie!"

"What?"

"The ID you used for the school forum!" Zhou Feng exclaimed. "So high and mighty. Brings back that awe-inspiring feeling from high school. Hey, when are we gonna go back to campus and show those squirts the magnificence of their seniors?"

The juvenile vibe Zhou Feng still kept after five years in the army rendered Ye Qin speechless. "Go by yourself."

Zhou Feng let out a long sigh. "Not yet married, no career. I don't have the face."

Ye Qin knew he put emphasis on "married." Lying on the bed, he found a comfortable position and waited for Zhou Feng to air his sufferings. "What, the class monitor's still ignoring you?"

"If only! He used to just slip away as soon as he saw me. Now he won't even let me see him. He gave my description to the guards at the school gate, and now they stop me before I can even set one foot on campus."

These days, Zhou Feng not only treated Ye Qin as a relationship guru but also a confidante, airing out all his suffering in front of him. Fortunately, Ye Qin had free time at the moment and entertained him in order to relieve boredom, as if listening to a series of jokes. Else he would have blocked Zhou Feng long ago.

"Can't you use your brain a bit and try some other methods? Like put on a disguise, make use of your job, or something?" Ye Qin suggested.

"I already thought of that. Last time, I tried to sneak in during the fire drill, but no success."

"Weren't you in the army? Sneaking in should be easy."

"Well, I'm not a firefighter! The station issued me a uniform with P-O-L-I-C-E on it! I wore a mask because I was afraid the guard would recognize me and the guy thought I put on a fake uniform and came looking for trouble."

"I bet you look too gross to be a policeman!" Ye Qin laughed.

"No way. My mom said I'm so much more handsome than

before I joined the army. I don't even need to put on makeup, and I could star in 'The Underdog Knight.'"

"All moms look at their kids with rose-colored glasses. You can't trust their compliments," Ye Qin said, before thinking of something and correcting himself. "Well, even though our elders' praises are a little exaggerated, you can trust them a little bit. They'll be happy, too, if you give them a reply."

Knew that he touched Ye Qin's sore spot, Zhou Feng stopped bantering with him and got straight to the point. "Actually...there's something I'd like your help with."

That weekend, Ye Qin finished work early at 3 p.m. After removing his makeup and changing clothes, for the first time, he didn't go back and hole up in his hotel room. Instead, he split a taxi with several members of the crew and carpooled downtown.

A female staff person asked him jokingly if he was going to see his girlfriend. Ye Qin straightened the hat sitting on his head and smiled until his eyes went small. "Jiejie, have you ever seen someone go see their girlfriend dressed so modestly?"

Happy at being called "jiejie" so sweetly, the female staff generously stuck a BB cushion into his hands. "I know you young bloods are timid and low-key nowadays. Here, the lightest shade. Just remember to give it back to jiejie when you return."

Ye Qin didn't bother to explain that he didn't have a girlfriend. Once he got downtown, he changed taxis and headed straight for a certain conference center in the city center.

After waiting in front of the building for about ten minutes, the gates opened and people came out single file. Ye Qin immediately caught sight of Liao Yifang with several books tucked under his arms.

"Class monitor!" Ye Qin shouted, taking his mask off and waving.

Liao Yifang looked over. He pushed the pair of black-framed

glasses up on his nose, then laughed.

They found a coffee shop nearby and ordered a latte each.

"So many years have passed! You haven't changed at all. I even saw you on TV last week, on that eyedrop ad."

Ye Qin got self-conscious whenever his job was mentioned. "That ad was shot three years ago, and they're still airing it on TV. The company probably isn't doing so hot if they can't even afford a more popular celebrity by now."

"No way," Liao Yifang said, smiling. "You have such big, bright eyes. The manufacturer must have found the ad quite effective. That's why they're still using it now."

For a moment, Ye Qin was stunned. Then, he also broke into a smile. "So many years have passed, and you also haven't changed a bit. Always able to see the bright side of everything."

The two chatted about their life in recent years. Ye Qin was on a special mission today and was struggling to find a good time to insert the topic when Liao Yifang asked a question.

"How did you know that I was here to attend a lecture?"

"I heard about it from a certain someone," Ye Qin replied immediately. "He knows your routine like the back of his hand. I can't not know about it even if I wanted to."

Ye Qin thought that Liao Yifang would get angry or at least a little upset. Then, he'd get a chance to dab on some color as he recounted everything Zhou Feng had done for him. Unexpectedly, Liao Yifang took a sip from the coffee cup, cast down his eyes, and let out a soft "Oh."

Confused, Ye Qin could only get straight to the point. "He wants to reconcile with you."

"Hm."

"He wants to marry you. Truly."

"Hm."

"You...don't like him anymore?"

Faced with someone as calm as Liao Yifang, Ye Qin began to feel more and more that he'd made the wrong decision agreeing to be a mediator for Zhou Feng. It'd be fine if the monitor held a lot of resentment, but Ye Qin was worst at dealing with people who seemed like they no longer cared. It was harder for him than fighting internet trolls for a whole day and night.

Liao Yifang pondered for a moment before shaking his head.

Ye Qing didn't know if he meant "No, not anymore," or "No, I still love him."

He was about to ask when Liao Yifang began, "As a teen, I always believed there were still a lot of youthful years for me to squander away. The most important thing was to feel happy, even if only for a day, even if I only got a moment's delight through effort that was clearly more than it was worth. I thought it was worthwhile. But now, I've gotten used to working after sunrise and sleeping after sunset. An entire year passes in the blink of an eye. I know now how precious time is."

Ye Qin blinked, not understanding his words.

Liao Yifang looked out the window with a small smile nestling at the corner of his mouth. "Perhaps you can say that I've become cowardly. I can't bear any waves. I don't want to take any risks. I just want to live a simple, peaceful life with my parents."

After Liao Yifang left, Ye Qin sat alone in the coffee shop for a while.

Apart from not knowing what to tell Zhou Feng, that simple exchange a moment ago dug up many memories that had been deeply buried.

Once, he had had many ways of obtaining happiness: spending money, drinking, cards, computer games. When was it that "Cheng Feichi" had become the words his life revolved around?

He knew he wasn't acting right. His family had fallen, his mother had passed away, he had gone into showbiz against his own will—all these things had nothing to do with Cheng Feichi, and Cheng Feichi wasn't obligated to make him happy.

And besides, in the year that he had spent with Cheng Feichi, he had already overdrawn his due share of happiness. Now that Ye Qin was an adult, he could no longer use the excuse of being young and naïve. He shouldn't put all his hope on Cheng Feichi, shouldn't be greedy even more so, wanting to both ask for forgiveness and reconcile.

Back then, he had only served as a burden for Cheng Feichi, whereas Cheng Feichi had added a backseat to his bike for him, had given up a prestigious school to choose C University for him, had even worked hard to earn money so that he could buy him a ring.

But what could he give Cheng Feichi now? A lot of debts, or a life of insecurity? What did he have that could possibly make Cheng Feichi happy?

Ye Qin walked on the road dejectedly. He remembered Liao Yifang saying in their conversation just now that he had sent that postcard to Zhou Feng for two reasons. One was to let him know he'd received his letter. The second was to say that he hoped Zhou Feng would let go of his obsession and move on with his new life.

Despite giving himself a giant blow, Ye Qin still had to sort out the words to relay to Zhou Feng. That idiot had staked so many years of hope on that precious postcard, and Ye Qin didn't know if he could stand hearing it all at once.

He took out his cellphone and was just about to call Zhou Feng when he got one from Tang Chong.

Ye Qin didn't have his number saved, but Tang Chong called him too many times. Although he changed phones from time to time, there were only ever so many numbers, and Ye Qin already had them all memorized. He rejected the call and

returned to the directory, planning to blacklist Tang Chong behind Zheng Yueyue's back. But then his cellphone rang again from the same number.

Unable to even get a moment to blacklist him, Ye Qin got annoyed beyond measure. He resigned to take the call.

"Qin-Qin, baby, are you are in S-City right now? I'm here too. Come hang out and have some fun."

As soon as Tang Chong opened his mouth, Ye Qin clenched his fist tight, regretting not having socked him harder. He should have knocked out several teeth before shedding all pretense of cordiality.

"Oh? Not talking?" Tang Chong switched to speaker and raucous laughter echoed in the background. "Why don't we let President Cheng come on the call? Our President Cheng's got a lot of face. Who knows, maybe he'll even get the superstar to come over."

Ye Qin's eyelid twitched. "Cheng Fei... President Cheng is there?"

"Of course. We're discussing business. President Cheng, there's a call for you. President Cheng?" Tang Chong's voice faded away. After calling Cheng Feichi several times and getting no response, he came back. "He drank too much and passed out. Aren't you old classmates? You're not going to come and pick him up?"

Glossary

- *A-, Xiao-*: friendly prefixes attached to a person's name to show closeness.
- *-tongxue*: "classmate", added as a suffix to a school peer's name.
- *Ge, gege*: literally "older brother", but also used between people as a friendly nickname, or occasionally flirtatiously between romantic partners.
- *Di, didi*: literally "younger brother", but also used between people as a friendly nickname, or occasionally flirtatiously between romantic partners.
- *Jie, jiejie*: literally "older sister", but also used between people as a friendly nickname, or occasionally flirtatiously between romantic partners.
- *Mei, meimei*: literally "younger sister", but also used between people as a friendly nickname, or occasionally flirtatiously between romantic partners.
- *Da-ge, lao-ge*: literally "eldest brother" and "older brother, but also used as a friendly nickname between peers.
- *Laogong*: a term used to refer to one's husband.

Cheng Feichi x Ye Qin

Falling
Volume 02
An imprint of Via Lactea Ltd.

Copyright © Yu Cheng

ISBN 9781774085219